Billion Dollar Daddies

-JENNIE-

By
Breanna Hayse

©2018

©2018 All rights reserved.

This is a work of fiction. Names, characters, businesses, places, events and incidents are either the products of the author's imagination or used in a fictitious manner. Any resemblance to actual persons, living or dead, or actual events is purely coincidental.

No part of the book may be reproduced or transmitted in any form or by any means, electronic or mechanical, including photocopying, recording, or by any information storage and retrieval system, without permission in writing from the publisher.

Published by Breanna Hayse and Twisted Hearts Productions.

Hayse, Breanna
Billion Dollar Daddies: Jennie
(Book 3 in Billion Dollar Daddies©)
Cover Art by Twisted Hearts Productions

This book is intended for adults only. Spanking and other sexual activities represented in this book are fantasies only, intended for adults. Nothing in this book should be interpreted as Twisted Hearts' or the author's advocating any non-consensual spanking/sexual activity or the spanking of minors.

CONTENTS

CHAPTER ONE 1
CHAPTER TWO 10
CHAPTER THREE 26
CHAPTER FOUR 44
CHAPTER FIVE 56
CHAPTER SIX 79
CHAPTER SEVEN 90
CHAPTER EIGHT 105
CHAPTER NINE 118
CHAPTER TEN 129
CHAPTER ELEVEN 145
CHAPTER TWELVE 158
CHAPTER THIRTEEN 171
CHAPTER FOURTEEN 183
CHAPTER FIFTEEN 197
CHAPTER SIXTEEN 219
CHAPTER SEVENTEEN 228
CHAPTER EIGHTEEN 239
CHAPTER NINETEEN 249
CHAPTER TWENTY 266
BREANNA HAYSE 274
TITLES BY BREANNA HAYSE 276

Chapter One
(Jennie)
∞ ∞ ∞

My hands shook as I slipped the set of stolen car keys into my pocket and slung my travel bag over my shoulder. Catching my reflection in the dressing mirror, I touched the faded bruise under my eye. Hopelessness reflected in the eyes of the stranger who stared back at me. The shiner was a warning not to 'bite the hands that fed me' when I refused to comply with what they considered a *simple* request. It was also the promise of something much worse if I was caught during my escape. A sense of powerlessness thudded in my heart knowing I had to accept the help of a man I barely knew if I wanted to survive.

Several hours earlier, I 'appropriated' a cell-phone from the back pocket of an inebriated house guest and dialed the number I committed to memory two years ago.

Would he remember me?

He answered promptly, his voice laced with worry when he immediately asked me how I was fairing. When I replied affirmatively, the concern in his voice caused my heart to ache. Thankfully, he didn't push for an explanation regarding the reason for my call, rather he took the bait and asked if I wanted to 'meet up' with him during his upcoming visit to the area. When I explained that I was *seriously* busy, and stuck until I finished my assigned chores, he put his incredible acting skills to work. His disappointment weighed heavily in his voice as he claimed to be missing his 'little girl' and begged me to *seriously* consider changing my mind.

I inhaled deeply with relief. He recognized my use of the safe-word—a term that indicated the presence of danger or potential harm, and the promise of protection. The man was astute, thank God, because if the house security team had tapped into the phone and heard the wrong thing, I'd already be dead.

Dressed in a pair of jeans and a hoodie, and wearing a long blonde wig from my closet of 'fantasy' accessories, I tip-toed through the enormous living room of the silent house. Holding my breath, I stepped over several bodies sprawled out on the floor following an all-night party of drugs and alcohol. Some of the faces were familiar, particularly those who I was lent to as a gift in the past. Others were strangers. They came from all over the world, had power and wealth, and expected my owners to cater to their every need. The latter spoke volumes in itself. These people served an essential role in business arrangements that entailed things I was better off not knowing.

At four o'clock in the morning, the bouncers had retired from their duties, leaving only the security monitors to watch the goings-on. By the time they noticed I was the thief and escaped their clutches, I would be far out of their reach.

At least, I prayed I'd be.

Every sound sent a tidal wave of fear through me as I helped myself to the contents of several pockets and wallets, as well as the community bucket that held the keys to the multiple vehicles parked in the long driveway. I hoped that the little act of sabotage would delay some of them from traveling and cause enough confusion to distract them from looking for me.

My teeth chattered as I trod through the thin layer of snow until I reached the vehicle at the farthest end of the driveway, and fumbled through the keys until I found it's match. Slipping the gears into neutral, I released the emergency brake and rolled down the steep slope to the street below. The only sound heard in the darkness of the early morning was the ice crunching beneath the tires and my own shallow, terror-stricken breathing. Punching in the gate's security code would alert those in the guard shack, giving me less than twenty seconds before the gate closed and locked me in. I had to move quickly and not look back.

I switched on the ignition and glanced one more time at the dark house behind me. My hands shook as I counted down the seconds as the gates opened.

Twelve... Thirteen... Fourteen... I waited anxiously for the gates to open wide enough to squeeze the car between the iron posts. Now! I stepped on the gas when a house light shone in my rear-view mirror and skidded east down the dark, empty road.

For the second time that night, I dialed the man's number. The risk that my conversation would be recorded, and a manhunt ordered, was high, so I still selected my words carefully. My quaking intensified when he answered the phone.

"Hi," I chirped, feigning cheerfulness. "I borrowed a car and am on the way out of the neighborhood. I made some noise on the way out and might have woken up everyone. I don't want them to worry and have to start looking for me, so I can't stay more than a few hours."

Please read between the lines.

"I completely understand. In fact, I'll take you home myself when you're ready."

"Thanks, *Daddy*, but I'll have to get the car back in case it's needed. Where are you staying?"

"This was a last minute trip, so I didn't make reservations. Do you have any recommendations?"

"Did you try the airport? I'm sure there are plenty of hotels there."

Catch the hint!

"That's a good idea. How far away are you?"

"Roughly forty minutes. The weather's pretty bad, so I might lose reception. I need to call home when I get into the city so that no one will worry."

"You can always stop and use a payphone."

"*Daddy*, don't be silly. We don't have phone booths around here anymore."

"I'm dating myself. Do you want me to ring your family and let them know where you are?"

"That would be wonderful, thank you. Just wait a couple of hours in case they went back to sleep. The party ran late last night, and the house is full of tired people. Oh, I hope you don't mind, but I brought my hedgehog with me. The heater in his cage isn't working, and the only way to keep him cozy is to tuck him in my bag. I'd leave him home, but he's majorly *aloft* with people who don't handle him regularly."

Will he be able to figure out where I'm trying to send him?

"A hedgehog? I thought they were illegal."

"There are a lot of illegal things here, but no one reports them out of fear of retribution."

"It's the way of the world, darling." He paused. I heard him typing in the background. "I'm sorry, I'm trying to wrap up my work before I see you. I need to get a room, too."

"I can help you find one. I'll see you when I get there, okay?"

"Perfect. Drive carefully, and no talking or texting while on the road."

I disconnected the phone and sighed with relief. What could I say about that man except he was a marvel? It amazed me how he was able to pool together my cryptic comments. My fear dissipated a bit as I merged onto the highway. He would help me escape, and I'd never have to deal with my past mistakes again. I drove a few more miles and then changed direction. Call me paranoid, but if the phone could be monitored, it could also be traced. They would hear my plans to go to the airport and think I was trying to dupe them when they saw I headed in the opposite direction. My decoy was complete when I tossed the phone into a plastic bag filled with air and threw it into a large, swift-moving river. I watched the bag bob in the current for a few seconds and smiled to myself. The contents of the basket of keys followed. With all the cars in the way, it would be impossible for security to pull a vehicle out of the garage and follow me.

It felt good to have some control again.

I returned to my original route and parked the stolen car at the far end of the lot belonging to the Aloft Montreal Airport hotel. With Hobo snuggled warmly inside the bag on my shoulder, I exited and tried to keep my footing on the ice-covered pavement. A moment of panic hit when I saw no one at the entrance. *Where was he? Did he miss my hint? What was I going to do?* I had money I 'appropriated' from the semi-comatose guests, but without an ID or a passport, I was stuck.

Calm down; I coached myself. *I can buy a throw-away and call him. Breathe…*

"Ma'am? Is that your silver BMW over there?"

Startled, I turned to the sound of the voice. "Pardon?"

The man smiled and handed me a card and a paper bag. "You made mincemeat out of the sides. What did you do? Drive through a wrought iron fence or something? Don't look so scared. I'm here to help you."

"Who are you?" My heart pounded wildly in my chest. This wasn't the man with whom I had spoken.

"A friend. There's a cell phone in the bag. Call that number while I'm hooking the car to the tow truck."

I narrowed my eyes. *Trust no one.*

"I'm not doing anything unless I get some information first."

The man raised an eyebrow, took the cell phone, and punched in the number before putting it on speaker.

"Graye."

"Master Graye, your client needs some reassurance. Would you please speak with her?"

"Of course. Give her the phone and remove that car immediately."

"Yes, sir. Keys?"

Numbly, I dropped the set of keys in his extended palm. He handed the phone to me and waved as he left.

"Jennifer? Are you there?"

"Yes, Mr. Graye. I'm so glad you were able to tell I was in trouble. Thank you."

"How are you holding up?"

"I'm confused, overwhelmed and scared to death. I'm also freezing."

"I'm sure you are. Let's get you out of the cold—I can hear your teeth chattering. I'll explain everything once I get you on the road. Do you see a white SUV with dark windows next to the sign for valet parking?"

"Yes."

"Run over there and get inside. The driver doesn't know anything other than he was called to pick you up and take you to another hotel. Take me off speaker. I don't want him privy to anything I say to you. Likewise; be careful with what you share out loud. Once you're settled in the car, text me the address of where you were staying."

I was more than happy to follow his directions. I hadn't brought a coat and was feeling the icy wetness seep through my clothes. The air inside the vehicle was warm, and it only took a couple of minutes to stop shivering. I checked on Hobo and smiled when he flipped over when I rubbed his tummy with my index finger.

"I'm in. Thank you so much for all of this."

"You're most welcome. You can give me the details later, but for now, this is the plan. The car you appropriated is being transported to a remote area where it'll be gutted and then impounded. We also set a false trail at the airport. My people found a look alike, gave her an ID and put her on a flight to New York and then Hawaii. She'll take multiple cabs and change her wigs and clothing to throw any sniffers off your path. As we speak, one of our teams is on its way to disable any exits from the house and deactivate all means of communication."

I texted a message:

Sent live phone down river in baggie after changing direction in case of trace- also took IDs/passports/CC/money to delay travel. Threw car keys in river, driveway blocked.

"Smart girl! I didn't even think of doing that." His praise felt good.

"I don't know what to say. Thank you. I'm astonished that you were able to pick up on my hints, especially since they were so vague. Did you know anything about what happened to me?"

"Given what I do, it's necessary to know how to read between the lines. We also try to keep close tabs on the girls who've applied for Manor training so we can help them find what they need. When I saw you made a sudden move to Canada without a word, and we couldn't find any information matching the people you were staying with, my radar started bleeping. I wish you would've contacted me two years ago."

"I couldn't. Getting a signal in that part of the world is impossible. Someone told me that the nearby radio tower and all the wrought iron fencing and gates might have interfered with the transmission, but I always thought that being on top of a hill and set back from the road would've helped. I was wrong." I eyed the driver. He didn't seem to be paying attention, but I wasn't going to take my chances.

"I'm sending that description to the team. You were under house arrest, weren't you?"

"Yes, I have a very overprotective family," I suddenly started to tremble. When they discover my escape, I'll be placed on a hit list. Mr. Graye must've heard it in my voice.

"I need you to stay calm. There are a lot of people watching out for you. If one of mine approaches you, and you're concerned, ask about the weather. They'll comment on how gray the skies have been." He didn't wait for my acknowledgment. "You're going to be dropped off at another hotel in a few minutes. Go to the front desk and let them know you have a reservation under the name of 'Merry.' They'll have a small suitcase with a change of clothes waiting for you. I want you to go to your room and take a hot bath. Once you're done, order from room service and have them leave the food in front of your door. I'll call as soon as I'm alerted to the charges and give you more instructions."

"Okay, thanks. You're incredible." My throat tightened with emotion. Kindness in this world was something I believed no longer existed for me.

"You're safe now, sweetheart. I have the best man in the field who'll place you in a location where you'll be happy and cared for. I need to make a few more calls, so I'll talk to you later, okay?"

"Okay, *Daddy*. Bye."

I looked up to see the driver watching me in the rear-view mirror. I shivered as I quickly looked down and hid my face. *Had he been listening?*

Chapter Two
(Dorian)
∞ ∞ ∞

"Dorian, darling, it's almost two in the morning. Why are you still awake?" My wife asked as she walked into our lavish bedroom. I beckoned to her from the settee and patted my thigh in an invitation to sit. I wrapped my arms around her narrow waist.

"Mmm, you're so warm and soft. I could ask the same thing of you, Miss Meredith. It's hours past your bedtime," I advised, nuzzling her neck.

"If I had a bedtime, then you'd be missing out of a lot of after-hour play."

"This is true. So? Talk to me."

"Two of our first-year maids got into a fight. I broke it up, and Elias took over. He'll ensure it doesn't happen again."

"Was anyone hurt?"

"No, although they will be when your mean old Master-At-Arms is done disciplining them."

"As much as I'd like to take pity on our young ladies, they need to understand that rules are made with a purpose in mind. Your hard-ass brother doesn't have the word leniency in his vocabulary when it comes to dissension among the ranks, so I know those girls will walk away with a new understanding about life in the manor."

"Yeah, I know, but I don't have to like it. I've experienced many years of his bossiness, remember? Back to you. What's wrong?"

I stared into her eyes and felt my heart ache with love for the magnificent creature perched on my knee. The memory of meeting the chubby, sassy child on the playground trickled through my mind. I was barely fifteen and new in town when she provoked a fight between her brother and me. Elias, the town bully, learned a valuable lesson when he ended up eating dirt, yet I offered him my friendship. The three of us became inseparable from that moment on, and I soon fell in love with the little girl who grew to be a curvaceous, red-haired goddess and my first submissive.

"You're so beautiful. What did I ever do to deserve to have you as my wife?"

Merry frowned. "You were the perfect sadist and wouldn't let me come until I agreed to marry you, remember? Okay, love, it's clear something's going on. Can you talk about it?"

"I always tell you how beautiful you are."

"Yes, but you're usually drooling and taking off your pants when you say it. Ow! No pinching."

"This scrumptious backside is made for pinching."

"Yes, I know. Pinching, chewing, fucking and spanking. Please tell me what's bothering you. Maybe I can help." She ran her fingers through my hair and started massaging the back of my neck. It felt wonderful, as her hands always did, but there were pressing matters to take care of that didn't involve my needs.

"I just received a bizarre call from one of the girls who applied for training about two years ago. Do you remember Jennifer Hudson?"

"Wasn't she the little brunette with gorgeous teal eyes? She wanted to Middle for multiple daddies."

"That's the one. We didn't have what she needed here, so we asked her to hang on while we did some research. She then made a sudden move to Canada about three weeks after her interview."

"Oh, yeah! You were worried sick when you weren't able to find any information about her whereabouts or who she was with."

"I'm a worrier, especially when I can't help a submissive and she takes it upon herself to make things happen. Anyway, her phone call came out of the blue, and her words were very cryptic. It wasn't difficult to piece together the clues to realize she was in some sort of trouble and needed help."

"That poor baby. Do you think she's in danger?"

"Yes. I haven't had a chance to speak with her in detail yet, but I jumped right on getting her out of there. I just hope she was able to catch my clues. I was under the impression that the phone she used might have been monitored."

A frown settled on my wife's beautiful face, and I traced the line with my finger.

"What exactly did she say?"

"Well, she started the conversation by calling me *Daddy*, and then commented that the snow in Montreal brought back memories of how happy she was when she lived at home."

"Daddy? Snow? If I recall, she was a preacher's kid and raised in Beaumont, Texas. Does it snow there?"

"No, it doesn't. Her use of the term stopped me in my tracks. She spoke very quietly, and there was definite fear in her voice."

"She was crying for help. Smart girl. She grabbed your attention and gave you her location."

"I told her I was coming for a visit and asked if she wanted to meet with me. She said *no*."

"She lied to you, otherwise why would she have called?"

"Precisely. I told her I missed 'my little girl' asked her to *seriously* consider seeing me very soon. She told me everyone was asleep and she was afraid she'd wake them if she left the house."

"Dear Lord, she *is* in danger."

"Probably more than we suspect. I already contacted our connections up in that area to be on standby in case she's able to get out of the house and needs to hide. Until she calls me, it's a matter of waiting."

"You? Wait? Patience is not your virtue."

"Not when it comes to protecting our girls."

"How is she going to prevent anyone from following her?"

"I wish I knew. Until I get the address, my hands are tied." I gently massed her knuckles with my thumb and then lifted them to my lips.

"What do you have in mind?"

I fingered her pert nipple absently as she snuggled against me. "I'm going to assume the worse. I'll have to find out where she's heading, first. Once we get a solid hold of her, we can dump her car into impound and move her to a couple of hotels so that no one recognizes her. We still have the photographs of her on file, so I asked the agents in the area to hire a look-alike and use the decoy to confuse anyone who might try to pursue her. I know it's overkill, but better safe than sorry."

"It's not overkill, Dorian. It's brilliant. What are you going to do once she's safe?"

"I'm going to drag Max Tohler out of his warm, comfy bed and send him to Montreal with instructions to place her in the *Guardian* program. He's the best and, if there's a perfect fit for that girl somewhere on this planet, he'll find it."

Merry chuckled. "You realize that you're going to have to listen to him bellyache over how cold he is. He hates the snow."

"He'll get over it. A woman's life is in danger, and he's the man I trust to do everything possible to keep her safe. He's also going to be hypersensitive to the situation after going through what he and his brother did to protect their ward."

"Max's the best. Do you want me to wake him?"

"No, Meredith, you'll enjoy his griping too much. One of these days, that man's going to let his palm loose on your backside. You can't keep taunting him."

"Why not?" Her smile broadened as she turned to straddle my lap and pull my lips against hers. "He's like a big brother to me, and it's so enjoyable to get away with everything no matter how much I push."

I shook my head. "He's got the patience of a saint. I wouldn't tolerate a quarter of the crap you pull on him."

"That's why you're the Whip Master and Max is a Daddy Dom. I get to mess with him in a way I wouldn't dare with you."

Flicking her under the chin, I issued a warning. "You may mess with me in any manner you wish; you just might not get the reaction you want."

"It's no fun then. Come. It's time for bed," Merry said, taking my hand and pulling me off the couch.

"I need to be available if Jennifer calls me, sweetheart."

Merry's eyes twinkled as her clothes puddled to the floor. "Just lay back and enjoy. I'll do all the work."

I sighed. Merry was an *Unsatiable* and would collapse from exhaustion and still want sex. I've always appreciated her passion for my body, but tonight I was too tired to respond—not that my wife cared. Any of her orifices could outlast a thousand energizer bunnies!

"Would you accept an IOU? I'm sorry, but I'm beat. I've been going nonstop since five yesterday morning. Please don't pout."

"I'll make a deal with you. Get naked and hold me."

"There is no such thing as getting naked and just holding you, and you know it. You'll start rubbing that backside against me and not stop until my cock finds somewhere to visit."

"I'm not that bad." Her cheeky grin said otherwise as she unbuttoned my shirt. "Oh, don't scowl at me. I'm going to let you sleep until the phone rings again. Once you're done with performing your magic, I'm going to perform a little of my own. Is that reasonable?"

"Bless you, my love." I lifted her onto the bed and pressed my mouth to her lips as she eased my shirt over the broadness of my shoulders. Her hands glided down my chest, and she curved her fingers to run her nails over my solid abdomen. The fairness of her skin against my dark olive tan drew my attention.

"Are you sure you want to sleep?" she asked hoarsely as she unbuckled my belt and pulled it off with a loud *swish*. Wrapping the leather around the back of my neck, she pulled me closer.

"I love you," I murmured into her mouth. "Please, let me sleep."

"I'm not stopping you." She dropped the belt and returned her hands to the front of my trousers. "This certainly isn't tired."

Groaning, I gently pulled my disloyal cock from her warm hands. "Yes, it is. It's just too stupid to know it. I need to sleep, Meredith. I've running on fumes and am going to start making mistakes if I don't recharge. Please don't press me. I don't want to be cross with you."

Merry rolled her eyes and moved across the bed to give me room. "You're really no fun when you're tired."

"You know how I am, yet you still push. I promise to make it up to you."

"I'll make sure you keep that promise."

I grabbed the hand that inched over my cock and raised her knuckles to my mouth to kiss them. "I love you. Good-night."

Within seconds of the light being turned off, Merry's even breathing made me smile. I pulled her sleeping body against my belly and nestled her warm, soft bottom against my groin. *Brat*, I thought with a smile. *If only everyone could have a love like ours once in a lifetime.*

The ringing phone startled me to wakefulness two hours later. Slipping out of bed, I went into the adjoining sitting room and sat on the couch with my laptop. Jennifer reported being on her way and dropped the clue of the name of a hotel. As we spoke, I left word with my brother-in-law to activate the diversion plan that his security team put into place.

"Dorian?" Merry's sleepy voice called.

I held up a finger. "One second. I'm notifying Elias to initiate DEFCON Two."

"DEFCON Two? My brother needs a life. This isn't the military, and we aren't under a nuclear or terrorist attack."

"We might not be, but that little girl's life might be in danger if we don't act now. Besides, it makes him happy to label missions this way and keeps him from complaining. Look." I pointed to the computer screen and the spider web of functions that Elias' on-site team prepared to perform. "Defense readiness, condition two, means his forces are set to deploy and engage within six hours."

"Boys." Merry shook her head and leaned against my shoulder as I answered my phone.

The cheerful lilt of Elias' voice was replaced with that of a soldier reporting battle plans to his commander. "The team's in place and ready to implement my orders. Charles Murphy's already on a plane to HQ and will bring the girl to Max from the final coordinates. Did you get her address and ETA?"

"She's on the highway and will reach the Aloft hotel in forty minutes. I'll give you the address as soon as she and I can speak freely. I hope everyone there is too inebriated to think clearly and buy us some time."

"Are you sure she understood the directions you coded to her?"

"She's a clever girl and devised her escape on her own. I also have the feeling that reading between the lines is something she's quite accustomed to doing."

"Did she understand the possibility that any phone entering the residence might be tapped or connected for monitoring? The car could be as well."

"Yes, and unless they were listening for clues, nothing she said gave her destination."

"You figured it out. I'm shocked."

"Very funny. I give Jennifer credit for having a good brain in her head. These people aren't alert enough to suspect she's the mastermind of this operation yet. That's to her advantage since they'll be waiting for her to realize she can't live without them."

"If that girl reneges after all this, her little ass is mine," Elias grumbled as he clicked on his keyboard.

"We're not going to give her a reason to go back. I'll also remind you that I'm the boss, so I get her first."

Elias chuckled. "The boss, eh? Okay, Boss, impound's on the way to pick up the vehicle and my ground team's ready to dispatch to the location once it's given. Do you know anything about the layout of the house?"

"Not yet. What else do you have planned?" I asked.

"The crew is instructed to secure the property to prevent pursuit. They'll be cutting off the power to the house and jam any electric gates, disable all communications, slice fuel lines of any vehicles on site, and lay plexiglass planks of nails under the snow over the exits. We're going to make it impossible for anyone to leave the premises. There's no way in hell those fuckers are going to hunt down that girl on my watch."

He sounded pleased with himself which meant two things. The first is that, in his typical fashion, the old coot went above and beyond the call of duty. The second is if his plan worked, he'd be unbearable to be around for several weeks.

"You're incredible. Over the top, but incredible. We need to find a way to retain the residents and guests until I get information from Jennifer as to what's going on in that place."

"I've already got that covered. As soon as we get the coordinates, the team's running a false DEA raid with a SWAT team. We'll call in the local police if we find evidence to bust them. If she can get any additional information to you, that would help."

"Shall do. I want to keep Jennifer uninvolved in the legal issues if we can help it."

"We'll do what we can. Most importantly, we'll be able to hide her safely." Elias said proudly. "I sent you the list of hotels for transfers and the transport companies for untraceable payments. I just got a message that they're ready to mobilize at my word. I'll send you updates as they send them to me."

"I don't know what I'd do without you. Thank you."

"Don't thank me. Just call Max and get this kid to safety. We'll investigate further in case she has something she might need us to know."

"Perfect. Good job and bonus your team for their work. I'll call Max when we hang up."

"Tell the old bear 'hi' for me and that he owes me some time in the boxing ring."

I chuckled. "I'm not getting between the two of you. Don't forget that he cheats and will switch places with his twin to wear you out."

"Pft. Tell him anyway. I can take both of them down with my eyes closed and hands tied behind my back."

"Sure, you can. Keep me updated."

"Gotcha, Bossman."

I stroked my wife's tousled hair. "Go back to bed. I've got this."

"No. We're partners in taking care of these girls, so I'm going to lend emotional support if there's nothing else I can do to help."

"Very well. I need you to stay quiet while I call Max."

"I can do that."

"What are you doing, Meredith?" I lifted my eyebrow as she kneeled between my legs and started kissing the insides of my thighs.

"Lending emotional support."

"You just can't help yourself, can you?"

"Nope. That's why you love me," she grinned as her lips made their way to my rigid cock. "Should I stop? I know you love it when no one can tell you're coming."

"You're a brat. Do whatever you wish, but please don't interrupt while we're talking."

"Why would I do that when I have something else to focus on? Mmm? Just put the phone on speaker so I can listen in," she said, twirling her tongue around the mushroom-shaped head of my over-eager cock. She smized before pulling my growing shaft to the back of her hot, wet throat. *Damn thing*, I scolded mentally. *Whose side are you on, anyway?*

I inhaled through my nose to calm my speech and not give away the events occurring between my legs as I dialed the number of our oldest, and dearest, family friend.

"Did I wake you, Maxwell?"

"What the hell, Dorian. It's one-thirty in the morning." Max's voice registered his partially awakened state.

"Actually, it's four-thirty. You're getting old, Your Honor. Law school taught us to be alert at any time, in any place, and for any reason."

"We graduated from law school decades ago and if I'm getting old, so are you. I'm also not on the bench anymore, so dump the judge-stuff."

"Daddy? Who's that and why do you get to swear?" I heard a voice in the background.

"It's got to be Uncle Dorian. No one else would be such an asshole to call this time of night. That being said, Daddy has every right to swear," a second voice added. Merry winked at me as I smiled.

"Tell your Little and your brother that it's business and to go back to sleep," I ordered.

"Gimme the phone! Uncle Dorian? Why are you calling so late? We were sleeping."

"Is that how your Daddy and Uncle taught you how to speak to your elders, young lady?" I reprimanded, tightening my fist in Merry's curls as her mouth began to bob up and down my shaft.

"Well..."

"Mik? Please take Lonnie to her room and remind her about manners," Max requested.

"No!" the girl protested.

"Now. March." I listened to the remonstrations and held back my laughter. "Sorry about that, D."

"He's going to fuck her, isn't he?" I asked with a chuckle.

"That's very probable. Drawing that line between Big girl and Little girl time with her has been difficult for him."

"What about you?"

"Me? I'm good with separating the age-play from the D&S. My line is complicated because I keep messing up. I'm constantly having to learn how to make it up to her for being a jerk."

"Well, you're going to have some more practice. We have an urgent placement. I don't know all the details yet, but I need you in Montreal immediately."

"Montreal? If it's snowing here in Tahoe, it's going to be miserable there."

"Are you taking whining lessons from my brother-in-law? Wear a coat. This girl's in danger, and I need you to work your magic as the head of the *Guardian* program. We've no time to waste in this case. I'll send you her files as soon as I get everything pulled up." I winced as my wife responded to my words, drawing my cock into her throat with so much suction that it was borderline painful.

"What kind of danger?"

Breathe, I coached myself as my body began to tighten. "The kind of danger that Elias alerted the local team with a DEFCON Two. The girl's on the road toward the first pickup point and is driving a stolen car."

It was easy to visualize Max sitting up in bed. "Shit. Have the police been notified?"

"Not yet. Getting her out of there is my priority, and then we'll see if this is something that the legal team needs to handle."

"I don't understand."

"Do you remember the game we played at Cambridge called *Read Between The Lines*? This girl's a master."

"When you speak with her again, make certain she puts that aside when I interview her. I don't have the patience for games right now. Did you contact impound?"

"The tow truck's waiting for her to arrive, as is a taxi to transfer her to the next drop off point. Your regular driver's going to meet you up there. He'll escort her to the final location before the interview at your hotel."

"I need to get out of here soon if we're going to do this. The snow's starting to come down."

"The chopper will pick you up at dawn and fly you to Reno to catch the company jet. I'll also reserve an extra room at your hotel so she can remain close to you and Charles."

"Thank you. Do you have an idea for her placement?"

"That's your expertise, my friend. She's a Middle and desires a poly relationship. Men only."

"I'll figure it out. We've got Guardians all over the globe, and I'll find her the perfect family."

"Head's up. Charles has been ordered to treat this assignment as a Code Red and will be armed. The jet will be on standby to transport you to her placement as soon as you give the word."

"This certainly isn't our standard modus operandi. You've got my curiosity piqued. I'll get right on it. By the way, I have one more question."

"What's that?"

"Did you come yet? I know damn well that Merry had her mouth full of your dick during this entire conversation."

"What makes you say that, Maxie?" Merry asked, licking her fingers as she pulled away from my spent manhood.

"It's not difficult to deduce. First, you were completely silent. That never happens. Second, you and Dorian have played this game since I met you back in England. You give your husband a blow job, and he hides any hint of it in his voice and actions. I still don't know why you do it, or how he manages to disguise his response, but you've become very predictable."

"Why? Because we can and there's nothing you can do about it," Merry snickered.

"Regarding the second half of your question, the explanation rests in why I'm such a damn good courtroom attorney while you sit on the judicial bench," I said, stroking Merry's long red, curly hair.

"Very funny, asshole. I resigned from the bench to be home with my family, and you know damn well that I'm just as good in the courtroom as you are."

"Are you?"

"Fuck you, Dorian."

"I believe I already did it for him and we both enjoyed it immensely. Good night! We love you!" Merry said cheerfully while snatching away my phone.

"Now just you—"

"Oops. I think I just accidentally hung up on Maxwell." Merry blinked *not* so innocently. I took her hand and stood. "Where are we going?"

"Back to bed. To sleep. I'll deal with your naughtiness tomorrow."

"Really?" She clapped with excitement. "Are you going to spank me? Or maybe use the belt?"

I turned off the lights. Meredith might be a masochist, but I had my own sadistic moments. This was one of them.

"Neither."

"What?"

"Good-night."

"I thought you were going to punish me? Dorian?" She shook my shoulder. "Dorian!"

I turned to my side with my back toward her. "I am. You're getting nothing."

I could only imagine the expression of disbelief on her face!

Chapter Three
(Jennie)
∞ ∞ ∞

My head was still spinning with confusion, and I felt disoriented after falling asleep right after I finished my meal. A couple of hours later, I received a call from one of Mr. Graye's people ordering me to take the back stairs and leave through the storage rooms to meet a driver in a police car. Nothing was said as we drove to a distant parking lot and I was placed in a taxi-cab.

It was almost three in the afternoon when an enormous tattooed, bald biker wearing a leather jacket and jeans blocked my path as I headed toward the door after being dropped off at another hotel. Before I could say anything, he took my bag, grabbed my hand, and led me to a light blue Toyota. I knew he wasn't one of the house's people—the owners' would never have anyone who could be perceived as a gang member in their organization.

"Buckle up, buttercup. This is the last leg of the game. My name is Charles Murphy, and I'm your driver, bodyguard, and interpreter for when Judge Tohler starts speaking legalese as he explains the process of the program."

"Judge?" I swallowed dryly. "Am I in trouble?"

"No, dear. Mr. Tohler resigned from the bench, but he'll always be a justice of the peace in my eyes. In the world of Graye Enterprises, he's on the top of the food chain. There are some items in the bag on the floor for you to change into. Did you forget your coat? You're shivering."

"I left everything at the house when took off. I didn't want them to think I was gone for the long haul."

"You left everything?"

Busted!

I shrugged and gave him a little smile. I couldn't help but like the big, gruff teddy-bear of a man. "Well, I *might* have borrowed a telephone, a car, and a pocketful of cash and essential identifications. Oh, and all the car keys I could find. I thought it might help delay anyone from leaving and also give information about who these people deal with."

His laugh was as large as life. "Was that a drawl I heard sneak out?"

"Yes, sir. Beaumont, Texas—born and raised." The grin that stretched my face felt strange. I couldn't remember the last time I smiled so hard.

He touched the imaginary brim of a hat and faked an accent. "A fellow Texan bids you welcome, Miss Jennie. I'm here to serve."

I laughed so hard that I snorted. "I'm pleased to make your acquaintance, Mr. Murphy. If you ever need your pocket picked, call on me. It's my superpower. That and some quick knife work."

"You're my kind of naughty, little miss. Here's the agenda. Tomorrow, you'll meet Judge Tohler, and he'll walk you through the interview and answer all your questions about the process."

"Is he nice?" I suddenly felt very nervous.

"You met Mr. Graye when you applied for the Manor, correct? He trusts Judge Tohler to protect his girls. I promise you'll feel very safe with him."

I frowned. "You didn't answer my question. Is he nice?"

Mr. Murphy chuckled. "Judge Tohler is his own man. He and his twin brother share an adult little girl, so he can't be all that bad."

"You're scaring me."

"I'm messing with you. He's very professional and concise but has more love in his heart than anyone you'll ever meet. If you get nervous, look into his eyes. We're going to be arriving at the final location in a few minutes, so do some quick shape-shifting. Once we're there, we'll get you all cozied up, grab you some grub, and settle you down for the night. We want you to be rested and coherent so that you can make informed decisions when options are presented."

I lifted an eyebrow when I pulled the items from the bag. "You don't want me to dress in this, do you? Please say you're kidding."

"Got a problem?"

"A little bit." I pulled out a thickly knit burgundy pullover dress with dark green trim, light brown boots with dark brown leatherwork, and a pale pink long-coat with piping around the color. "These clothes don't exactly match, to start. I'll stand out like a sore thumb."

He chuckled. "You're not entering a fashion show. Put them on and then close your eyes."

"Why?"

"Just mind me."

I quickly obeyed, happy to be in warm, dry clothing. The dress fit snugly and ended at my knees, and the boots and coat fit perfectly. "I'm done."

"Are your eyes closed?"

"Yeah. Why?"

"What are you wearing?"

"Duh- a dress, boots and a coat."

"Describe what they look like. What color is everything?"

"The dress is dark purple, the coat and boots are white."

"Look at them."

"Holy moly," I whispered. "How did I get the colors all wrong?"

"Your brain remembers primary colors and will try to make sense of different shades. If anyone remembers you, they'll describe your clothes in the way their brain remembers. In a matter of days, it's likely your dress will be remembered as leggings and a sweater, and probably dark pink."

"Wow, that's cool."

"Yup. Slip those gold-framed glasses on, and your facial features will be remembered differently as well." Mr. Murphy pulled the car into an older neighborhood and drove by a dozen vehicles that matched ours.

"You guys are brilliant."

"Our chief of security and all his wing-men are special ops who've been trained in urban psychological warfare. We know how to blend into our surroundings and become forgettable."

"I'd never forget you," I protested.

"Oh, yeah? Without peeking over the seat, describe me."

"You're uber tall, dressed in biker gear, bald, and have a beard."

"What makes me different from anyone else? How could you pick me out of a crowd?"

"Your tatts, I guess. They go up your throat and over your head, and both arms are full sleeves with lots of colors." I paused. "You also have one ear pierced. I can't remember which side, though."

"My tatts are tribal, so no color. I'm also wearing long sleeves, so the only tattoo you saw was on the side of my neck toward the back. I don't have any on my head or throat. While I do have full sleeves, you never saw them. My earring's fake and I'm also clean shaven."

"How can I be so off?"

"TV, movies, pre-conceived notions—there are dozens of things that will alter your memory. That's why statements are taken by crime victims as soon as possible after a situation. Since you've only met me once, you'll completely forget any details within a week or two."

"You also managed to distract me from watching where we were heading. Is this it?" I looked at an older yellow and white two-story octagonal flanked by tall evergreens.

"Yes, ma'am."

"I thought we were going to a hotel. Where are we?"

"We trained your brain to automatically register that you were going to a hotel. We selected the other sites to make a pattern and mislead anyone who might try to follow you using the same type of psychology. They'll assume we're heading south toward the States and an easy border crossing, while this house is north. I hope your French is good. I believe that's the primary language spoken in these areas."

"I wasn't allowed to learn. It ensured my dependence."

"That makes sense in a captive situation. Watch your step. It's slippery."

"Who lives here?"

"Your costumed double. She got herself a first-class three-week vacation in Hawaii in exchange for the use of her home. Mr. Graye's going to have a construction crew come in after you're gone and make repairs as a surprise thank you for her help."

"That will make the neighbors think she's staying somewhere else while her place is being fixed, right?"

"You're catching on."

"How will you be explained?"

He wrapped a big arm around my shoulders. "I'm your new squeeze. After you, my dear."

The house was quaint with dated decor, quilts, and wallpaper that was probably the same from when it was first built sixty years ago. I turned to a clanking sound and watched Mr. Murphy unload his weapons one at a time on the wooden kitchen table next to a large gym-bag he had brought in with us.

"What the hell?"

"Orders from the boss."

I couldn't believe how many he had been carrying! "Your boss is a little overreactive, don't you think? Where did you hide all of them?"

He pulled a ten-inch blade from the side of his boot, flipped it in his hand and sent it twanging in the far wall. "There's no such thing as being overreactive when it comes to criminals. The address you gave us is unregistered and armed with so many security cameras that one would think they were guarding more gold than Fort Knox. What's going on there?"

"Drugs and human trafficking. The guests come from all over the world, but I don't know the details of their organization."

"We'll run the pictures on the IDs through the data base and see if we can get some hits. Your room's up the stairs, first door to the right. We'll have an early dinner so you can get to bed and rest up before heading in for your interview."

"Are you staying with me?"

"I'm just a phone call away. Guards are posted throughout the yard and along the street and won't let you out of their sight for a minute. No one can call over here without going through our switchboard, and we're photographing every license plate and face that comes this way. We even took care of your rat."

I scowled. "Hobo's a hedgehog, not a rat."

"He's a prickly rat that's wearing a little leather jacket with a tracking device."

"No way!" I opened the bag and started laughing. Hobo looked up at me with a leather 'jacket' carrying a Harley emblem over his fat little body and a tiny leather helmet on his head. "When did you do this? You turned him into a Biker Hog. He's so cute! Okay, do you guys think of everything?"

"We try, at least on the major things. Do you have any food allergies?"

"I'm deathly allergic to vegetables."

"You're not having ice-cream and candy for dinner." He tapped my nose. "My girl claimed she was also allergic to veggies when she first came to live with us. I didn't buy it—particularly since I had access to her medical records as part of her application to Graye Manor. Would you like a retry?"

Busted again. "I'm not really allergic to them directly, but I really hate the taste. They make me gag."

Mr. Murphy wagged his finger. "I'm a good cook, and you won't gag. That's also the last fib you're going to tell. Trust is everything in the life you're about to start. You won't ever have to worry about this again." He captured my chin in his palm and touched the faded bruise on my face with the pad of his thumb. His eyes were warm and filled with genuine concern. "But you will be sitting on a tender bottom if you're caught in another lie. I can guarantee that will happen no matter who you're assigned to. Be a good girl and don't disappoint me."

Biting my lower lip, I looked at him, suddenly wishing he could be the one who took me in. He made me feel safe, cared for and wanted—feelings that I've long-forgotten existed. An unfamiliar aching in my chest rose to my throat. I refused to cry in front of him. I wanted his respect, not sympathy.

"Does this mean I have to eat my vegetables?"

Kissing my forehead, he turned me around by the shoulders and gently nudged me toward the stairs. "Every bite. Fib again and I'll give you a double portion. March."

****

When Mr. Murphy declared an early bedtime, he wasn't joking. I was tucked in before the clock struck seven and given a loving kiss on the forehead.

"I'll be back to pick you up in the morning. Help yourself to anything you want, just stay in the house and keep away from the windows. Do you have any questions?"

I looked away and shook my head. The sound of rain and sleet falling from the darkening sky cast a shadow of gloom into the room and steadily increased my agitation. I didn't want to be left alone.

A big hand brushed my hand from my face. "Jennifer? You're awfully quiet. What's going on in that beady little brain of yours?"

"Nothing." The lies came so naturally after years of hiding my true thoughts and feelings. I quickly corrected myself. "I'm just tired and a little nervous. You must be exhausted. When was the last time you slept?"

"I'll sleep when I'm dead," Mr. Murphy said. "I'm going to check in with the team and get back to Judge Tohler and see if he needs anything. He's going through your files and making calls, but as soon as he's ready, I'll come and get you. Mr. Graye reserved a room for you at our hotel so you can be close to us after the interview."

"Will you be staying there with me?"

"I have a room, but if you need me, I'll be available."

"I want to go where you are. You aren't thinking about taking another girl, are you?" My voice was filled with hope. I knew he'd be the perfect guardian for me.

"No, honey. I'm sorry, but I do appreciate the confidence. My Dorothy is more than enough for Tim and me to handle. We're at the point in our relationship that she trusts our commitment to her and knows that we love her to infinity and beyond. She's been through her own share of hell and, like you, deserves undivided attention and affection."

I was disappointed but again refused to display my feelings. Emotions made you appear vulnerable, and I wasn't about to give up my control to anyone again. I chose the route of casual conversation. "Is Tim your brother?"

"No, he's my best friend and my husband."

I admit that the news surprised me. "You're gay? I never would've guessed. That's another example of how our brains interpret information based on outside influences, isn't it?"

"You're learning," he said with approval. "Tim and I are in a committed, monogamous relationship with Dorothy as our third. My husband is an accountant, very soft-spoken, clean-cut and handsome as hell."

"Are same-sex marriages legal in Texas?"

"Yes, but there are no guarantees that the couples will receive the same benefits. Fortunately, the Graye's have some bigwig friends in the justice department who do what they can to help the community. It's always one step at a time, but each one gets us a little further."

"You're fortunate to have friends like them to help you."

"Baby girl, we're all fortunate to have each other. That includes you, darling. Together, our community is strong and cohesive, and we leave no one behind."

"I guess."

"Whoa, did I hear doubt coming from those pretty lips?"

I hesitated to answer. I didn't want to hurt his feelings, but I also didn't want to lie to him again. Choosing my words carefully, I replied.

"I haven't had a chance to be part of your community, so I only know the life I've had. I'm not saying anything against you. I'm just—"

"—skeptical. There is absolutely nothing wrong with that. It takes time to build trust. There is one thing all the guardians have in common that might make you feel more confident. Each one is committed to three ideals. The first commitment is to the *Graye Way*. That means, in a nutshell, that the happiness, safety, and well-being of our girls are a priority above all other things—including ourselves. The second commitment is to the relationships we've formed both intimately and publicly. We work tightly together to build and grow on a solid foundation of support and accountability. The third commitment focuses on building the process and making what is good even better and introducing fresh thoughts and practices into our lifestyle under the sanctity of the first commitment."

"Are all the guardians Daddy-Doms?"

"The primary guardian is. Everything will be explained- I promise. You have the cell phone that Mr. Graye gave you with all our numbers. Use that if you need us. I picked out some clothes for you that I think will make you feel more confident when you meet the judge. I left them on the table downstairs."

"Can I keep the ones you already gave me?" I asked hopefully. He kissed my nose.

"You certainly *may*. I'll see you in the morning. You're going to go right to sleep and not even have a chance to miss me. What's wrong, sweetie?"

"I'm terrified," I admitted.

"I know you are, but it's almost over. Once Judge Tohler has you in his hands, you'll have nothing to be afraid of ever again. Go to sleep."

I waited until I heard the front door close and peeked out the window to watch Mr. Murphy slip into the shadows. Once he drove away, I padded downstairs and grabbed a bag of pretzels and the two packages and backpack that were left on the table. I double checked the locks on all the doors and windows and then returned to my room. I plopped back on the bed and sighed with relief.

"How are you holding up?" I asked the little hedgehog as I pulled him out of his travel bag. He yawned and looked at me with annoyance for waking him. He certainly didn't seem to be affected by all the travel or by his new accessories!

I put him down on the carpet to get some exercise while I unwrapped the first brown paper sack.

"Way too cute and so soft," I purred as I cuddled a pair of gray leggings and a matching cashmere sweater against my cheek. I giggled when I held the panties and bra in the air, imagining the expressions on the customers' faces when Mr. Murphy waltzed into Victoria Secrets and picked out his favorite undergarments. The second package held outerwear consisting of a soft teal sweater, light gray snow-pants and matching knit hat. The gray and teal backpack contained necessary toiletries and a pair of adorable gray and teal snow-boots.

The care that Mr. Murphy took in selecting my outfit for me left a warm glow in my chest. I started thinking about Mr. Graye and all the work he was doing to keep me safe and make me happy. It was easy to sleep knowing that there were people in the world who I could call friends.

****

Mr. Murphy called me shortly after I finished cleaning up and dressing the following morning.

"Did everything fit?" he asked.

"Well, hello to you, too." I twirled in front of the mirror admiring the selection of clothes. "It's all perfect and is too damn adorable. Thank you. I feel like a queen."

"I've got great taste, what can I say? I hope this will be the beginning of your journey as royalty, Your Highness. I'm on my way and will be there in about ten minutes."

"I'm all ready and so is Hobo."

Mr. Murphy chuckled. "You didn't happen to find the little red suitcase in his travel bag, did you?"

I giggled. "Where did you find that stuff?"

"The suitcase is from Build-A-Bear, but the other little outfits are compliments of yours truly."

"You sewed costumes for my hedgehog?" I was stunned.

"I'm a man of many skills with too much time on my hands."

"Do I dare ask where you learned how to sew doll clothes?"

"That's what daddies do when their little girls like to play with dolls. My Dorothy likes to pull out pages from magazines and dress her dollies in haute couture. We'd go broke if we had to buy them, so we both learned how to sew."

"That is the sweetest thing I've ever heard!"

He sighed. "That's because you're a girl. If Judge Tohler or Mr. Graye ever found out, they wouldn't let me live it down."

"That's sad. I'd think that, given what they do, they'd see how wonderful you are."

"They know how wonderful I am, but they're like brothers and can't resist harassing me. It's what we do.

I'm turning the corner and will come to the door to get you."

"We're ready. Thank you so much. You've made my day."

"Let me add a cherry on top. None of your old housemates have asked any questions about your whereabouts yet. Why? Well, someone planted a bug in their ears that you stole a car and are in custody after a high-speed pursuit when you were found to be driving under the influence. You're being blamed for the sabotage of the other cars and shorting out all the security equipment."

"Wow! I'm smarter than I thought I was."

"Right? For some reason, the electric and telephone company still can't activate the utilities, and there's no mechanic available to fix the vehicles. Oh, and one of the 'guests' had a bunch of credit card, personal IDs and passports hidden in his drawer. He denied taking them, but the guests are sure he also took and hid, the other missing ones. Bottom line is by the time they get their shit together and find a way to leave; you'll be long gone. I'm here."

The break in the sky allowed a glimmer of sunlight to shine onto the wet surface of the ground as I held his hand and skipped to the long, black sedan that was parked across the street. I gave him an enormous hug before sliding next to him in the front seat.

"Thank you for everything. Let's go meet Judge Tohler and get this party started."

"You look good enough to eat. Ants in your pants?" Mr. Murphy asked, glancing at me with a smile as I fidgeted in the seat.

"Too much coffee on top of my nerves. I just want to get out of this town."

"If everything goes as planned, you'll be on your way by this time tomorrow. We try to arrange the meet up within a day or two of the interview."

"Do you know where I'm going?"

"Not a clue, babe. Excuse me. Murphy," he answered the car phone.

"Good morning, Mr. Murphy. Did you pick up the package?"

"Yes, sir, Mr. Graye. She's right here and is as cute as a button." He winked at me. "Say hello to Mr. Graye, Miss Jennie."

"Thank you so much for everything, Mr. Graye. I don't know how I can ever repay any of you for all you've done for me."

"I do. You are to take full advantage of this opportunity and make the best of every moment. I want you to be happy, healthy and whole. You're getting a chance to make your dreams come true. It's also a chance to help someone else's dreams come true as well. Whoever Mr. Tohler put you with will be seeking the same kind of relationship that you desire. It might take some work and a little discipline, but well worth it if it's the right match."

"I want the kind of relationship that you and Mrs. Graye share. I've never seen two people so deeply in love before," I admitted.

"They worship the ground the other walks on. Nothing is too big or too small that they can't handle together," Mr. Murphy added.

"We have a strong support system and don't hide the truth from those we trust. Mr. Tohler sat day and night with my wife as she battled cancer and was a rock for both of us. He's going to be your fairy godfather."

"I thought I was her..."

"Put a plug in it, Murphy."

I giggled as Mr. Graye interrupted. "All of you are wonderful. I'll do my best to make you proud. I promise."

"Just be happy, my girl. Charles? Meredith wanted me to relay a message to you. She said she's sending you a care package full of swatches of material that she received from one of our clients in Japan. Why is Jennifer laughing?"

"No reason, sir." Mr. Murphy shot me a look. "Please thank the missus for me."

"Shall do. Call me later with an update."

I continued my laughter when the call ended. "Does Mrs. Graye know about your hobby?"

"Not unless my girl told her. I know my secret's as safe with her as it is with you."

"Thank you for trusting me. You know—I can't wait to see Hobo's next outfit. He'd look adorable in a tux."

"Are you blackmailing me?"

"Who? Me?" I snickered.

"After all the wonderful things I've done for you, is this how you're going to treat me?"

"You made me eat my vegetables. Payback's a bitch."

"You need a good spanking," he grunted, steering the car into the valet lane of the Ritz-Carlton Montreal.

"You wish. Ow!"

"What? I just clapped your thigh." He didn't even try to look innocent.

"That hurt."

He exited the car and walked around to open my door for me. As he helped me out, he whispered in my ear. "It would probably be wise to remember how heavy my hand is, Miss Smarty-pants. I've been doing this Dom stuff for a long time and can always tell when a subby is trying to provoke a paddling. If you need it, ask. There's nothing to be embarrassed about, and it will be much more pleasant for you to take that route than if you got yourself into trouble."

I looked at him with confusion. His eyes crinkled while he lifted his right eyebrow. A tiny smirk rested on the side of his mouth. *Was he amused or annoyed?* A quick peck on the tip of my nose and a wink assured me of his delight. He handed the car keys to the valet, took my hand in his giant paw and led me to the elevator.

"We still have time," he said as he punched the button.

"What are you talking about?"

"If you need a spanking, we have time. It might relax you."

I blinked dumbly. "Relax me? How?"

"Once I'm done, you'd be more concerned with sitting comfortably than your nerves."

"I've never been spanked before," I admitted shyly. "I have no experience in your lifestyle. I'm sorry."

"*Our* lifestyle," he corrected. "You're aware that Graye Manor is a submissive training facility, correct?"

"Yeah, but I never connected it with stuff like spanking."

It was his turn to look confused. "What did you think it was?"

The elevator opened before I had a chance to respond. "The Royal Suite?"

"Mr. Graye thought you'd be more comfortable if he dialed it down a bit," Mr. Murphy chuckled.

"This is dialing it down?"

"For him, yes. Between you and me, I think the posh effect is just something that's expected to come out of Graye Enterprises. It's strange because Mr. and Mrs. Graye are two of the most down-to-earth people you'd ever meet."

Another voice joined our conversation. "Personally, I think Dorian does this with the sole intent to harass me. He knows I'm a country boy at heart and more comfortable in a log cabin than a penthouse. I heard voices in the hallway and came out to see if you were getting cold feet."

Chapter Four
(Jennie)
∞ ∞ ∞

I whipped my head around to the sound of the low, melodic voice. The big man standing in the hallway was mouth-wateringly beautiful with eyes that warmed the chilly air.

"Why, in the world, would Mr. Graye what to do that?" A huge smile spread across Mr. Murphy's face.

"Simply because he can. I'm Max Tohler." He held out his large hand to me.

"Jennifer Hudson. Sir." The quaking I had been pushing down was threatening to rise. "It's good to meet you."

"You're shaking." He placed his other hand on top of the one he held. "There's no need to be afraid. I'm here to help you. Come inside and sit next to the fire. Charles? Would you mind bringing our guest something hot?"

"Yes, sir. What would you like, Miss Jennie?"

"Coffee would be wonderful. Thanks."

"Hot chocolate it is. I'll be right back."

"Daddy Doms have a thing for hot cocoa," Max chuckled. "How are you holding up? You've had quite an adventure these last two days."

"I'm a little overwhelmed, but trying to hold it together. Your Honor," I added, unsure of what to call him.

The handsome older man rolled his eyes. "I resigned from the bench several weeks ago so I could spend more time with my brother and our girl. Please just call me Max."

"Yes, sir."

"Try to relax, okay? I don't bite."

"That's not what Lonnie told me," Mr. Murphy said as he handed me a cup of steaming chocolate.

"That's a different kind of biting and you know it." Max laughed. "The Graye's intervened with Lonnie's placement and hijacked my heart. I loved that woman the second she walked into my chambers at the courthouse."

"What?" I was confused.

"It's a long story. I'll tell you about it later. Let's get business out of the way. Charles? Please stay. She's comfortable with you."

"How can you tell?" I asked, looking back and forth between them.

"Judge Tohler's an expert at reading body language."

"I'm not a justice anymore, Charles."

"You are to me."

"I give up. This is one of the most stubborn men you'll ever meet in your life," Max said, pointing at the enormous biker.

"Not stubborn. Consistent."

"Let me guess—that's the newest phrase your Dorothy has adopted."

"You guess correctly, but it's not as bad as Tim's. His latest is the promise to twang her butt and ring her bell."

"I'm just going to ignore you. I hear you brought along a little pet. May I see him?" Max asked. Relieved to have a reason to hold Hobo, I pulled him out of his travel bag and gently handed him over.

"Hello, little guy. Nice collar. I want you to cuddle your mommy and keep her calm while we talk, okay?" Max said as Hobo sniffed his palm before looking up at him. My prickly pet was handed back to me where he was held to my chest. "If you have any questions, feel free to interrupt and ask. This interview is to help me find the place that you'll be the most happy and feel safe, so don't worry about formalities."

"To be honest, anywhere is better than where I've been. I don't care where I go, as long as it's far from those people," I said quietly.

"I understand, but *I* care where you're going. I need to know more than what I've read in your application files. Let's start with what happened after your interview with the Graye's two years ago. Take your time and remember that we're on your side."

"Do I have to?" I suddenly felt intimidated by the two men in front of me. I didn't want to tell my story or admit that I brought it on myself for being impatient.

"Yes. Telling me the whole truth is nonnegotiable. I'm not going to judge you or make any assumptions, I promise."

"Jennifer? You've put up a great game face the last couple of days, but we can see right through it." Mr. Murphy's voice was low and firm. "This is the day you get to wipe the slate clean and start over. We've pulled girls out of jail, drug dens, and off the streets. Every one of them had applied to the manor for training and weren't honest with us because they were ashamed or prideful. There's no room for any of that garbage here. Did you decide to put your fate into your own hands because you were too impatient to wait for the Graye's to help you?"

I looked down and nodded.

"Did you also lie to them about your living arrangements?" Max asked softly.

Hot tears threatened to show if I didn't get my emotions under control. "I'm an adult and responsible for myself. I just needed to find a job."

"You were homeless, weren't you?" Mr. Murphy asked, his tone loaded with disapproval. "They would have taken care of you, child. What were you thinking?"

"I refused to be a burden to anybody. I pull my own weight and don't want any handouts."

"Is that what you think you did? Where did your pride take you?"

"Easy, Charles. Give her a chance to answer before you lose your cool."

I flashed a burning glance in Mr. Murphy's direction. "Do you really want to know where my pride took me? I sold myself to the cartel, okay? They promised me the moon and I was a stupid fool to believe them. Once they had me in their grips, they used me as a reward for their clients. I was a fucking virgin when I got there!" I was shouting at him, desperately trying not to let go of those tears. "They gave my virginity away as thanks for one of their most powerful drug smugglers and laughed as the disgusting troll and his goons dragged me off for a gang bang. That's where my goddamned fucking pride took me."

"Jennie, it's okay, honey. Breathe." Max coaxed.

I jerked away from his hand and distanced myself from them. "I was their pet to share with anyone who wanted me—for a price. Each time a client came into town, I was given a note with his, or her, fantasy to fulfill. If I failed, this happened." I pointed to the faded bruise on my face. "They made sure to keep me healthy and prevented pregnancy, but that was to increase my length of service to them. I was isolated from others, rarely spoke the language of whoever had me for the time, and never allowed to go anywhere without a guard. Do you know what they called me? Do you know? The Palace Whore!"

The tears broke through and I started to weep uncontrollably. Hobo placed his little paws on my chin and licked a salty tear as the men sat silently in their places.

"I started not caring about living anymore and they put me on suicide watch. Not because they were concerned for my life, but because I was in such high demand. Hobo was a bribe to keep me engaged. They knew I was desperate for companionship and left him in my room while I was sleeping. It wasn't out of kindness, either. It was to have something else to hold over my head. Once I had bonded with him, they used him as a weapon. His life for my cooperation."

I started to hyperventilate and found myself being scooped up by a set of heavily muscled arms. Mr. Murphy sat down and held me on his lap while I sobbed against his shoulder. He began to rock me back and forth while kissing my hot temple and softly humming.

"Drink this, baby girl," he coaxed, holding a glass of sherry to my lips. The liquor warmed my chest as I sipped.

"Do you need something stronger, sweetheart?" Max asked, his brow wrinkled with concern.

I shook my head and hid my face in the sweet-smelling leather of the biker's coat.

"They're international drug dealers. " I finally forced out. "Their clients are high profile and very wealthy, and they have smuggling connections all over the world. Everybody who comes into the house is given a false identity and a traceable phone, just in case there's a raid. I know several politicians are involved, but I don't know their names."

"Jennifer? I need you to look at me," Max said. His voice demanded obedience even though I didn't want to make eye contact with him out of pure shame. "If we get enough evidence on these animals, we can shut down their operation and lock them away for life. Would you want that?"

"More than anything."

"Would you be willing to testify if we needed you?"

I nodded and felt Mr. Murphy hug me.

"Good girl." Max nodded his approval. "Let's change the subject. Are you still interested in a poly relationship?"

"No women. Just men. Kind, trustworthy and loving men," I whispered.

"I wouldn't have it any other way. Is there anywhere in the world that you refuse to live?"

"Yes. In a tent in the middle of the desert and here. I melt in the heat."

"Spoken like a true Texan." Mr. Murphy laughed.

"I wish I could say we don't have any guardians who don't have desert tents, but that would rule out several of our participants. I also won't put you where there's either a language barrier or that could hurt Hobo."

"Thank you. He just needs to be able to stay warm. We're not high maintenance," I said, locking eyes with the prior justice of the peace. Mr. Murphy had been right about his eyes. This was a man I could trust with my life.

"Would you object to living off the grid? There are amenities, of course, but the area I'm considering is very isolated. There's only one road in and it's typically closed down in the winter, limiting access to only small planes."

"I'd prefer to live as far away from crowds as possible. I think I'd feel safer if I knew I couldn't be found."

"None of your personal information will be recorded in any transactions. Our transportation is private and the location is under heavy protection by the town's owners."

"May I ask, why?"

Max leaned back in the overstuffed chair and crossed his long legs. "Northern Lights is a community that's operating under the umbrella of Graye Enterprises. Extensive property was purchased in the Denali National Forest in Alaska and built up to house a company of professionals involved in various occupations, but all are involved in wildlife preservation and research. Only members of the community are permitted access."

"Are you saying you want to send me to live with tree huggers?" I didn't know if I was amused or frightened by the thought.

"These gentlemen are far from tree huggers, darling. The town's owners were born in Fairbanks and have a cultural heritage with the native Athabaskan tribe through their grandmother. They earned billions as platinum recording artists and then recruited others in their same financial state to invest in the land and protect what they could from political influence. Without going into detail, the lift of the hunting ban on denned wildlife in Alaska and changes in the oil drilling laws of federal property sparked reasonable concern. I honestly have no idea of how many thousands of acres belong to Northern Lights, but I do know that they've spared no expense in building the dream and protecting what they love."

"What aren't you telling me? Start with why this place falls under the protection of Mr. Graye."

"Dorian was right about her. She's very intuitive," Max said to Mr. Murphy. "Northern Lights is a community that focuses on polyamory living arrangements. Most of the households consist of a minimum of three men and all have vetted guardians. The brothers wanted a place where people didn't have to hide their lifestyle from the other residents. The Athabaskans and Dorian worked together to indefinitely secure the private property under tribal law to protect it from federal seizure in the event some jerk decided he wanted to drill on it."

"I told you that you needed my help in translating legalese. Northern Lights is a town filled with Daddy Doms who are looking for their own adult little girls, and they answer to no one outside of their community except Mr. Graye."

"I'll go."

"It's not that easy, honey. You need to meet the primary guardian and decide if you're comfortable with him and—"

I interrupted. "Nothing can be as bad as what I've lived through. Being snowed in with strangers is no different than being locked in a room to be used as a sex toy for two years."

"I understand that, but there are some things we need to discuss. This program offers you a new beginning. Your guardian is placed to help you meet your goals and provide a life that your deserve. You aren't under any obligation to engage in a physical or romantic relationship either, although that is the hope we have for all involved. The only restriction that might arise is that the participants go in as a team, and most of the men are very close. We don't want those relationships being threatened because a ward is only interested in a monogamous lifestyle."

"I'm not."

"You haven't met your guardians yet. You might be attracted to one, but not to his best friend or his brother. You're also not obliged to remain with the placement once your term of service is complete."

"How long is that?"

"It varies depending on the situation, but basically runs for three to five years to give the ward time to attend school and make the changes in her life to be happy. She's strictly monitored and held to a high degree of accountability and responsibility in completing her part in the arrangement."

"What's should I expect?"

"If you wish, I'm sure my girl will be happy to speak with you, but every situation is different. In a nutshell, you are accepted into an established household as a ward. Your guardian will give you rules, chores, and instructions that he expects you to follow. As Mr. Murphy stated, most of our guardians are involved in an age-play dynamic, so those terms will also be discussed."

"Will I be allowed to make decisions for myself?"

"To a certain extent, yes. This program teeters on a fine line of trust, dominance and submission."

"Our girl, Dorothy, says we're a nondictatorial dictatorship," Mr. Murphy said with a chuckle.

"Your Dorothy knows the perfect way to describe imperfect things. The purpose of the program is to give you a voice and decide a path to happiness under the guidance of men who genuinely care."

"Let's do it. I've done nothing but fuck up my life and will do whatever is needed to make things right for myself."

"You do realize that this program will involve the minimal elements of domestic discipline and might progress into BDSM, don't you?"

"Yeah, and I don't care."

Mr. Murphy pointed at Max. "Did you see that wince? Judge Tohler loathes the word 'yeah' and is a stickler for lady-like language outside of the bedroom. Apparently—"

"That's enough, Charles. Jennifer doesn't need to hear a blow-by-blow description of my love life."

I looked at the expression on Mr. Murphy's face and bit my lip. He was trying so hard not to laugh. Max, however, didn't so much as twitch an eyelash.

"I'm sure it has its *ups and downs* and might be a little *hard* going *back and forth* like that. It must be a pain in the ass for your poor girl." I tried to appear innocent. "Why are you laughing? Was my question hard to swallow?"

Not even one muscle moved on Max's face as Mr. Murphy started to snort. "Watch out before he gets a *boner* to pick with you."

"Must I deal with children?" Max rolled his eyes. He pointed to Mr. Murphy. "You I can send away but this one will fit very well across my knee. Don't encourage her."

"What did I do?" I asked.

"Charles? Do you think it's safe to take her shopping for some clothing while I call Northern Lights? They'll have all her information and supply the specifics that we can't get here, but I don't want her freezing during the transfer."

"Shall do, Boss. I'll take her for lunch, too."

"Excellent. We'll have dinner here and, if the landing strips are clear, we'll take the jet to Fairbanks."

"You know what? Dorothy and Tim are having some alone time, so what if I take Miss Jennie for the transfer and you head on home?"

Max tapped his finger on the chair. "I can't step down from my responsibility."

"I promise it will be fine. Your family needs you, especially after your little one's stunt."

"What happened?" I asked.

Max raised as eyebrow. "Lonnie had a tantrum and ran off. She's in big trouble and I'm the last person she wants to face right now."

"You're the one person she needs to face, though. I insist, Max. Don't make me pull out the big guns?"

That actually got a reaction from the somber man. "Do you think you can beat me?"

"I wasn't talking about these guns, and yes—I can beat you." Mr. Murphy kissed his biceps. "I was threatening to call Mrs. Graye."

"I'm not afraid of Mrs. Graye."

"No? Hand over the phone."

Max scowled at the big man. "You're a prick, Charles."

"Thank you." He turned to me. "That was an admission that I won. Let's go shopping. You can leave Hobo here with Judge Tohler if you wish. He'll be safe."

"I'm not a judge anymore," Max grumbled.

"I know, but calling you that annoys you."

"I don't know why your husband puts up with this crap."

"It's for the same reason you do. You love me. Ciao!"

Chapter Five
(Jennie)

∞ ∞ ∞

"Wake up, sleepy head. We're getting ready to land." The voice seemed so far away, as though it were a part of my dreams. A warm hand rested on my knee and gently shook my leg. "It's time to rise and shine, Jennie-girl."

"We just left." I yawned groggily. "How can we be in Alaska already?"

"You passed out the second the jet started down the runway. Are you feeling okay?" Mr. Murphy looked at me with concern.

"I think that was the deepest I've slept in two years. I didn't even have a nightmare."

"Have you been experiencing many of those? You should have told Judge Tohler." His brow line crinkled.

"He really hates you calling him that. I've had nightmares every night since the real nightmare began. But I'm free now, right? They can't touch me again."

"You're free, baby girl. I need to reinforce something about meeting your guardian. You aren't obligated to go with him if you feel any sort of discomfort. He won't take it personally."

"What if he doesn't like me?"

"This is about you and you alone. Remember the only obligation is that you're provided an opportunity to be happy—with or without them. You may leave once you've been given the tools to thrive, and there will be no hard feelings."

"But won't it waste his... their time if we're not compatible?"

"That's a risk these gentlemen are willing to take. I'll let you in on a little known secret. Judge Tohler has a perfect record. The only time he doubted a placement was when he was given Lonnie. He fell for her right away and thought he'd have to assign her to someone else. He didn't even know that the Graye's had sent him to get her for himself."

"Wow. Do you think this will be good for me?"

"I want you to have a voice and take back some control in your life. You started by escaping that prison. You then chose to pursue this path, sight unseen. It's not too late to back out. You may refuse until the second the door of your transport closes and you're on your way."

"What if I change my mind after I get there?"

"We'll ask you to give it some time. It's not unusual to get cold feet once you take the step. No pun intended," he gestured to the snow-covered mountains below.

"I can do this. I have to do this," I said.

"You're calling the shots. Excuse me." Mr. Murphy held up a finger as his phone rang. His face was etched with worry. "Are you sure? Damn it. Let me call you back after I speak with her."

"What's wrong? Did they change their minds about me?"

"Not at all. We just hit a snag. The exchange site is a ranger station located in the middle of the damn forest. The weather's turned and they're worried about being snowed in very shortly. They have to send a plane instead of a truck, and then transport you via snowmobile."

"So?"

"So that means I can't come with you to help you with the adjustment. The plane is a two-seater and will only fit you and the pilot. By the time we're done with the back and forth, the pilot doubts he'd be able to get me out of there before they're snowed in."

My heart pounded with fear. I couldn't back down now. *Where would I go and how could I protect myself?* I knew it was only a matter of time before the goons started looking for me.

"I can do this on my own. Don't worry about me, okay?" I hoped I sounded more confident than I felt.

"My job includes worrying. There's another factor in the mix that might be a deal breaker for you. The home consists of four men and they are tightly knit. Three of the men are already at the house, but the fourth is out of the country. They haven't told him that you're coming."

I bit my bottom lip. "Is it safe?"

Mr. Murphy nodded. "I'm certain of it. No one can enter Northern Lights without being thoroughly vetted. The men are old service buddies and partners in their business. They're also part of the package. This type of relationship's been something they've wanted for years"

"Are they like the rest of you?"

"They're experienced dominants and pro age-play, but I don't know what role they'd take at the house. That's part of the introductory discussion."

I made a face. "Let me get this straight. Max picked out two guys to take care of me who are into this program-thing and they live with two other guys, one of which is out of the country and knows nothing about me. All four of them are involved in the dynamic, and I can chose whether I want them or if I have to mind them?"

"I didn't say that, you little weasel. Once you're in the home and under his care, your primary guardian will lay out the rules. That includes what he expects of you with the other men. He will not, however, order you to be involved sexually with anyone- including himself. That will always be on you to make the first move if you're interested."

"What if they aren't interested in me?"

"Then they aren't. I wouldn't worry about it, though. You're beautiful, smart and funny. What man wouldn't want you?"

I looked down. "That's how I felt at the other house. I don't want to be a piece of meat."

"Look at me, kid." He chucked his finger under my chin. "You'll always have a choice and you'll never be punished for saying the word 'no.' I promise."

"What if—"

"No 'what-ifs.' I get plenty of those from the judge. If any problems arise, you have our numbers. We might not be able to get you out of the town right away, but we will get you to safety. Deal?"

"Deal." I shook his hand.

"We need to get permission before I can let you go on your own. His Honor won't be happy about it."

"Too bad. It seems that I have a very small window of opportunity here and I don't want to miss it."

"Gotcha. Give me a second."

I listened to Mr. Murphy speak to Max, assuring him that the additional men were safe and vouched for, and that their profiles were on the way for him to review. He also spoke up for me and supported my decisions as being the beginning of my healing. Once he ended the call, he contacted the guardian. I dug my nails into my palm as I listened to him speak, trying desperately to hear the voice of my new caretaker.

"Well?" I asked.

"Deep subject."

"Do you always think you're funny?"

"Yes, but that doesn't mean anyone else agrees with me. Here's the plan. The actual flight from Fairbanks to Denali air field is only about fifteen minutes or so. Your guardian will meet you at the ranger station and take you home. It's about an hour inland."

"No cars?"

"Not for entry into Northern Lights. They specifically made it so that no one can drive, fly, or boat in. Anyone entering on foot, snowmobile, ATV or sledding will be redirected."

"What if there's an emergency?"

"The entire town is self-contained. I wish I could go with you. I'd love to see what they've done there."

"Me, too." I whispered as the private jet landed on the long runway. "When is the pilot going to be here?"

"He has my number and will call when he lands. Let's go grab something hot to drink. It's a bit nippy out here."

He took my hand and led me into the tiny airport. Several enormous taxidermied animals stared down at me as we walked toward a small coffee shop.

"Whatcha thinking?" Mr. Murphy asked.

"Just that being a big animal in this state isn't a good idea. I'm not into hunting and I don't care for people who hunt for trophies."

"Believe it or not, that's one of the questions in our vetting process. Men who are into taking down animals as prizes are disqualified. We want people who value life. We do agree to have some who hunt or fish for food, especially in remote areas."

"That's cruel."

"I'm not a hunter, so I tend to agree with you. That's when I found out the hunting conditions barred traps, snares, aerial take-downs, or poison. The hunters in Northern Lights share their kills with the community in exchange for services or fresh fruit and vegetables from the hydroponic gardens."

"I still think it's cruel."

"As I said, I get it. Tim, my husband, pointed out something to me one day when we were out at McBride's Steakhouse. I was sucking down a ribeye when he asked me where I thought my steak came from."

"I hope you told him from the refrigerated section of the grocery store."

"That's exactly what I said. Steak hasn't so appetizing since then. It's different when the animal is allowed it's freedom and is taken down by a bow or an atlatl. Our hunters only use guns for protection or for mercy kills."

"It doesn't make it right."

"Are you vegan?"

"I'm a flexitarian."

"What's that?"

"I eat meat when I'm in the mood AKA I'm a total hypocrite." I admitted with a grin plastered on my face.

"Yeah, well, so am I. I like my steak. Drink up."

"You're letting me have coffee? I feel so privileged," I teased, lifting the cup as a toast.

"Enjoy it. If your new family is anything like the rest of us, this might be the last taste of coffee you'll have in a long time. How are the feelers?"

"I'm excited and scared. I—" My vision fell on a woman's face across the room. I quickly ducked my head and focused on my cup.

"What's wrong?" Mr. Murphy whispered, touching my arm.

"The woman across the room wearing the red coat and glasses. I know her."

"How?"

"I think she might have visited the house."

"That would be a very strange coincidence. Maybe she just looks like someone you've seen. Remember what I taught you about hiding in plain sight? That red coat and knitted hat would fit the profile. Add the fear factor and chaos that you were surrounded with, and it's more than likely your brain is redirecting you."

"Maybe you're right. I'm a little paranoid."

"Given what you've been through, you have every right. Keep telling yourself that you're no longer there."

We chatted for a while, but I kept glancing at the woman. I was certain she also looked at me but the more I observed her, the less certain I was toward her identity. It didn't matter, either way. Even if she did recognize me, no one would know where I was going or how to find me. I'd also be protected by the impenetrable fortress of Northern Lights. Between them and the Graye's, no one could hurt me again.

I don't know who cried more when I boarded the private plane—Mr. Murphy or me. The pilot finally had to pull us apart so he could get me buckled in and get on our way. My heart ached as we left the ground and Mr. Murphy's bald head disappeared out of sight.

If my guardian was a quarter like my new friend, I'd be a very happy girl.

Everything below seemed to be enveloped in a gray cloud as we progressed to the landing strip near my new home. I was unloaded from the plane, reloaded onto a snowmobile and taken to the ranger station. After a quick apology for having to leave me unattended, the pilot returned to his plane and left me standing in the wooden building and staring out over the snow-covered forest below.

"I never get tired of a fresh fall of snow. The first real snowfall of the season is a bit late this year, but is always so special. It's beautiful, isn't it?"

I turned to the man's voice and felt my breath catch in my throat. *This couldn't be him, could it?* Indigo blue eyes smiled as playfully as his relaxed, white-toothed grin. The crisply ironed khaki and olive green park warden uniform emphasized his broad-shoulders which tapered to a slender waist. Long sleeves couldn't hide the flexing of hard muscles beneath the material. His neatly trimmed light brown hair framed a strong jaw and flawless, smooth cheeks.

Damn, he was scrumptious!

"Ryder Watkins." He introduced himself with a welcoming hug. As though his appearance wasn't enough to catch my interest, he also smelled of fresh pine and a hint of cinnamon. *I was a goner!* "Max didn't tell me that you were so beautiful!"

I felt my face heat up as he looked at me with appreciation. "Thanks, Mr. Watkins."

"Call me Ryder. We don't hold to formalities in our neck of the woods. Welcome to Northern Lights."

"You're a guardian?" I forced out.

"Not *a* guardian. I'm *your* guardian. I also head up the ranger station on this side of the mountain when I'm not home making sure my kid brother isn't getting on the boss' nerves and my best friend isn't being turned into wolf chow. Do you like animals?"

I've never been into small talk, but was grateful to him for instantly placing me at ease. "Yes. I have a pet hedgehog who's staying toasty on a battery operated electric pad right now." I lifted my bag.

"I've heard all about Hobo. We'll make sure he's taken care of as well as you are. I know the circumstances of this meeting are atypical for this program, but I'm so happy that you decided to give us a try sight unseen. It took a lot of courage."

"Life's about adventure, right? Judge Tohler and Mr. Murphy wouldn't steer me wrong."

"They're good people and so are the Graye's. I don't mean to rush you, but we should get moving. Night comes quickly to these parts and we don't want to be out after dark. I'll get your bags for you, sweet girl," he said in a voice that reminded me of melted butter on a cinnamon roll.

After bundling up in coats and gloves, he straddled the large snowmobile and patted the seat behind him. "Hop on up and hang onto my waist. We need to swing by the town to pick up a package on the way, but we'll be home before you know it. You'll get to meet the rest of the squad and get settled in."

Home. The word sounded good to my ears. "What did the others say about my coming?"

"I've never seen them so excited. The boss started planning dinner and my brother grabbed his tool belt to build something. I don't think I've ever seen that boy move so fast in his entire life," Ryder said with a warm laugh. "Hang on."

My grip tightened around Ryder's waist while we zoomed over the snow-covered slopes. I buried my face against the center of his back and felt him squeeze my hand. That tiny gesture made me smile and snuggle in closer to his body. He paused the snowmobile at the top of a hill and turned to me.

"How are you doing back there?"

"Good." I realized I was still holding on to him and quickly pulled away. "Sorry. I didn't mean to cling."

"You may cling to me anytime you wish. I'm the hugger of the group. See that trail of smoke over there? That's our place. If I know Lex, he's making you a welcome home dinner in the hearth. That's also my cue to get the lead out. Lock and load, baby girl."

I giggled as he flexed his muscles and restarted the snowmobile. Within a few minutes, we drove into a quaint little town that instantly reminded me of Santa's Village. Candy-striped gas street lamps lined the main street and tiny white lights sparkled within the branches of the evergreen trees. Several snowmen guarded different shops, donned in the apparel of the shop keeper.

"This is so cute!" I said as he parked on the side of the snow-covered road. A snow-white horse pulling a red open sleigh stopped beside us. In it were three handsome men and a stunning young woman with bright pink cheeks.

"Watkins! I heard the Grayes came through for you. Congratulations! Introduce us to this lovely lady," The driver of the sleigh said with a large grin planted on his face.

"They certainly did. This is my ward, Jennifer Hudson. Jenn? Allow me to introduce you to the Markford brothers and their wife, Lena. They're the founders of Northern Lights."

"It's good to meet you," I said politely as I inched closer to Ryder.

"Is this your first time in Alaska?"

"Yes, sir. It's very beautiful."

"It's also mega cold, but we have fun during wintertime. We always have lots of things to do," Lena squealed as she bounced in her seat.

"Did someone get into the candy apples again?" Ryder asked.

"How did you guess," one of the other men groaned.

"I *love* candy apples. Daddy? Can Jennie come over to play? Please?" Lena asked, tapping the driver with the arm of the Teddy-bear she held in her arms.

"Absolutely, sweetheart. She's welcome anytime her daddies want her to visit."

Daddies?

"Tomorrow? Can she play tomorrow?"

"We need to give her and her new family some time to get to know each other before we kidnap her to play with you."

"Look at that pout!" Ryder exclaimed. "I promise that we'll bring her over as soon as possible."

"Promise, Uncle Ryder?"

"Northern Lights Daddies never break their promises. In fact," he leaned over the edge of the sleigh, "if I find out you've been very good, I'll have

Uncle Lex make you his famous *Come Hither* red velvet and chocolate chip cake."

"Really?"

"Really, truly. Now, if you'll please excuse us, we need to pick up a package and then get home before sunset."

"Civil twilight is hitting fast, too. By the way, are you planning to take the family on the campout during Christmas?"

"We wouldn't miss it for the world. I can't say the same for our antisocial friend. He's been moping since he was sent on his newest assignment. He pissed off some bigwigs on the hill with his conservation protests, got tossed in jail, and was sent off to Tokyo on a Diplomacy mission. He wasn't even allowed to bring his dog, so that should tell of the kind of mood he's in."

"I didn't know he spoke Japanese."

"He doesn't. Yet. Give him a week and he'll be fluent enough to piss off some more representatives." Ryder sounded proud of his friend.

"When's he due home?"

Ryder covered Lena's ears. "When, and I quote the Major, when he gets his head out of his ass, pulls his shit together, and finishes his job. Not necessarily in that order, either."

He kissed Lena's forehead and freed her ears.

"You know I can still hear every bad word you said, Uncle Ryder. You owe two dollars to the swearing jar."

Ryder sighed, pulled out his wallet, and handed her the money. "You're becoming quite a shrewd businesswoman, Miss Lena. You're sure making bank on me."

"Then stop cussing. It's that simple."

"Lena, watch your manners."

"Sorry, Daddy. Back to Uncle Slater, I bet Jennie can make him smile. She's really pretty and he needs a little girl to cuddle who doesn't have four legs and drools," Lena nodded confidentially.

"I bet you're correct, and be careful not to say that around Mollypup. You'll hurt her feelings. I'll give you guys a ring later and update you on our plans. Lena, you be a good girl for your daddies."

"I'm always a good girl. Hey!" she scowled as the three men snorted at once. Ryder laughed and grabbed my hand as they drove off.

"After you, my dear," he said, holding the door to the a small store for me to enter.

"Man! It's like stepping back in time at the North Pole. Mmm, it smells like caramel apples and cinnamon in here."

"Ambiance is everything in this town, and if it's something that makes our girls happy, we do it." Ryder lifted a bag with his name on it from the counter, grabbed several items off the shelves and tossed them in, and then jotted a note. "Okay, babe. Let's get going."

"Don't you have to pay for that?"

"Northern Lights doesn't use money as an exchange. This community runs on old fashioned values and trust, so we help one another as an extended family would."

"Is that why Lena calls you guys *uncle*?"

"Yes. I saw your reaction when the word 'daddies' was mentioned. Did you see the welcome sign when we entered town?"

I shook my head. "I was distracted by the decorations."

"It reads *It Takes A Village*. We're all responsible for one another. We'll talk about all this stuff after dinner, okay? Please remind me to speak with the guys about the camp-out."

"You go camping in the snow?"

"Heck, yeah. We go ice-fishing, build igloos, ice-skate and loads of other things. Why the face?"

"I don't like cleaning fish."

He tweaked my nose. "Not to worry. We draw straws for fish duty. Ready?"

The sun shimmered on the horizon and cast a pink hue upon the snow banks. I forgot about the cold as the shadows from the trees stretched over the landscape and stars twinkled in the indigo blue sky. We rounded a corner and the house came into view.

"Oh, my God," I whispered as Ryder pulled the snowmobile onto a dock. "I'm speechless."

"This baby is the brainchild of Judge Tohler's brother, Mikaal."

"He must be a genius." I gazed at the multi-story log and stone lodge raised on stilts. Windows covered every wall, including that of the high-pitched roof and a cylindrical look-out tower.

"He is. The design takes advantage of the full panoramic view of the property from Denali to the lake. That entire forest region to our right is a designated wolf enclosure. We also have a workshop, greenhouse and a cold meat locker. This device allows us access to the snowmobiles in the event of a snow-in." He unhooked my bags and gestured with his head. "We always enter through the mud room. Lex is a neat nick and has a fit when we track mud and slush onto his floors. Don't tell him I said this, but he's our Den Mother."

I heard the sound of male voices approaching the room as we hung our outer wear on hooks to dry, and placed the snow boots on a metal screen.

"Ryder! Where's our girl? Fuck! You're gorgeous."

"Jenn? This is my kid brother, Simon. Please excuse his language. He's the class clown of our unit and directs Northern Lights Engineering Corp."

"What's that?"

"It's a fancy term for handy man. Simon can build, fix and invent anything anyone could ever need," Ryder explained. "He's brilliant. Just ask him."

"I sure am and don't you forget it. Simon says, give me a hug." The bear-sized man with a contagious smile ordered.

"I can't breathe," I gasped as he squeezed me.

"I'm the cuddler, so get used to it. See you guys later!" Simon announced, taking my hand and pulling me into the main house.

"Get back here, you turd. This is Lexington Becker, communications and data systems expert for the town. He's also the commander of this pile of misfits. That big, furry thing sleeping through this whole introduction is Molly."

"We're so happy that you chose us, sweetheart. This is a great group of guys and I'm sure you'll be comfortable here in no time." Lex squeezed my hand gently. "I understand you have a little friend with you?"

"His name's Hobo. He's tucked in his carrier and is happy as a clam." I lifted Hobo out of his bag to show Lex.

"Hello. I bet you're hungry, buddy. May I?" Lex asked, taking my pet from my hand. My mouth literally fell open when Hobo flipped over for a tummy tickle. "You're going to like it here, too. In fact, Simon built a heated hutch just for you."

"He did?" I was stunned.

"As soon as Ryder told us that you were coming, Simon got to work making your little friend a safe, warm place to live."

"I don't know what to say. I can't get over how incredibly kind and thoughtful you all are." Tears glazed my eyes. *Could this be real?* They were almost too perfect.

"I know what you can say," Simon said. "Repeat after me. *Lex, feed me. I'm hungry.*"

"You're always hungry. One of these days it's going to catch up with you."

"In your dreams. This bod is going to stay gorgeous just like my face."

"He's delusional. Do what the rest of us do, and ignore him," Ryder explained. He handed the canvas bag he was carrying to Lex. "Here are the things you needed from town. Have you heard from Slater today?"

"Yeah, he called earlier. He's pining over being confined to the embassy and worried about those damn wolves like they were helpless pups. Your buddy needs a life." Simon rolled his eyes.

"Give the guy a break. He's been in a crappy mood since the incident in DC and is pissed because I sent him away to work and cool his jets. He doesn't need any more harassment from you," Lex scolded.

"I'd be in a crappy mood if I ended up in jail again, too. He's damn lucky he has you to pull strings for him."

"Why was he in jail?" I watched as the guys glanced at each other.

"Slater's a bit obsessive about the wolf population here. He has this Dr. Doolittle thing with dogs. Long story short, he's been fighting Washington because the present administration lifted the hunting ban in this state and are screwing with the National Forests. He swore to go after anyone who he discovers is den hunting, with the promise to dismember that person piece by piece and feed their parts to the grizzlies. If he was just an ordinary green peace type, they would have ignored him, but Slater's anything but ordinary."

"Not only is he capable of following through with his threat, but he has the resolve to ensure it's done," Simon added. I could have sworn I heard a touch of satisfaction in his voice.

"He also has the resources to protect himself when he's being a dumb-ass." Ryder shook his head. "The man's got a heart bigger than the universe and a temper twice that size. No one and nothing comes between him and his dogs without facing serious consequences."

I swallowed dryly, wondering how this Slater person would receive an outsider. Vetted or not, he didn't sign up for the Guardian program like Ryder and Simon. At least Lex seemed to be on board as he squeezed my shoulder and looked down at me with warm, brown eyes and a sweet smile.

"Don't fret over him and just take anything he says with a grain of salt. He probably won't be back for a bit, so you'll have time to adjust to the three of us before Hurricane Foxx descends upon us."

I realized I was holding my breath, completely overwhelmed by the three handsome strangers as we stood in the warm cedar mudroom room.

Lex noticed. "I'm so sorry, baby. Let's get into the house and give our girl some space before we scare the poor thing. I bet she'd love to see her new room and Hobo's hutch."

"Shall do, Boss. When's dinner going to be ready? I saw the smoke signals from the mountain."

"Give it about thirty minutes."

"What are you roasting? A moose?"

"Very funny. You know that cooking straight from the hearth takes much longer if we want it to come out well. Complaints?"

"I'm no dummy. I won't mess with perfection, and that starts with your chow."

"Smart man. Jennifer? Go with Ryder to your room. There's time for a bubble bath if you wish."

"That sounds heavenly. Thank you."

"Let me know if you need help. I'm really good at scrubbing backs. Ow!" Simon volunteered.

"Show some manners," Lex ordered after popping his friend on the back of his head.

"This place is amazing," I said, twirling around.

"Those rooms belong to Slater and me," he pointed to a hallway. "Lex and Simon are down there. The entrance to the guest level is through those doors. We've got six extra rooms for when family comes to visit."

Ryder chuckled as he led me through the beautiful, spacious house. He paused before a spiral staircase that was partially surrounded by a curved wall and multiple vertical windows.

"We all agreed that you should have the best view from the lodge and, since you're our princess, you deserve to live in a tower."

"I might be a royal pain in the ass, but I'm no princess."

"We'll see about that," Ryder chuckled. "Ladies first."

"This is mine?" I asked after ascending the stairs and walking into an enormous, circular room with curved bay windows on every wall. A white wood-burning stove set on light brown bricks flickered with orange flames from the far end of the room. The color scheme matched that of the downstairs with honey-colored wooden floors, thick throw rugs, and raw cedar ceilings. The furnishings were white-washed with pale beige and gold upholstery. Filmy, white curtains were held by gold tie backs and the four-poster bed was covered with thick down comforters and large fluffy pillows trimmed in gold.

It was a room fit for royalty.

"Every bit of it. Here's your bathroom. Simon put all this in himself."

'This' consisted of white and camel marbled countertops with brass bowled sinks; a large jetted tub surrounded by a multi-level cedar deck; and a rain shower with environmental control. From the cedar ceiling hung an elegant brass and crystal chandelier that twinkled with tiny white lights. Ryder opened another set of doors that led into a walk-in cedar closet filled with clothes.

"How in the world did you manage this in just one day?" I choked out, overwhelmed by the beauty.

He looked incredibly pleased with himself. "We had the room ready for a ward about a year ago. The moment we were told of your arrival, I contacted a personal shopper with your information and received all of this the following day."

I shook my head and touched the soft leather of a turquoise blue jacket. "I don't know what to say. Ryder? How I can thank you enough for all you guys have done? Please tell me what I can do to show my appreciation."

He cupped my cheek in one of his big hands. "The best thanks would be to see you make the most of the program and fulfill your dreams."

"You've already said something like that. What else?"

"When the time is right, let your guard down. I know you've been hurt and you're scared, but you don't have to stay that way." He took both of my hands in his. "We all want the same thing as you do. Happiness and love. Each of us has something special to offer you, including the commitment of our friendship and the desire of a permanent arrangement."

"I don't even know where to begin. I'm out of my element."

"Give yourself some time to know each of us as individuals as well as a group. It's going to be strange as you discover your place in our family, but we're here for you. Years ago, we were in your shoes and had to learn what made each other click and how to bring out the best in who we are. We did that by serving in the military where we fought together, bled on each other, and spent plenty of nights beating ourselves up for the stupid decisions we've made in the past when we were too arrogant to seek accountability."

"How long have you known each other?"

"Over ten years." Ryder chuckled. "We were specialists in Force Recon and sent on a vanity mission which guaranteed that one, or all of us, would die. Simon and I met Lex after being shoved into a cattle car. We were scared and angry, but determined to live to show headquarters never to use us as decoys again. We vowed to watch each other's backs for the rest of our lives and never let anyone, or anything, come between us."

"What about Slater?"

"He joined us about a week into the mission as a civilian. With his bare hands, he put down an entire enemy camp and saved our lives without even knowing our names. Once we were out of danger, our promise was shared with him. He grumbled about it, but we haven't been able to get rid of him since. We haven't been separated from then on."

"Put down as in killed?"

"It was them or us. If he had let them survive, they would have shot us in the back the second they lifted their guns."

I didn't know how to respond. Killing was murder. I need to change the subject. "How did you manage to stay together?"

Ryder winked. "Intel Officers have ways of getting things done. Lex is the best computer geek in the nation and the Corps wanted him to extend his commission and complete a valuable project he had started. Between you and me, I think Lex planned this all along—he negotiated an unbreakable contract that would transfer to DoD once the period of fulfillment was up. By the time he finished negotiations, Lex was promoted to major and commanded an untouchable

Recon team. He also got each of us huge pay raises and other perks like school, housing allowances, and so on."

"So, he picked Simon and you. What about Slater?"

"Slater is—" He paused. "Intense. He doesn't always play well with others, but none of us would be alive if not for him. As Lena mentioned earlier, the only way he could love us more was if we all had four legs, were covered with fur, and drooled."

"Are you saying that if I want his attention, I need to be a bitch?"

Ryder snickered. "As long as it's not the kind of bitch he's had to deal with in the past. Are you hungry? I'm famished and am about to turn into a grizzly bear."

"I thought Daddy Doms were more like Teddy-Bears."

"That's Simon."

"I have a question." I stopped him before we went downstairs. "Am I supposed to call all of you 'daddy' like Lena does?"

"That term of endearment is earned, not demanded. I know Lex and myself would be thrilled to death. Simon doesn't care about a title as long as he gets to play. Slater? He's, well, Slater."

"It doesn't sound like he would want me here."

A flash of sadness crossed Ryder's face. "Slater moves at his own pace in his own time. He's been hurt. Badly hurt. The three of us know what's best for him, but until he accepts that, he's going to fight us. In a way, it's good that you have time to settle in before he arrives."

"Is there anything I can do to encourage him to come to know me?"

"Be yourself and try not to take anything he says personally. He's a great guy and a vital part of our family, but tact isn't his forte. He's also my closest friend and I'd give anything to see him be happy. There's a good chance you might be exactly what he needs."

"I'll help however I can. I promise."

"Thank you, sweetheart. Let's go eat."

Chapter Six
(Ryder)
∞ ∞ ∞

I smiled as Lex and Simon fawned over Jenn to ensure she was warm, comfortable and well-fed. I imagine that all the positive attention was somewhat unnerving for the girl, but I had to admit that she was a good sport and behaved much better than any of us would have in the same circumstance. I could also tell that she was extremely good with masking her feelings. The years of being forced to disguise her pain and fear were ingrained in her, and that needed to be fixed before she imploded.

She sat quietly as Simon fed her Lex's 'fireside special' of fire-roasted duck, baked potatoes, and caramel apple dump cake. A smile only crossed her face when the giant, black Newfoundland nuzzled her leg while begging for food.

"How are you holding up, sweetheart?" I asked, sitting on the couch and wrapping my left arm around her as I stole a piece of cake from her plate.

"I feel like I'm walking in a dream that I won't wake up from."

"A good dream or a bad dream?"

She popped a piece of cake into my mouth and allowed me to pull her closer.

"A bad dream," she answered quietly.

"Is it me? Am I chasing you away? I'm sorry."

"No, Ryder. It's not anything that you've done. I'm just afraid to wake up and find that it's all gone."

"We're not going to abandon you, baby. I promise that you'll never be alone, even if we are called away to work. If it's a team thing, you will go with us, or we'll refuse."

"What if something happens to you?"

"You'll always be loved and cared for. You don't have just this family, but an entire town to take care of you. Lex also promised us that he wouldn't accept any more dangerous missions once we had someone worth coming home to."

"You belong to us now, Jenniebean. You don't have to worry about anything ever again," Simon piped in.

"Please don't be afraid to talk with us about anything. We're listening, and none of us will judge you."

"Are you going back to playing our unit psychologist, Dr. Becker?" I asked.

"I do what I do best, Mr. Watkins."

"Are you really a psychologist?" Jenn asked.

"I am. We're all multi-faceted which is why we're so good for you. At least one of us can help you in whatever direction you want to pursue. Speaking of which, I'm issuing a direction for you right now, and that's to bed. You've had a very long day and need to get some sleep."

"But I'm not tired."

"I don't believe that's a factor, my dear. We have a rigorous regimen here because of limited daylight hours and will get you on a routine with us right away. Simon? Go make our girl a bubble bath and lay out her pajamas. Ryder? Prep your potion to help her sleep. Hop to it, gentlemen." Lex clapped his hands twice.

"I see where this is going. Now that we have a pretty young lady in the house, you're grabbing the chance to be bossy," I teased.

"The Den Mother doesn't need a reason to be bossy. It's as natural as breathing for him," Simon added. "Ow!"

"Smacking you upside the head is as natural as breathing for me, too. Move it."

I chuckled as Simon left the room. "You'd think he'd know better than to talk back after all these years."

"I'd say the same about you. Jennifer? If you'll please excuse me for a moment. I need to run a parameter check before I close up for the night. I'll be up to say good-night when you're ready for bed."

"Okay, thanks."

I helped the girl to her feet and led her by the hand to the kitchen. "Stand by me while I make your potion."

"What is it?"

"It's just a mix of warm milk, honey, cinnamon, butter and an infusion of chamomile. It's the only thing that works to help Slater sleep when he's home." I poured the ingredients in a saucepan. "I know it's easy to say, but try not to let the thought of Slater get on your nerves. I promise that once you get to know him, you'll love him to death."

"He's killed people, Ryder. With his bare hands!"

I sighed as I stirred the milk. "Please don't condemn us for doing our jobs. None of us have ever taken any delight in hurting anyone. I can't tell you how many tears I've shed over the years because of it. Slater's suffered the most. He's had to look his opponents in the eye before taking them out."

Jenn was quiet for a moment. "Is Lex really in charge of this house?"

"He's our commander, and we follow his orders. He's the brains of this operation, and we trust him to keep a level head no matter what occurs. He's the one to go to when you have a problem making a decision. Taste." I held up a spoon to her mouth.

"That's delicious."

"I can make it more delicious with a splash of rum, but I don't think Daddy Lex would approve," I said with a chuckle.

"We can let Daddy Lex know I'm an adult and can have a drink if I want. We could also not tell him."

"That's not how things operate in our home. We hide nothing, and we don't lie to each other. Trust is the foundation of this family and something none of us would betray. We know that this way of life is new for you, and we're going to help you with the transition as best as we can, but we are also very serious about maintaining discipline." I looked at her straight in the eye. "Were you briefed about what to expect?"

"A little bit. I was told that every household functions differently."

I handed her a mug filled with my potion. "Let's get you into bed and then we'll give you a run-down."

"I thought I was going to get to have a bubble bath? Didn't Simon go upstairs to make me one?"

"Silly me." I chuckled, starting toward the stairs. "I'd never deprive my girl of her time floating in the clouds. I should warn you that Simon makes a tub of bubbles like nobody's business."

"I can't wait to see it."

"It's going to blow your mind. He won't give away his secret, either. Will you, little brother?"

Simon rose from the settee and smiled heartily. "You must be talking about my bubble mountains. She's got a doozy in there. Go on, Jenniebean. Take a look-see."

Jenn entered the bathroom. "Oh, my."

"She's speechless. What did you do?" I asked, looking over our girl's shoulder. I repeated her words. "Oh, my."

"It's pretty awesome, don't you think?" Simon asked proudly as he stood next to a thick mound of bubbles that was a good three feet high.

"I have never seen anything like it," Jenn answered honestly.

"The secret's in the love."

"There's more to this than love," I said, facing my brother. "Give it up. It's not fair that you can give this to her and no one else knows how. What if you go away on an assignment? Should she be deprived of her bubbles for months on end?"

"You're going away for months?" Jenn asked, her voice filled with worry.

"Not anymore. The Major said any assignments he sends us on would be short-term and not dangerous. He wants us to pack up our weapons and stay home with our girl."

That was news—good news—for me. I was tired of the jungle, and risking my life to end someone else's fight without so much as a thanks. I've served my time. We all have. Besides, we had Northern Lights, and the community residing in our little town, to protect now.

"This is divine," we heard Jenn purr from the back of the steam-filled room.

"Where are you?"

"In the tub. I wasn't about to wait for either of you to help me get in. Now, if you will please leave and give me some privacy. If you'd lock the door behind you, I'd really appreciate it."

"See what you did? I could have seen her naked. Ow!" Simon grunted as I smacked him on the back of the head.

"Ryder! Don't hit Simon. You were thinking the same thing. Now, out!"

"I'm putting your potion on the side table next to your head. Can you see the red and blue buttons?" I asked, placing the mug on the heating element. "This will keep your drink hot or cold. Just press whichever one you want."

"That's awesome. Did you design this too, Simon?"

"Yeah." I heard him answer from the other room. He sounded upset.

"It's absolutely brilliant. You knew exactly what I dreamt would be the best bubble bath ever. Thank you."

"You really like it?" His voice brightened.

"I love it. Including the rose petals. Ryder, out now, and don't forget to lock the door."

I pinched her cheek gently. "I see what you're up to, you little minx. It won't work."

"What are you talking about?"

"Pft, I wasn't born yesterday."

"Oh, I know." She broke into a giggle. "You're old enough to be my daddy."

"Not likely, little one, but that doesn't stop me from being your daddy anyway. Do you like that idea?" I asked, sitting on the dressing stool.

"I might. Does being my daddy mean I get spoiled?"

"Absolutely. You'll also get lots of loving."

"Hmm. I like that." She reached for my hand and squeezed. "Thank you for taking me in. You guys saved me from the pits of hell."

"When you're ready, I want to sit down with you and get as many details as possible so we can go after those animals."

"I took the passports and IDs of nearly all the guests that were on the floor when I left. I'm sure they're fake, but they do have photos. I'm hoping that will help."

"Did Mr. Graye tell you to do that?"

"No, I thought of it myself. I also stole a phone that eventually got floated down-river in a zippy bag in case they were tracing it and tossed every car key I could find in right after."

"I have a strong feeling that you are going to fit into our unit perfectly. Do you play chess?"

"I've never learned."

"I suspect you'll do very well. We have tournaments in town every Saturday after our BBQ when the weather's clear. I'll teach you to play."

"That's sound like fun."

"I'll even give you an incentive."

"What kind of incentive?" Her voice dropped to a lower register.

"What kind would you like?"

"Being that you've given me everything I could ever hope for, let's be more practical. Brush my hair, a massage, paint my nails- girly things."

"Who said I wouldn't do any of that anyway?"

"I'd feel less guilty if I won them from you."

"You wouldn't have to reciprocate, you know."

"What if I wanted to?"

I was elated! At least I wasn't the only one feeling an instant sexual attraction to the beautiful woman, but it was too soon, and I didn't want to take advantage of her vulnerability.

"As much as I'd love that to happen, I don't want you to do anything you would regret. You just met me."

"Are you worried about my honor, Mr. Watkins?"

"No, I'm concerned that I won't be the kind of Daddy that you deserve straight from the get-go. There will be plenty of time for grown-up stuff if you want it." I kissed her palm. "Finish your bath. Today's the first day of the rest of your life, and I want you to enjoy it."

She squeezed my fingers as she leaned back against the tub. I couldn't see her through the bubbles, but I could tell she was smiling.

****

"Is everything all right?" Simon asked as I exited the bathroom and locked the door behind me.

"She's an incredible girl. Get this." I shared with him the details of her escape before meeting up with Dorian Graye's people and the diversions.

"She came up with that all on her own? Impressive. Does she play chess?"

"Not yet, but I'm going to teach her. If she can get up to the master level, she can join the town's planning committee. It would be great to have a woman involved as a voice."

Simon chuckled. "I can see it now. Excuse me, Mr. Watkins? Does this little girl belong to you? She just told the entire commission to go jerk off because we're too old and set in our ways to listen to the idea of a youngster with no life experience."

I laughed and played along. "Well, Mr. Commissioner, Sir—since you're the one who uses the chess tournaments to decide those with the greatest strategic foresight, then you'll have to accept that she's here on your terms."

"Cheat? How could she cheat? You supervise the tourneys. You know what? Pull out your set and let's have a showdown right here and now. An old, grumpy Admiral against a young, fresh-faced civilian."

"She'll so kick his ass," I said, plopping on the bed.

"In our dreams. I love the guy outside the tactics room, but when he's in his high and mighty commander mode, I want to hurt him."

"Yet he and Slater get along like old school chums." I grunted. "I'll be back in a bit. I need to feed Mollypup and then let her out."

"She needs a good romp in the pool, too. We don't wear her down as Slater does and she's getting antsy." Simon leaned into me and whispered. "I caught her chewing on Lex's boot this morning."

"Oh, shit. How did she get hold of it? He's meticulous about putting his stuff away."

"She's learned how to open closets. She's still a puppy and needs attention. She probably felt a change happening with bringing Jennie home."

"I'll take care of her. Keep your ear out in case our girl needs something. See you in a bit. Oh, and Simon? Hide the boots. If he finds out, we might be having Molly Casserole."

"Already done. This is between bros."

I eyed him. "You left the door to his room open for her, didn't you?"

"Why would I do that?"

"I know you. You pulled that shit on Dad every time you got pissed at him. You knew Mom's stupid cat would take a dump in his office chair."

"You're getting old. You're the one who did that. I switched the hot and cold water in his shower and rewired his television so he couldn't get his favorite channels."

"Okay, you got me there. Then how did she get in Lex's room?"

"Maybe he just left his boots in the hallway outside of the mudroom." Simon shrugged.

"He's going to have your head for this, you moron."

"He'll have to find out, first. I'm not going to say anything. Are you?"

"Never. He'll find out eventually, though. He's got a nose like a bloodhound, and the only one who's been able to pull anything on him has been Slater."

"Too bad he's not here. We could blame him." Simon snickered.

"We'd both have our necks in a noose for that. We'll worry about it if and when the time comes. Meanwhile, Lex should be distracted by our girl for a bit."

"He should. She's already got him wrapped around her finger, and she doesn't even know it."

"She's going to be good for all of us. You'll see," I promised.

Chapter Seven
(Jennie)
∞ ∞ ∞

I sunk under the thick bubbles and sighed as the hot water covered my body in a delicious embrace. It was the first time I had been alone long enough to process the last couple of days and the houseful of handsome men that were now part of my life. I smiled as I heard Simon and Ryder talking outside the door about Molly eating Lex's boot. They sounded like two little boys plotting together to get out of trouble with their dad. It was beyond cute and showed me the depth of the family and the love they shared.

Simon's laughter filled the room. He was the youngest of the group and, by far, the largest. He reminded me of a happy lumberjack with a contagious smile that never left his face. Like his brother, he had dark blue eyes and short light brown hair. There was a strong sense of tenderness and caring about him, so the discovery of his military specialty shocked me. He was a trained killer—a sniper who shot people from an unseen perch. Call me the worse Texan on the planet, but I've never been comfortable around guns or the people who used them. I also couldn't shake the curiosity of what it would feel like to be held in his massive arms and feel his lips against mine.

Then there was Dr. Lexington Becker—the eldest, and clearly, the most cultured of the group. He was tall and lean, with rich brown eyes and some premature gray in the dark brown hair of his temples. His 'hot geek' look was darling, especially when he slipped off his silver wire-rimmed glasses and chewed thoughtfully on the end of one of the earpieces. I honestly wasn't surprised when he admitted to being a psychologist, especially after seeing him direct his 'boys' and enforce decisions. It was as easy to picture him as 'Daddy Lex' as it was to imagine the feel of his hands over my flesh.

Thirdly, Ryder. *My Ryder.* My lips twitched as I recalled our initial meeting. He was breathtaking, with piercing deep blue eyes and a smile that made my knees wobble. Resting my cheek against his broad back while snowmobiling through town left me feeling safe, and the frequent squeezes he gave my hands reassured me. Underneath his sweet exterior, there was a hint of a bad boy that I found incredibly sexy. *How would he feel inside of me? Would he take me from behind and fuck me like an animal or would he be slow and gentle?*

I frowned. *What was wrong with me?* After all the abuse I've experienced, I quickly learned to hate sex. Hell, I've never really been kissed other than the gross, sloppy attempts while being groped at like a plastic doll. I wish I could say they were all cruel and inhumane, but they weren't. They were just incompetent, drunk, and clumsy. Those who had hurt me lost any privileges to use my body, but that didn't erase the memories.

"You're going to get all pruney in there, Jenniebean," Simon called from the other side of the door. "It's time to get out."

"I don't want to, yet. You made the perfect bath," I called back, sinking deeper into the tub.

"I'll make you another one tomorrow night. Come, now. You don't want me to have to come in there and fish you out."

"You wouldn't dare," I said with a snort. "Hey! How did you get the door open?"

"I designed it, remember." Simon flashed a mischievous smile and yanked a big towel off the rack. "Need some help?"

"No, thank you. Are you pouting?"

"Maybe just a little. Does that mean you'll let me help?" he asked eagerly.

"No. Turn your back or get out of here."

"Do I have to?"

"If you don't, I'm telling Lex."

"That's cold, little girl. Where did you learn to be so mean?"

"It's called survival."

"You're sassy."

"I suspect that you like that characteristic. Turn around!"

"What's going on in here?" Lex's voice asked from the doorway. I sunk deeper under the bubbles. It wasn't that I was shy about my body—modesty had been stripped from me long ago—but I didn't want these guys to form the wrong opinion of me.

"I was just trying to get our little fishy out of her bowl."

"Jennifer?"

"I just wanted some privacy as I got out of the tub. The word *no* seems to be foreign to him."

"Ow! Stop doing that," Simon complained as he, once again, was popped in the back on the head.

"Let the girl have some space. We'll be out here waiting, sweetheart."

"I need something to wear," I said after he closed the door.

"Go into the closet. I put some jammies on the center table for you," Simon advised.

I chuckled as Lex scolded Simon about his manners. Another voice, Ryder, joined in. A wave of guilt hit me hard as I heard the defeat in Simon's voice. This was my fault.

"Excuse me." I stuck my head through the doorway. "Simon? I can't find a robe, and I'm cold. Would you help me?"

Like a bulldozer, he shoved his brother and Lex out of the way and happily entered the bathroom. He then froze when he saw I was only wearing a towel.

"You're naked."

"All of us are naked when we aren't covered in something. I'm sorry I got you into trouble. That wasn't my intent."

"I'm always getting hollered out. I—holy shit," he gulped when I dropped the towel and walked into the dressing room.

"You said you wanted to help. So help."

I loved the way he looked at me! In the past, the men who've lusted after my body left me feeling dirty and repulsive, but not Simon. I felt like a piece of art in his eyes.

"You're beautiful," he whispered.

"I'm also very cold. Did you put a heater in this room?" I asked, squeezing the water out of my long, dark hair with the towel. He nodded mutely and flipped on a switch. His brazenness suddenly turned to bashfulness. It was not only as cute as hell, but it gave me a sense of power that I've never had.

"I, uh, the stuff's there," he stuttered, pointing to the accessories table and averting his eyes.

"What's wrong?" I asked casually, slipping on the soft pink, flannel PJs.

"I need to leave before I do something stupid."

"Wait. I didn't mean to embarrass you." I grabbed his arm. His huge muscles were hard under my hand.

"You didn't. I tend to be spontaneous and more reckless than the other guys, and I don't always think ahead."

I felt my face flush. "I need some spontaneity in my life," I admitted. "My every breathing minute's been dictated for the last two years and—"

His mouth crushed mine in a shockingly powerful kiss that instantly stole my breath. My hands crept to the back of his neck as I opened my lips to him. He tasted like honeysuckle with a touch of rum.

"Simon!" Lex pounded on the door. "Jennifer needs to get to bed. Move it."

He reluctantly pulled away, mumbled an apology, and quickly left the room. I touched the tips of my fingers to my tingling mouth. My legs still felt a bit rubbery as I made my way to the bedroom where the guys waited for me. I couldn't look at any of them in the eye, suddenly feeling remorseful about the stolen kiss. I hadn't even been here for one day and already was causing problems.

Simon didn't behave any differently, though. He jumped on the bed and propped his head on his hand as he flipped down the blankets.

"Beddy-bye, little girl," he said, patting the mattress with a smile.

Lex helped me onto the bed, took off the robe and tucked me under the blankets. He sat on the edge while Ryder eased himself next to his brother.

"Did you like your bath?" Lex asked, slapping Simon's hand as it crept under the sheet.

"It was nice. So was the potion. Thank you."

"You're welcome." Ryder's smile made me tremble. "I told Lex what you and I had discussed so he could lay out the ground rules."

"You already know that I run a tight ship. It's not because I'm a control freak—"

"Bullshit. Ha! Missed me!" Simon snickered, ducking Lex's hand.

"But because that's how things work best for us as a unit and as a family. We each have our specific jobs and responsibilities to ourselves, our home and our community. The motto 'it takes a village' means that we all look out for one another, and every man in this community has vowed to protect the women as though she was his own. There's nothing hidden here, either. That means we keep no secrets from one another."

I glanced at Simon and saw him wink.

"While each of us has different expectations and requests as individuals, there are some general and unified rules. Rule number one—at no time will you put yourself in any dangerous or precarious situation. This is non-negotiable. That includes going anywhere without telling one of us or leaving a note in plain sight, using proper equipment and covering if you go outside, and staying away from any of the areas posted as restricted."

"Restricted areas mark either glacial slides, soft snow, black ice or dangerous animals," Ryder explained. "The Northern Lights wolf pack resides in this area. We installed a double gate system to keep the wolves a safe distance from the lodge, but it's not full proof. There's also a monitoring system that alerts us if anything bypasses the fencing along the parameter."

"Just a word of warning, Jenniebean. The puppies are Slater's pride and joy. We don't go anywhere near them without his okay out of respect and fear for our lives. They're dangerous animals and not ones to be trifled with," Simon added.

I nodded, noticing that the other two didn't even flinch when he used my new nickname.

"Rule number two is respect. I don't expect you to call me 'sir' unless I'm in a position of having to exert my authority. Not all the Doms in the town agree with me, but it's important for you to understand that you don't belong to them. You're ours and ours alone which means our rules come first and foremost, and you are not obligated to obey anyone other than us unless it's a safety issue. Understand?"

I couldn't help myself. "Yes, sir."

"Good girl. Rule three. All four of us are firm believers in two aspects of the lifestyle. The first is domestic discipline. Broken rules will result in consequences, and dispensing discipline is all of our responsibility. I'm the head of the unit, so if you break a house rule in the presence of two or more, we will hold a family tribunal, and I will decide the outcome and be responsible for the execution. I don't enjoy that part of my job, but it's necessary, and I will make certain that I'm thorough enough that you'll think twice before making the same mistake again."

I swallowed dryly as I felt my stomach turn. I didn't doubt for a second that Lex was capable of all he promised. A trickle of healthy fear joined my resolve to not push my boundaries with him. Simon slid his hand under the covers and squeezed my thigh.

"Finally, rule four. Talk to us. We are always available to you and are open to discussing anything that concerns you. If the discussion involves something that you're in disagreement, but that we believe is for the best, we're open to hear you out. That doesn't mean we'll change our minds. In this regard, temper tantrums, name-calling, lying, and other such behaviors won't be tolerated."

"Which now brings up the second part of the lifestyle that we support. Age-play," Ryder said as he rested his warm hand on my leg. "Have you ever engaged in the dynamic?"

I shook my head. "No. It's something I've always been drawn to but have never been in a situation to explore it. When the Grayes interviewed me, Mrs. Graye said I was a Middle."

"That only means that you might have teenage tendencies. We will support, nurture and encourage that part of you in every way we can, but we do have some guidelines that we want you to understand. There's a line we draw between you, as an adult and your age-play persona. This means that we handle situations in an age-appropriate manner."

"What do you mean?"

"We keep the two sides separate. If you approach something as an adult, you'll be treated as an adult.

Likewise, if you're in your Middle, that's how things will be."

"You're not making any sense."

"What my brother is trying to say is that when we're your daddies, you're getting daddies, not lovers. We don't cross the line and have sex unless you're in an adult state of mind."

"Simon!" the other two men spat.

"What? She knows we aren't going to make her do anything she doesn't want to do. She also knows that we want the same thing that she does. We want a wife, and she wants multiple husbands. Am I right?" He looked directly at me.

"Yes," I whispered.

"She's a smart lady. There's no reason to beat around the bush and play guessing games," he added. "She needs to know exactly where she stands right from the beginning so that she feels safe and cared for. I'm going to break the ice and lay down the law. Jenniebean? When I'm not kissing those gorgeous lips, I want you to call me Daddy. Got it?"

My mouth fell open in surprise. I wasn't anticipating him to be so assertive.

"I asked you a question, baby girl."

"Yes, Daddy," I whispered. The words felt good on my lips.

"Good girl. Kiss me good-night."

I bit my lower lip after he gave me a quick kiss on the mouth and left the room. Lex sighed.

"Well, I guess Simon summed everything up for us, didn't he? I think the same request applies to both Ryder and myself. Yes?"

Ryder nodded in agreement. "I know it's awkward, but it will get easier in time."

"It will. Go to sleep, sweet cakes. We'll put together your routine in the morning and then show you around."

"Okay. Good night." I offered a tiny smile as I placed a kiss on his soft lips. The touch sent a shiver of desire through me. "Thank you, Daddy."

His pleased smile reached his beautiful eyes. "You're welcome. Ryder?"

"I'll be down in a bit," he said. After Lex left, he stretched out on the bed next to me. "How are you holding up, darling?"

"I'm not sure. My emotions are all over the place."

"Come here and put your head on my shoulder." He pulled me against him, and I inhaled his scent. It was delicious, and it felt so good to be held. "How did you feel when Simon kissed you?"

"It was sweet," I answered with hesitation.

"I'm not talking about the good night kiss."

"You know?"

"My brother isn't good at hiding his enthusiasm," Ryder said with a chuckle. "His pupils were dilated, and he had a goofy smile on his face. The only time he looks like that is when he's had a real kiss or had a great night of sex. He also had a massive hard-on when he left the bathroom. Well?"

My face grew hot as I looked away. "I'm sorry. It just happened."

"Why would you be sorry? We want you to connect with each of us naturally."

"I don't want to cause problems between any of you."

"If you're worried about jealousy, don't. That beast doesn't live in this house. We're a group package."

"Do you guys ever share, like in, together?"

"As a five-some? Hell, yeah. Singles or multiples, watching or participating, we're okay with whatever role we play at the moment. What we don't do is sneak around." A mischievous smile crossed his face. "Notwithstanding impromptu rendezvous."

I grinned back. "You're bad."

"I confess that I'm the defiant member of the team."

"I don't believe that."

"Yeah, believe it. I'm not proud of it, but Lex says that's one reason I'm so good at what I do. I don't always follow the rules, and certainly never in the order given. It's allowed me to think outside the box."

"Does that mean I can be defiant, too?" I asked in a low voice as I traced the veins in the back of his hand.

"A little, maybe, but be selective in what you chose to challenge."

A black and green curve peeked out from under the cuff of his shirt. "What's this?"

"Our Code of Honor. We all carry the symbol to unify us. We've had a piece added for every mission we've shared."

"May I see it? Please?"

He nodded and stood to remove his shirt. My hands flew over my mouth as I stared at his naked torso, unable to decide what drew my eye the most—his tightly muscled body or the magnificent tattoo that wrapped entirely over his right shoulder and stretched over his arm and along his ribs. I sat on the edge of the bed and reached to touch it.

"What does it mean?"

He took my fingers and ran them from his wrist to the top of his bicep. "This is the sword of truth. It stands for the promise we share never to allow anyone or anything to divide us. The pommel is the Celtic symbol for our brotherhood. We got this after our first mission."

"And this?" I rubbed the pad of my finger to follow the flow of the glimmering green and gold serpent that wrapped its body around the blade.

"Slater fulfilled his promise to his masters to bring his brothers to the temple to meet them. We were prayed over and each given a symbol of protection. I received the snake; Lex was given a panther; Simon—an eagle; and Slater—a wolf. We were blessed, and our brotherhood celebrated." Ryder looked sad as he turned his arm and studied the snake. "This is a bitter-sweet memory for Slater. It marked the end of his old life and the beginning of a new one."

"What happened?"

"That's his story to share if, and when, he wants to. Anyway, after the celebration, we were taken to a room in the temple where four traditional tattoo artists waited. Our protectors were blazed using original bamboo tattoo methods. It took twenty-four hours from start to finish."

"Straight through?" He nodded. "That must have been excruciating!"

"The pain was nothing compared to not being allowed to get up to pee or having to listen to Simon's stomach growl." He chuckled. "He was suffering big time."

I giggled. "I can't imagine how he survived. What about the rest of these?"

"Different places and different events. See this?" He placed my hand over an empty spot on his chest. "This will stay blank until we complete our largest, and most important, mission. It's saved for our future wife."

I looked up into his eyes as he pulled me to my feet. His kiss was soft and gentle, but I sensed something was wrong. I pulled back and looked at him with confusion.

"Ryder?"

"I'm sorry. I'm so sorry." He shook his head and stepped back while quickly pulling on his shirt.

"Ryder! What did I do?"

"Nothing. You did nothing. I—" He stopped at the French doors and grabbed the frame with his back toward me.

"You what? Oh!" I gasped as he rushed back and slammed his mouth against mine. He lifted me in a hungry embrace, kissing me with a passion that I've never experienced. When he broke away, he was breathless.

"This isn't like me. Simon's the spontaneous one. I'm so—"

I placed my fingers on his mouth as he lowered me to my feet. "Don't. Please. This isn't like me, either, but I'm not going to apologize for how my body responds. I feel something with you that I've not felt before."

"What about Simon?"

I glanced down and nodded shamefully. "Him, too. I even felt a tingle with Lex. I don't understand any of this myself. I didn't think I could feel desire for anyone after what I've been through." I sat heavily on the bed and studied my hands. "I'm not a whore. I've never given myself away to anyone. You guys gave me hope that there was a chance I could be loved for even a single day. Don't ever apologize for that."

"Do you really feel something with us?"

"Yes. Is that horrible of me? I just met you."

His eyes glazed and he knelt on the floor to take my hands. "Horrible? Dear Lord, no. If the chemistry is there, then it's a dream come true. I'm so afraid of scaring you. The four of us have faced death too many times to waste time on trivial matters or playing games. That's one reason Simon and I signed up for the program. We knew that we needed someone who thought the same way we do. We want to date and romance you, to fall in love, to plan a future together, and we know that will take time. But other things, like sharing our needs, isn't something we take lightly even if it happens spontaneously. Am I making any sense?"

I squeezed his hands back. "I don't scare easily. As long as I know your motives and I know the rules, I'll be okay. I don't do well with guessing games and, to be honest, patience isn't my forte. I've lost over two years of my life because I was impatient and it doesn't seem to have changed me at all."

He kissed my knuckles. "Nothing's been lost. You've just become wiser and more discerning. There's nothing wrong with that. I'm glad you're here. Get some sleep before the old man has a fit, okay?"

"Why do you call him that? He can't be much older than the rest of you."

"Lex has an old soul. He's thirty-seven. Simon's thirty-three and the baby of the group. Slater and I are both thirty-four. We even share the same birthday."

"I guess I'm the baby of the group now. I'm twenty-two."

"You're going to love being our baby. I promise that we'll erase everything bad that's ever happened. If you need me, my room is down the stairs and the second door on the right. Good night, sweetheart."

"Good night, Ryder."

"Call me Daddy."

I smiled. "Good night, Daddy. Sleep well. May I have one more kiss?"

At that moment I knew I could stay locked to his lips for the rest of my life.

(Ryder)
∞ ∞ ∞

"Does it ever stop snowing? It's been over a week!" Jenn asked, pointing at the window.

"Mother Nature's making sure we have plenty of time to get to know each other. If you're bored, we can go work out or something," Lex suggested as he looked up from his computer.

"I'm not bored. I'm intrigued. Can we go outside?"

"Not when it's like this. We even put Molly on a long lead so she doesn't get lost. Do you want some more hot chocolate?" I whispered in her ear.

She wiggled closer to my chest and gave me a quick kiss on the lips as she twisted to look at me. "Can I have some Kalua in it?"

"No, you may not," Lex answered quickly.

"How did he hear that? I barely whispered."

"He hears everything he's not supposed to," I whispered back. "He probably has one of those surveillance mics pointed at us or something."

"Or something," Lex muttered under his breath.

"You're a party pooper. I have an idea. Let's play strip poker!"

"Simon!"

The girl giggled. "You guys don't have to yell at him every time he speaks without editing. I've heard much worse. Plus, he's kind of funny. I like that you make me laugh, Simon."

I rolled my eyes as a huge smile lit my brother's face. The big, old sap was already falling in love!

"I don't approve."

"I don't think it's really up to you, Lex," Jenn spoke gently. "Isn't it about whether or not I'm the one who's offended? I promise that if I'm uncomfortable, I'll say something directly to Simon when we're alone. Is that okay?"

"That's a reasonable argument, Major. Give her this," I added.

"Very well. I want you to see the best part of us." Lex looked abashed. Jenn wiggled off my lap and planted herself on Lex's knee where she delivered a quick kiss and a big hug.

"Seeing you as you are is the best of you. Thank you for watching out for me."

I raised my eyebrow and winked at Simon as we watched the two share a long kiss. I frowned and shook my head as Simon pointed to his crotch. *Moron*.

"I'd like some love today, too," Simon said after a few minutes of silence.

Jenn grinned and walked over to him, glancing over her shoulder with a hint of pride that she left Lex with a raging hard-on. *Brat*. Placing her hands on her hips, she let her eyes rove over Simon's powerful body.

"What kind of love do you want?"

"I thought you'd never ask," he said, snatching her up and cradling her head in his hand so he could plant a big kiss on her sweet lips. Jenn wasn't satisfied and quickly straddled his lap and held his face in her hands.

I leaned back on the floor next to the crackling fire and watched her kiss my brother into a state of silence. When she was done with him, she slithered off his lap and returned to me.

"What are you doing, young lady?" I asked with amusement.

"Me? Nothing. I'm just curious to see if he can walk with that boner," she said, pointing at Simon.

"Jennifer!" Lex and I said at once.

"What?"

"I think there's a little bit of a Middle showing her face on this lovely morning," I said with a firm hug. "How would you like to hang out with me today? I have a bunch of things I need to work on for the campout next month."

"Is there something you forgot to tell us, Mr. Watkins?" Lex asked.

"Yes, Sir. It's for White Ice Night. The town's going to have an igloo building contest this year, and I want to design something that the girls will go nuts over."

"Why the girls?" Jenn asked.

"The ladies are Ice Princesses for the whole weekend, and we cater to their every whim."

"That sounds like fun!"

"It is. The weather's supposed to be perfect, too. It's the peak of the season to watch the sky dancers."

"Huh?"

"The Northern Lights," I explained.

"Are we going to have a fishing contest, too?" Simon asked.

"You're not interested in the contest; you just want the fish. It's always about food."

"So, what? Molly likes bacon, but you don't pick on her."

"She's a dog, Simon."

"What exactly is White Ice Night?"

"WIN is the celebration of when Northern Lights was granted sovereignty under a tribal government," Lex explained. "The Markford brothers are blood members of the Athabaskan tribe and, with the help of the tribal elders and some very influential politicians, lawyers, and historians, Northern Lights was granted a permanent place under the Athabaskan nation as *Yoyekoyh*."

"It also falls on Christmas Eve, so the town spends three whole days together and celebrates," Simon added.

"I haven't had a holiday since I left Texas." Her voice dropped.

"I think we need to make a special Christmas for our girl, gentlemen. Any suggestions?" Lex suggested.

"It'll be a blast! Can we do everything homemade?" Simon looked like he was about to jump out of his chair with excitement. "Please?"

"When we were growing up, our folks insisted on keeping Christmas humble and family focused," I explained. "Everything involved was done by hand. Mom made us cookies, Dad carved toys, and we—"

"Almost had Christmas canceled on many occasions. Ryder made bombs, and I shot wild turkeys."

"And the head off the neighbor's garden trolls."

Jenn started to laugh. "You two must have been hell in a handbag for your parents."

"Yeah, and yet they still miss us."

"His father wished me luck after handing them over to me." Lex groaned. "I was the perfect child. Quiet, scholarly, and never got into any trouble."

"You lie like a dog," Simon snorted. "How many times did Homeland Security show up on your doorstep after you hacked into government computer systems?"

"I was exploring my potential," Lex insisted.

"How old were you?"

"Thirteen. I looked at coding like a video game. Dad started entering me in video wars to keep me from being tossed into geek jail. That backfired, though. I not only won, but I was able to break into the guts of the games. After I sold my first virtual reality program, the government decided it was better to use me on their team than to fight against me."

"No way!"

"Yep. I got a pretty pocketful of change plus royalties, a full scholarship and all the hardware I would ever want."

"Except a cybernetic girlfriend," Simon snickered.

"I didn't need a cybernetic girlfriend. I had plenty of real ones, thank you. My problem was they were too immature, lacked in the brain department, and didn't like the fact that I'd blister their backsides if they got mouthy with me."

"You didn't really do that to your girlfriends, did you?" Jenn's mouth fell open.

"We all did. There's something wired in us to be that way. Poor Slater suffered the most in that department because he wasn't released from his training until later and had no experience with women until he met us."

"Ryder popped his cherry."

"Simon!"

"I'm not even going to ask what that was supposed to mean." Jenn hid her face in her hands.

"I was dating this gal who wanted a threesome, so I coerced old Slater to join in. He took to it like a fish to water. He insisted it was his *Chi* that made him such a great lover. He didn't know that the girl wanted to explore D&S, so she started to provoke him. He naturally took control. The poor girl was never rude to him again."

Jenn bit her lip. "Was that a veiled warning not to cross Slater's path?"

"There's nothing veiled about it. He has power behind his swing that none of us can match. Remember that time when we were pestering him about the things he learned in his training, Lex?" I asked.

Closing his laptop, the Major walked over to join us on the floor. He leaned his back against the couch and played with a strand of Jenn's hair.

"We were hanging out around headquarters for the debriefing following our first mission. Slater was pissed. As a civilian, he was recruited to the unit through some unique channels, and we were trying to get information about him. He was very private and reserved, and the only thing obvious was that the dude had superhuman strength and could order Chinese food in Mandarin."

"I assumed he was an MMA fighter," Simon added.

"Your guess was the closest to the truth. He finally admitted that he was branded by the Shaolin's as a warrior, which opened up the door for us to tease him about having our very own Kung-Fu Panda."

"In all fairness, we didn't even know the order still existed other than for tourism, but some of them escaped the government's influence and continued to teach in the old ways," I added.

"Slater's a monk?"

Lex shook his head. "Not in the spiritual sense. He was made for something outside the temple, and his masters knew it. He was pushed harder than the others because of his temper, and it shamed him. The man's a strange mix of humility and pride, tenderness and indifference, and love and apathy. The three of us were insensitive boneheads, and at an age where seeing was believing, so we harassed him like most guys would in any normal situation. Keep in mind; we didn't witness what he did to the enemy soldiers who captured us, so we had nothing to weigh his words against."

"Lex has a way of winding people up if he wants to, and he found a nerve that he started to poke," Simon said.

"It was the dumbest thing I've ever done in my life." Lex sighed. "I started taunting him to show us his kung-fu moves. It was a case of stereotyping coupled with stupidity. By looking at him, you'd never put Slater in the category of a warrior monk. He's too tall, muscular and intense."

"He looks more like my brother than the twerp does." I gestured to Simon, who shot me the finger.

"What happened?" Jenn asked.

Lex continued. "Slater asked me very politely to stop."

"Twice," I added.

"Twice," Lex nodded. "On the third time, he shouted to cut it out and brought his hand down on the cement picnic table. I swear to God that the damn thing cracked right through the middle."

"He was so angry with himself that he left. We didn't hear from him for two weeks. He only came back because his masters told him that he had to return and show humility to his new brothers after losing his temper."

The room grew quiet for a moment as the big Newfoundland pushed herself between Lex and me and whined. "I miss the jerk. So does Molly."

"Yeah, so do I," Lex added. "Slater adds something to our team. I'm starting to feel guilty for sending him away."

"He screwed up, Major. His temper's going to hurt the wrong person one of these days, especially if I'm not there to calm him down."

"He sounds like the Incredible Hulk," Jenn commented.

"In a weird way, he is, and I'm Thor."

"No, you're Batman. I'm Thor and Lex is Ironman," Simon announced.

"You guys are dorks," Jenn giggled. "Hey, no tickling!"

I poked another finger in her side and made her squeal. "Like this?"

"Or this?" Lex asked, pinning her to the floor and attacking her ribs.

Simon stuck his face over hers and planted a big kiss. "Jenniebean! Can you cook?"

"Stop! I can't breathe," she begged. "Does macaroni and cheese count?"

"If it's food, and has bacon, it counts."

At the sound of the word *bacon*, Molly joined us and looked down into Jenn's face. I couldn't resist.

"Molly! Give kisses."

"No! Yuck! Gross! This is disgusting. Dog breath! Daddy, save me!" she squealed as the dog plopped down on the floor and held the girl's head between her paws while she groomed her with her big tongue.

"I got you," Lex said with a laugh as he pulled her onto his lap and used his shirt to wipe her face. "You look like a wet chicken."

"Payback, Ryder. You just wait," she threatened me.

"You're cute when you're mad."

"Pft. You haven't seen me mad yet. Why did Simon want to know if I cooked?"

"He lives to eat and always wants something new. Unfortunately, his cooking is limited to boiling water and opening MREs. Slater is vegan and stays raw when he can. I'm pretty good with breakfast, but Lex is our gourmet chef—especially over an open flame."

"That reminds me; we need to take a basket over to Lena. She promised me a man-sized jar of persimmon jam for fixing her dollhouse," Simon said, smacking his lips.

"I also promised her one of Lex's *Come Hither* cakes if she was good for her daddies."

Jenn was smiling again. "Did you still want me to hang out with you? I'm up for anything, especially if it means getting outside for a bit. When are we leaving?"

"We can't go anywhere until this blizzard clears. Lex? What does the monitor show?"

Lex hopped to his feet and went back to the computer. "The station's predicting a cease-fire sometime tonight, but there's another front coming in right after. If it's clear in the morning, you can go out, but no dawdling."

"Yes, Dad," I groaned, rolling my eyes. "Since you're going to bake that cake for Lena, you can make some extras for us, right?"

"If you ask nicely."

"Daddy? Will you bake me a cake. Please?" Jenn blinked her pretty turquoise eyes as she sidled onto his lap.

"Do you really want a cake?"

"I love cake. I love kisses, too." She pressed her mouth to his and pulled him against her. Lex's face was flushed when he broke for air.

"I've never had anyone who loved to kiss the way you do." He stroked her cheek affectionately.

"I've never been kissed until I came here. I swear I could do it all day."

"Well, you have plenty of lips who'll take you up on your offer. Did you want to help me bake?"

"Yes! Can I lick the bowl?"

"Of course."

"No way! That's my job!" Simon protested, following them into the kitchen.

****

"Tired?" I asked on our way out of town. "You had a long day."

"Too many people and names and things to see. I'm cranky, hungry and cold."

"We'll get you into a hot bath and feed you; then you can go to bed."

"Just because I'm worn out doesn't mean I need to go to bed. I just need some down time."

"It's a different environment, and it's important to establish a sleep schedule. Simon rigged the house to follow normal day and night hours year-round using artificial sunlight and window filters. Sleeping's an art in itself in this part of the world, and it's vital to survival here."

"I'm not going to be put to bed every time someone sees me yawn."

"You'll go to bed when you're told to go to bed." I felt her loosen her hold around my waist. She was getting angry. "Save your stubbornness for some other time, okay? You need to trust us to steer you in the right direction. You're not accustomed to this environment."

She didn't respond, but I could sense that she was a ticking bomb by the time we arrived home. Lex was waiting in the mudroom and frowned as Jenn stomped silently passed him after throwing her helmet, jacket, and boots on the floor.

"What happened?"

"Nothing significant. She's just throwing a tantrum about bedtime."

"That didn't take long." Lex picked up the gear and put it up to dry. "How do you want to handle it?"

"Let it go for now. Her body will start to rebel against her attitude in another few days."

"Yes, but she's been here over a week, and it's already messing with her circadian rhythms. She's under a tremendous amount of stress due to all the changes she's gone through, and a lack of sleep is asking for more problems."

"You're preaching to the choir. Let's have Simon increase the light intensity in the morning and see if she adjusts naturally."

"Okay. Are you hungry? Dinner's almost ready."

"Thanks. Let me get changed and I'll join you." I started toward my room when Slater called me on my cell phone.

"What's wrong? You sound upset," he asked.

I sunk into my favorite chair and shared the situation with him. Before he could say anything, I added "I know it takes time to adjust. We need to give it to her."

"She's been there long enough to see how things run in the house. Hear me out. If a wolf bites because it's hurt or afraid, you allow it time to adjust. But, if it bites because it doesn't want to be led, then the alpha needs to enforce his position."

"She's not a wolf, Slate. She's a scared little girl who doesn't know which way to turn."

"I told you the motto of my masters years ago. Do you remember what it was?"

I wrinkled my brow. "*In defense, like a virgin; in attack, like a tiger.* So?"

"I've shared the art of the temple with you, and you've taken it into your heart with honor. There's another part that you must learn and take into your head. You're a warrior. Do you only use your body to fight, or do you use your mind as well?"

"She's only been here for eight days," I reminded him as I changed into sweats.

"Only eight days and yet she feels safe enough to defy you. You need to prove to her that your displeasure isn't expressed by giving black eyes or bloody noses."

I sat on the edge of my bed and sighed. "I hate it when you're right."

"No, you hate it when I'm right, and you didn't listen. The real problem is that you aren't angry. You've never been in a situation that you've had to delay discipline or go through the formalities of approaching the transgressor. It's quite different than when the situation occurs spontaneously."

"That's very true." I sighed. "I don't like this one bit."

"It's part of being a Daddy Dom, Ry. It's who you are."

"You haven't seen this woman yet. She does something to me."

"That's even more of a reason to be firm. If you care, you want the best for her, right?" I didn't respond, so he continued. "Have you stopped to consider that she might be testing you to see if you're legit?"

"That's ridiculous."

"Is it? I seem to recall three grown men antagonizing me to prove I was who I said I was."

"We were just talking about that. This situation is different."

"No, it's not."

"Go away," I grunted.

"I am away, and yet I still know how to get under your skin. Do I have to remind you that this is what you've wanted since the day we met? It's your chance to have the family you've always desired. Don't let it slip by because of an uncomfortable practicality."

"It isn't just about me."

"No, it's about all of us. You're her guardian. Show her a daddy's love and make her feel secure. I'll call Lex to tell him to keep a dinner plate warm for you. Good luck, brother."

Chapter Nine
(Ryder)
∞ ∞ ∞

I stared at the disconnected cell phone and tossed it on my bed. Slater was right on all accounts, and it pissed me off. I mounted the stairs and frowned as I twisted the knob and found it locked.

"Jennifer? Open the door. You and I need to have a little talk."

"Talk to yourself. I have nothing to say."

"I'm going to count to three, and if you don't open this door, I will take it down. One..."

"Will you just leave me alone?"

"Two..."

"It was a mistake to come here. Just go."

"Three." I turned to go downstairs and noticed Simon's claw hammer on the top step. The jerk could've given me the key just as easily, but I guess he thought removing the doors would make a stronger statement. After popping the pins from the hinges, I lifted the pair from the frame and walked inside.

"What are you doing!" Jenn screeched while stomping her foot. I marched over to her, grabbed her hand, and swung her onto a chair.

"Sit down and listen up, young lady. We both signed up for a program that is based on a dynamic founded on obedience, respect, trust, and discipline. You're acting like a brat, and there's no reason except you're not getting your way. Are you trying to test me?"

"You need to get out of my room."

"No, what I need to do it put you across my knee and smack the sass and defiance out of you. Don't make me go there." Her wide eyes narrowed, but she kept quiet. "Would you care to tell me what's going on in that pretty little head of yours? I'm intuitive, but I'm not a mind reader."

She merely glared at me. If Slater were here, he'd point out the obvious—the discussion was turning into a battle of wills.

"Alrighty, then. It seems that you want to play hardball. Go stand in that corner until you're ready to talk about the reason for this tantrum."

"I'm not standing in the corner."

I leaned into her and locked eyes. "You will either go stand in that corner, or I'm putting you over my knee and spanking that little backside until it's the color of the sunset. I'm tired and hungry, and it seems that you're pushing my buttons for no other reason than to test my limits. If that's the case, you better stop this minute."

She sat frozen in place. Her internal struggle was evident, yet I still didn't quite understand what she was looking for.

In defense, like a virgin; in attack, like a tiger

"We've clearly met an impasse," I told her with some reluctance. "I also think I understand what's happening between us. You need set boundaries to feel safe. That's perfectly normal and I completely understand."

"You don't understand anything."

"No?" I pulled a chair in front of her and sat back while crossing my long legs. "When I sniff out a minefield, I always have to find the parameter of safety before I proceed with clearing it. I do that by detonating hidden bombs. The sound of the explosion and the eruption of the air and ground awakens my senses and keeps me focused on reality. Knowing the placement of the invisible fence, however, is a false sense of security, so I push further out to see if I can get a reaction from something hidden beneath the surface. When I find something, I receive a sense of satisfaction that I didn't take the easy way out and assume the way was clear. It also gives me peace because I saved my family from being turned into popcorn."

"What are you saying?"

"I'm saying that you need to see how far it's safe to go before this dream blows up in your face. You also know that the mine-field of trouble has multiple parameters, and each one is dependent on us." Her lower lip started to tremble, confirming I nailed the issue.

"This isn't my dream."

"Don't lie to me. Wanting this life is nothing to be ashamed of. If we didn't share that desire, we wouldn't be here."

She broke eye contact and looked down. "I'm sorry I was such a bitch to you."

"You're forgiven, but I don't think it's wise to ignore your needs, either. Lex runs this house, but I'm your primary guardian and ultimately have the final say in how things are going to progress. Starting immediately, there will be no more attitude. If you're tired or don't feel well, you'll excuse yourself. If not, we'll immediately assume that your Middle is seeking attention and will handle you accordingly. Am I understood?"

"Yeah."

"Pardon?"

She visibly gulped. "Yes, sir."

"That wasn't hard, was it? Use your words."

"No, sir," she whispered.

"I'm well aware that you're a virgin to this lifestyle, but that's no excuse for rudeness or disrespect. We already discussed this."

"I'm not a child," she mumbled.

"Yes, you are. I'm not speaking about the legalities of adulthood, rather the experience in a healthy and happy D&S household. You're also an age-player. Your need for an authority figure who loves and cares for you is strong. Why?"

"I don't know."

Her voice took on a younger persona. I was getting through to her. "What was your home like when you were growing up?"

Tears filled her eyes. "It was perfect. My parents loved each other and us kids with everything they had. We weren't wealthy, but we never lacked for anything."

"How many siblings did you have?"

"Nine. I was the youngest."

"Nine siblings? Did your dad have time for you?"

"He made time. He was my hero and could do nothing wrong in my eyes."

I already knew her history from reading her application and interview for Graye Manor, but words on paper never did justice to the emotional aspect of interrogation. I needed to find her foundation and build from there. "Tell me about him."

"He was a deacon in the church, and everyone loved him. There wasn't anything he wouldn't do if it meant helping someone who was in need. Mom was right there at his side and always had a smile on her face and loved to give."

I watched as she pulled her arms over her chest. *She was closing herself off, but why?*

"How did you find the Graye's?"

"I was the black sheep. My parents loved me, but they didn't understand this longing I had was for something other than religious laws. I started doing things to see how they'd react. I disregarded curfew, went to drinking parties, and skipped class."

"Typical teenager rebellion."

"Yes, but I didn't do it to rebel. I did it to see if they'd treat me differently than my brothers and sisters."

"Did they?"

She shook her head. "It was always the same thing. We'd sit down and talk, just as you and I are doing right now. They'd pray for me, kiss me on the forehead, and tell me they loved me. I know it sounds stupid, but I hated it. I felt like a paper doll from the book *How to Raise The Perfect Child.* I wasn't perfect, and I hated being stuffed in the same box as all the other deacons' kids."

"It doesn't sound stupid at all. We all come to a time in our life that we want to be treated like an individual instead of a number. My parents were talkers until I turned twelve and blew up Dad's truck with a home-made bomb."

"Oh, my God. On purpose?"

"On purpose. Only Simon knew that, though. We lied and said it was an accident. Neither one of us expected the folks to go ballistic."

"How did that feel?"

"Good. We finally got to see the passion in the love they had for us."

"That's what I was looking for. Nothing I did could break through the tenderness and care. It's not that I didn't love that about them, but I needed to see something more. Something that showed they weren't passive when it came to my life."

"Is that when you applied for the manor?"

"Yes. I started perving through dating apps and reading about the D&S lifestyle. I was in a chat room when I got a private message about the Grayes."

"Go on," I urged.

She looked down. "I made it all the way through the process and met them for the final interview. They were so sweet and understanding when they told me that the manor didn't have what I needed, but that they'd look for the perfect place for me. Then they sent me home."

"But?"

"I couldn't return. I already embarrassed my family by running away and then lied to them and said I got married and was moving out of the country. Even then, my parents kept calm and promised to pray for me. I was livid and said some horrible things about them and myself. I finally got a reaction, but it wasn't the one I expected."

"They told you not to come home, didn't they?"

"Yes. Since I had lied to the Grayes about my living situation, I had to find a way to survive. That's when I saw ads for submissives on the website. I grabbed the first offer, and my life went straight downhill from there. Those people took everything from me, including my ability to apologize to my parents. It wasn't until a year later that I pocketed a phone and called them."

"What happened?"

"Nothing. They moved, and the present deacon wouldn't tell me where. That was the last time I was able to get my hands on a phone, too. The punishment for that scared me away from trying again."

"May I ask what they did?"

Her eyes grew dull. "My greatest fear is being left alone. They backhanded me in the face and locked me in the closet of my room. I was only allowed out to get ready for a client or go to the bathroom, and then locked back in. They finally let me out when one of the clients complained that I looked sick."

"We'd never do any of that. You have my word."

I don't know if she heard me as she continued. "My life consisted of polar opposites. One end was with a family who loved me so much that they pushed their emotions away and replaced them with God, while the other end had people who used me for self-gain and showed nothing but anger and contempt. I must sound like a total idiot. I'm sorry."

"Please stop apologizing for how you think and feel. Look at me. You have my permission to explore your emotions. You also have my permission to think whatever you want except if it's something negative about yourself. Got it?"

"Yes, sir," she whispered.

"I'll also work on finding your parents so you can have some closure."

"You will?"

"Yes. I don't want you to start a life here and be worried about loose strings. It's not healthy."

"What if they don't accept my apology?"

"If they are the Christians you say they are, they will know the power of forgiveness. If not—well, I've seen enough frauds in my life that have done nothing but turn me away from believing in anything except myself and my brothers."

"I don't think they're frauds. They're just hurt."

"Yes, and if you extend an apology, then the ball is in their court to show what they're made of. I'm sure you heard that lesson in Sunday school."

"Constantly."

I entwined my fingers and leaned forward with my elbows on my thighs. "This is where we stand, kiddo. The past can't be erased, but it can be overcome. We'll help you with that. The present is another story. Did you or did you not deliberately provoke me?"

"I don't know."

"Go stand in the corner until you come up with an answer. Move it."

This time, she didn't argue with me. Hanging her head, she dragged her feet across the room and faced the single corner between the bathroom and curved picture window. I rose to feed Hobo and check the temperature of his cage, folded down the blankets on the bed, and tossed the laundry down the chute; all the while musing that her Middle was in full force when it came to tidying up.

I sat back down and chuckled as I glanced at my cell phone. Slater had sent me a gif of a mama wolf shaking her naughty pup by the scruff. A tiny piece of me hoped that my girl wouldn't cross the Wolfman's path—leniency was a word stripped from his vocabulary the day he was taken into training. Then, again—he'd understand her past better than the rest of us.

"Have you come up with an answer yet?" I asked when I felt my stomach rumble. She knew that she was between a rock and a hard place, so if she denied trying to provoke me, she'd be lying. If she confessed to the deed, she'd be in trouble for her attitude. Either way, she already admitted her needs to me, whether or not she acknowledged it.

"Can I plead the fifth?"

"No, you may not. Should I call the others up here and have Lex hold a tribunal?"

"No! Please, no."

"Come here, then." I took her hands and looked up into her fright-filled eyes. "The truth, baby."

"I provoked you. I'm sorry. It was stupid and childish and completely unwarranted."

"That's a very mature revelation for a little girl."

She blinked at me. "It's true."

I touched her face. "Yes, I know it's true. It's also in conflict with your big girl side and your Middle. Which side do you think is responsible for that mouth?"

"I don't know."

"No? How old were you when you started rebelling?"

"About fourteen."

"You were twenty when you applied to Graye Manor, right?"

"Yes, sir."

"Interesting. This is what I see. That mouthy, argumentative and defiant young lady is the teenager who's looking for love and security. The reserved, mature and thoughtful young woman is just a mask that hides the fear that her Middle has more influence in her life than she's comfortable with. Your Middle scares you. Why? Don't you dare say you don't know."

"Why don't you just tell me what to say, then?" she snapped. Her hands covered her mouth as I cocked my eyebrow.

"You don't like being told what to do, do you?" I slowly rose and looked down at her.

"I'm sorry," she whispered again.

"So am I, sweetheart. From this moment on, you'll be treated as a Middle until we tell you otherwise. There will be no more masks or pretending from you. It's time for a do-over in your life. With our help, you'll not only get what that little girl needs, but you'll learn to love the part of you that scares you the most."

"No! Let go of me!" Jenn kicked as I tugged her across my lap and held her firmly in place with my left arm. I pushed her sweater out of the way of her firm, round bottom.

"These aren't going to give you much protection, but I'm allowing you the dignity of keeping them up this time only." My voice was decisive and commanding, and I instantly gained her attention. "Tonight you're going to learn how much a Daddy can love you."

The clap of my hand against the thin material covering her backside brought about a gasp followed by a piercing squeal.

"You can't do this! You're hurting me," she protested, moving frantically to avoid another exacting smack.

"Sometimes Daddy's have to do things that hurt to keep their girl's from being harmed. I never, ever want you to be harmed again." My voice caught in my throat as I released my hard palm against the sweet undercurve of her beautiful ass. I slowed my pace as she fought against me. My purpose wasn't to cause her pain but to teach her my love language. Firm discipline tempered with soft words.

"You're a smart, beautiful and caring girl. You've never been able to give your heart to anyone because no one has earned your love and respect. I intend to do both. I will do whatever it takes to convince you that you're worth more than anything in this world. Am I understood?"

"Yes, Daddy." She sobbed pathetically as her movements slowed.

"All of us are going to love that little girl so much that she'll never feel alone or scared again." I placed my hand on her trembling rear end and felt the heat through the leggings. "Do you believe me? Tell me the truth."

"I want to believe you. I really do."

"In time, baby girl." I lifted her to sit on my lap and wrapped her tightly in my arms. "You're starting with a clean slate. I'll do everything I can to make you happy, but I need some help. Can you do that?"

"I'll try," she sniffed.

I kissed her head. "That's all I can ask for."

Chapter Ten
(Jennie)
∞ ∞ ∞

I've never been more embarrassed in my entire life than when Ryder made me come down with him for dinner. Simon looked at me with sympathy while Lex's lips were set in a determined line.

"I thought it would be nice if we started eating at the table as a family," he mentioned as he pointed to the dining room.

"We were waiting for you two to come down. I missed you today," Simon said, kissing my hot cheek.

"You didn't have to wait," I whispered. "You must be ravenous."

"I could eat."

"You can always eat," Lex said as he pulled out a chair. "Sit."

I winced at the word and then carefully lowered myself onto the hard wood. He walked around the table and sat directly across from me and stared at my face.

"Did you learn your lesson?" His question was bold and very loud.

"Lex, don't."

"Why not?" He looked at Simon. "We're all adults. At least, some of us are."

"Don't be an ass, Becker."

"Don't be a pussy, Watkins." Lex's brown eyes landed on me again. "I repeat. Did you learn your lesson?"

"Yes, sir," I whispered.

"Good." He turned his attention to Ryder. "What's the update about WIN next month?"

My brow creased with confusion. *What was that about?* He might as well have been asking if I was wearing matching socks. I looked at Ryder and saw him wink. *Was this what he meant by being forgiven and forgotten?*

"Try this and tell me what you think," Simon said, nudging my arm. He held a spoon of dark yellow liquid to my mouth. The light spicy flavor warmed me to my toes.

"It's good. What is it?"

"Coconut and curry pumpkin soup. Open."

"I can feed myself."

"I like feeding you. Taste this."

I sighed and let him place a piece of bread in my mouth. "This is delicious."

He looked pleased. "Athabaskan fry bread with dried wild berries and homemade goat butter. Are you still feeling adventurous?"

The flavors had awakened my appetite and provided a great distraction from my aching bottom. He spooned some piping hot stew into a bowl, picked up a fork and blew on it before bringing it to my lips.

"What do you think?"

"I'm not sure what to make of it. If it's whale or seal, please don't tell me."

Simon chuckled. "We don't do sea mammals. We wouldn't even do large game if we didn't have to. It's Brotherhood Stew."

"It's vegetarian Sisterhood Stew. You're eating tofu," Lex said with a snort. "It took Slater seven years to get us whimps to try the stuff."

"We still don't care for it except when Lex disguises it with actual flavors. It's better with moose or caribou, but Friday night is Slater's pick which means no meat."

"But he's not here."

"He's always here in spirit, so we keep our tradition. We wanted to give you Thursday nights since that's when you joined us. I'll make you anything you want."

"Really?"

"Don't get too excited, baby," Ryder said with a chuckle. "We have to do the dishes on our night. If I'm tired, I pick peanut butter and jelly sandwiches."

"I don't know why you're complaining. Just do what I do," Simon said, leaning back and rubbing his stomach.

Lex frowned. "Letting Molly clean the dishes is disgusting and pisses off Slater. It also gives her gas."

"I wash them afterward. You also forget that I've been in foxholes with you guys. That wasn't exactly pleasant."

I let Simon feed me as the three chatted about their day. He placed his hand on my lap and whispered in my ear.

"Do you need some lotion? I'm very gentle."

"I don't think Ryder will approve, but thanks." His offer was so tempting, but I was too humiliated to accept it.

"I'm your guardian, too. Remember? I'll be up when you're ready to go to bed."

"The bedtime discussion is what got me in trouble in the first place."

"I can make it so you'll beg to be put to bed every night if you'll let me."

"I can't. Ryder said that I'm not allowed to be an adult unless I'm told otherwise."

"If I told you otherwise, would you want to be my big girl?"

My body wanted to scream *YES* and seek a moment of playful distraction with the handsome man, but I stopped myself. "It's too soon, and I barely know you."

"You're worried about my perception of you, aren't you?" he asked knowingly. "Guys? I'm going to take Jenniebean for a walk before bedtime. We'll be back in an hour."

"But..."

"Be careful, son, " Lex ordered. "Stay away from the fences. We haven't dropped any carcasses for the wolves in over a week, and they might be looking for an easy meal."

"Keep her warm and dry. Jenn? Remember what I told you."

"She already said that you want her to remain in her Middle unless she's told otherwise."

"Yes. I'll catch you up later on all of it. Don't forget to adjust the inside lights."

"I'll take care of that right away. Thanks for dinner, Lex. I'll see you guys in the sandpit tomorrow." He helped me to my feet and led me out of the room with his big hand on the small of my back.

"Simon? I'm really not ready for anything intimate," I said as he punched in the lighting adjustments on the electrical panel in the control room.

"I know. I get my kicks in fucking with their heads. You have my word that I'll be a total gentleman if that's what you want. Just promise not to share that with the guys."

"You're going to get me into trouble, aren't you?"

"I hope so." His breath tickled my neck before nipping me with his teeth.

"I don't want to get in trouble again. It's horrible."

He kissed me lightly on the lips. "That's a bad kind of trouble. Mine is a good kind of trouble. Let's get bundled up. We have another clear night so the sky should give you a nice show."

"Will we be able to see the northern lights?"

"Probably not—it's too early in the season. The best time is in March, but if the conditions are right next month, we might see a rainbow of colorful sky spirits play and dance under the smile of the beaming moon."

I blinked dumbfoundedly. "That was beautiful, Simon."

He chuckled. "I wish I could claim the words, but the Markford's grandmother comes to the campout every year and shares the stories of the Athabaskan nation around the bonfire. Her people believe that the northern lands are a place to dream, and she brings those dreams to our town."

"You really love this place, don't you? Why?" I asked as we walked outside and adorned our snowshoes.

"Come." He lifted the Coleman lamp and started walking. The land was dark as shadows from the trees blocked the light of the rising moon and the snow glittered with a dark sapphire hue. He helped me up the steps to a large, wooden platform with benches built around the edges and an iron fire-pit in the center. After blowing out the lamp, he wrapped his arms around me from behind.

"You asked if I loved this place and why. It fills the senses like nowhere else in the world. Everywhere you look, it's perfect. Can you see how the lights from the lodge reflect on the frozen lake?"

"It's breathtaking. I feel so small up here."

"Close your eyes and breathe." He turned me around in a slow circle. "The snow on the ridge smells differently than the snow on the mountain."

I inhaled deeply. "This is amazing. It even tastes different. Why?"

"The ridge is open and kissed by the sun and the wind. Love warms its heart. The mountain is hidden in the trees and blocked by the shadows. It's cold, sharp and bitter."

"Grandma Markford?"

"Yes, ma'am. Her words speak life into the land, and we honor her beliefs by doing the same." He turned me to face him and pulled the balaclavas away from our mouths and cupped my face between his heavy gloves. "Words can build and nurture, but they can also wound and destroy. None of us are immune to that single word that can crush our hearts or make us jump for joy."

"W,why are you telling me this?" I asked, my lips trembling as he drew closer.

"I want you to know our hearts, that's all."

"If you think I'm angry with Ryder for hitting me, then you're right. It wasn't necessary."

"He didn't hit you—he spanked you as a form of discipline, and you're lying to yourself, not to me. I took you out of the house because I know my brother. I wanted to give him a chance to process his feelings and find a place of peace. He's crying his heart out for having to cause you pain."

"Why?"

"Because that man has more love in his little finger than there are stars in the sky. He holds nothing of himself from his family, and will give up his own happiness for any of us."

"I'm a selfish brat, aren't I?"

"You've never experienced the kind of love you're going to find with us. You also won't appreciate it until your walls are broken down." His mouth came closer. "Ask yourself where you'd rather be—on the ridge, exposed and vulnerable, but covered with love or on the mountain, hidden and cut off from life."

His kiss was warm and deep. It rattled me as much as the poetic words that flowed from his mouth. I suspected there was much more to the big Teddy bear than he let on.

"Will you help me?" I asked when he released me.

He nodded while adjusting the warm material back over my exposed face. "Name it, and it's yours."

"Teach me how to play." I could see the surprise on his face by the light of the partial moon.

"Are you sure you want that? It could get you into bad trouble."

"I need to stop being afraid and let go of my control. I feel like I'm on a giant playground and don't know how to swing. Is getting a scraped knee worth learning how to laugh and maybe even love?"

"That's the Jenniebean I want to see. I'm proud of you. Let's go home and put you to bed."

"But I'm not tired," I teased.

His hearty laugh echoed through the silent valley.

****

"Don't leave," I whispered after Simon took me to my room. Everyone else had already gone to sleep, and the lodge was silent except for the occasional popping of a fire.

"I can't stay here. You're too tempting."

"We don't have to do anything. I don't want to be alone tonight. I hate being alone; it scares me." I suddenly felt very bold. "You promised to rub lotion on me, remember?"

"Sweetheart, you're playing with fire."

"Please?"

He ran his fingers through his thick hair and glanced at the stairway. My doors were still off the hinges from earlier. "This isn't a good idea."

"You said I wouldn't be judged if I was myself. Truthfully? I hate sex. They used me." My voice was flat as I turned from his gaze. "I was a receptacle, nothing more. If I didn't participate, I was punished, so I learned how to put on a mask and pretend to save myself from being hurt. Please try to understand—I didn't want to do any of it."

"Shh," Simon whispered, drawing me into his strong arms and holding me to his chest. "You don't have to explain yourself to me."

"You deserve to know the truth. I was their pet— the prize they handed out to their top clients. Nothing was off limits except they had to respect the toy by using good hygiene and not leave permanent or visible marks. The things that were done to my body made me wish for a nearby cliff so I could end the pain and degradation. I survived by learning to cut myself off emotionally and imagine it was nothing more than a nightmare."

"Nightmares are pretty horrible places, darling. None of that's going to happen to you here."

I knew he was telling the truth. I hadn't had one nightmare since moving in with them, but there was more I wanted him to know. "I've been with multiple men. I can still feel their sweaty hands on me, smell the alcohol and cigarettes on their breath, and hear the sound of their disgusting grunts. I swore that if I ever escaped, no one would touch me except on my terms."

"What are your terms?"

"My terms?" I repeated. "I'm not really sure. I never thought I'd be in a situation that I wanted… I mean that I could…" My words were stumbling over my tongue.

"Hey, don't hurt yourself," he teased, snuggling me closer. "You didn't know that your body would respond to anyone. You also never expected that you'd have four hot boyfriends who treat you like a princess."

"Boyfriends? That word never even crossed my mind. I'm a commodity, Simon. Nothing more. I'm not trying to be difficult, I swear. There's just no way you can understand where I'm coming from."

"Listen, babe—I've seen men who've treated their women like throw-aways. They disgust me; especially the ones who target hurt and lonely girls and give them false hope of being loved. There's no escape because the gal is stuck. If she tries to stick up for herself, she's ridiculed. If she tries to leave, she's mocked or threatened. If she tries to kick out the loser, she faces a lifetime of being alone even though she ends up being alone anyway, whether he's there or not. Yeah, I understand where you're coming from. I also know that you're one of the few who got out. Others aren't as lucky."

"Yeah, I guess not."

"You *guess* not?" He poked my side. "You guess not?"

"No tickling!" I shrieked as his big fingers sought my rib cage. I twisted to escape and then whipped around to find myself looking up into his eyes.

"What?" he asked.

"Your eyes. They're the same color as the sky on the horizon. Almost indigo."

His kiss left me devoid of control or rationale. Desire raged and consumed me. I wanted him to touch me, to hold me, to chase away the monsters that mocked and scorned me in the shadows of my mind. I hated the need that welled inside of me, and I hated that I was too weak to snuff out my longing for him.

This was wrong.

"Simon, no. You're right. We're playing with fire. You have to go." The words came in short, raspy pants. Every one of them was a lie, too. I hoped he had more strength than I did.

He sighed. "Go put your jammies on, and I'll tuck you in."

"I'd like that. Thank you." I backed away and fought to calm my breathing, and then raced to the bathroom. Splashing cold water on my face didn't slow my pounding heart. I found a pair of fleece pajamas in my closet and slipped them on. Little pink and yellow unicorns would help remind both of us of the roles we were supposed to play for now.

Maybe.

The lust in his eyes twinkled as brilliantly as the stars in the winter sky when I returned to him. His gaze never left my face, making my attempt to distract him a colossal failure. Not that I complained. His big hands rested on my waist, and he leaned in to touch my mouth. There was no going back if I didn't stop him.

"We can't. Not yet," I whispered as I pulled him closer and parted my lips to let him fuck my mouth.

"It's too soon," he whispered in return, pushing me against the wall and pinning my arms above my head. His solid, muscle-bound body pressed against me and I could feel his cock against my stomach. I shivered as my panties grew wet.

"Much too soon. What will the others say?" I tilted my chin to give him my neck. A series of tiny bites traveled up the column of my throat.

"Only that they wished they could be here and taste you, too." He grabbed a handful of my hair and seared my lips to his.

"Honest?"

"Honest."

That was all I needed. I unbuttoned his soft, flannel shirt and dragged my hands underneath the material. My fingers followed the lines of his powerful muscles and revealed a sharply, sculpted chest and abdomen. His skin was soft and warm, and I entwined my fingertips between the silky curls of hair that lightly covered his chest.

I felt his hand inch under my pajama shirt and slide its way over the span of my back before sliding down and slipping inside my pants to clutch the entirety of my ass. I gasped as his strong fingers kneaded my skin, a combination of strength and tenderness. I bucked against him, his mouth still clamped on to mine, and ran my palms along his sides and down the rough material of his jeans.

I groaned as he touched the tender skin on the backs of my legs. He came close but never touched, the secret space between my thighs that yearned being discovered.

"Simon, please—"

"I do love the sound of begging." His low chuckle vibrated against my throat. "However, I made a promise. I'm a man of my word and refuse to break it by putting my needs first."

"What?" My mouth hung open in shock as he took a step back.

"I promised to rub lotion on someone's spanked bottom." He grinned as he produced a bottle of creamy liquid and sat on the edge of the bed. "Put that pretty little thing across my lap."

I scrunched my nose and slowly bent over the tree-trunk sized thighs.

"My, my… what cute panties you have," Simon said, lowering my pajama pants to my knees. I twisted around to look at him.

"The better to tease you with, my dear," I said with a devilish smile. "Eek! Why did you do that?"

His hand rubbed the area he had just swatted. "Because I wanted to. Are you sure you want me to unwrap the package?"

"Only if you want." I rested my chin on my hands as he peeled my thin panties away from my ass with agonizing slowness. "Are you trembling?"

"I've never seen anything so small and perfect," he whispered, cupping my entire backside in one hand.

"I aim to please."

"Unfortunately, so do I."

"Why did you say that?"

"Because I'm a spanker and nothing turns me on more than red, hot cheeks."

"Oh, shit! Ow! Stop it," I protested, stuck between laughing and squealing.

"This is too much fun," he said gleefully. "You have just enough puff to bounce and jiggle. Don't you dare let this get any smaller, hear me?"

"Owie! Okay, I won't. Simon! Please let me go."

"Now that I have your attention, there are some things I can share. First, I like being in control in the bedroom. We all do."

"Okay! Now, stop." I kicked half-heartedly as he started alternating back and forth. The spanks were hard enough to leave a delightful sting, and make me incredibly horny.

"Nah, I'm just warming up. Let's bring it up a bit."

"Nononono! Hey! That hurt," I whined, twisting again and glaring at him.

"I didn't feel a thing."

"Of course, you didn't."

"Hmm, are we getting a tad sassy? Okay by me."

"Fuck!" The air hissed out of my mouth as he landed a heavy smack across both cheeks.

"Shh, no swearing," Simon reprimanded as he rubbed the lotion over the point of impact. The hand that had just delivered pain now soothed and aroused my flesh. His fingers brushed the back of my pussy. "You like this, don't you?"

"This part. Not the spanking."

"You can't have this part without the spanking."

"Yes, I can. OW! Simon!"

"You're right. You can, but I can't." He shifted so that I could feel his engorged cock pressing against me. "I bet you've never had an orgasm by spanking. Jenniebean? Jenn? What's wrong, babe?"

"Nothing," I said. His hand ran gently down the back of my thigh.

"You stiffened up. Whoa—have you ever come during sex? That was a stupid question. Just ignore me."

"I've never come. Period."

"Never? What about when you've played with yourself?"

"I've never done that. My parents were really religious and believed that masturbation denied the intimacy shared between a husband and wife. They compared it to adultery in the heart. I know I sound like a hypocrite after what I became.'

"Not at all. Remember what I told you about words. There are some that can never be removed from the memory." He patted my backside.

"Are you stopping?"

"You need to sleep."

I slid off his lap, pulling up my pants at the same time. "Why are rejecting me?"

"I'm not, baby girl. I'm saving you for something incredibly special when the time is right. Trust me."

I shook my head and climbed into bed. I turned my back to him as I fought back the undeniable urge to cry. He walked around the room and turned off the lights and then sat on the bed.

"You're mad at me."

"No. I'm hurt. Please go away, so I don't cry and embarrass myself."

"That's not going to happen."

"What are you doing now?"

"Move over. You wanted me to stay with you, didn't you? Come here." He didn't wait for me to turn over and pulled my head to rest on his massive chest. He cradled me warmly. "Will you love me again if I show you my surprise?"

"I didn't stop loving you. I mean, I don't love you—we just met. It's not that I won't love you one day but…"

"You're really going to hurt yourself if you keep doing that to your brain," he said jovially. "Do you want to see my surprise?"

"Not if it has anything to do with sex."

"It's sexy, but it's not about sex. Comfy?" He kissed my forehead. "Here."

"A remote control? Is there a TV in here?"

"Yes. Press the center button."

"Oh, my God…"

"I did good, huh?"

I was speechless. The ceiling opened to reveal a planetarium view of the sky. Dense clusters of stars shone down on us in a shimmering display of multi-color diamonds.

"Hit the green button and keep your head down," he instructed.

"A telescope? Seriously?"

"Not *just* a telescope. This is the Top Secret, military-grade BWF Compuscope with a 3D screen and recorder. It's so strong that it can count the hairs in a flea's armpits on the other side of the universe."

"No way."

"I'm exaggerating a bit, but this is the strongest long distance surveillance device in the world. That's Saturn."

"It looks so clear. How did you get your grubby paws on something like this?"

"We made it."

"Say what?"

"BWF stands for Becker, Watkins, and Foxx. The military paid us a shitload of bucks for this puppy. This is the research version."

"Is there a combat version?"

"If I tell you, I'd have to tickle you. Forgive me?"

"Yeah. It's hard to be angry when looking at the universe."

"That's my girl." He took the remote from me and retracted the telescope to its cabinet in the wall behind the headboard. "Good-night, Jenniebean."

I cuddled against him, still staring at the sky. "Good-night, Daddy. Thanks for understanding."

I could feel the smile stretch across his face.

Chapter Eleven
(Ryder)
∞ ∞ ∞

I was relieved to see that Jenn was a little more relaxed around me the following morning. I never thought I'd be grateful for my little brother's intervention, but he stepped in and diffused any animosity that might have developed had she been left alone after our first disciplinary session. Part of me was sad for him, though. Despite his bluster and pomp, Simon was relatively shy and a little insecure when it came to women. Too many had underestimated him and took advantage of his gentle nature, and left him hurt and abandoned, and I wanted him to be the first among us to know Jenn intimately. He didn't seem to be bothered—in fact; he was rather chivalrous about it when he shared the details of their interaction.

I still couldn't believe that she had never orgasmed before. Neither could Lex.

"I can't imagine the things that are flying through that girl's head right now," Lex said quietly as we sat in Slater's meditation room and sipped our coffee after our morning workout. I sighed and looked out over the dark landscape. The weather finally settled and left behind a sparkling blanket of glistening snow. This was my favorite time of day, the minutes before civil twilight started to shadow the land and everything remained a mystery.

"We've got our jobs cut out for us. Until we know the degree of her brokenness, we can't help her. Any ideas?" Lex asked.

"I'm already the mean one, so don't ask me."

Lex looked at me straight in the eye. "Confidence and strength are the things she needs most from us right now. If you start second-guessing yourself, you're going to blow all the good work you can do. Stop it."

"I feel horrible, that's all."

Simon rolled his eyes. "Dude! You didn't even leave her little bottom the tiniest shade of pink. What's wrong with you?"

"I'll tell you what's wrong. He's already falling for her, and he's letting his heart sway his better judgment." Lex leaned back in his chair and stared at me as I lowered my head.

"She's different than any of the others I've been with. She's innocent and vulnerable, and all I want to do is protect her from more pain."

"I understand that. I really do. But, tell me something, son. If Slater was here yesterday, what would have happened?"

"I spoke with him before I did anything," I admitted. "He would've put his feelings to the side and focused on what was best for the girl. Come on guys, you know me. Have I ever shirked from my responsibilities or my duty? This woman's got me thrown for a loop."

"Hey, calm down. Don't beat yourself up over this. We'll work it out together, as a family, just like we do everything else."

"I know what you're really afraid of," Simon announced gently. "She told you about her parents and the lack of passion. You don't want her to think you don't care by being lenient, but you also don't want to take advantage of your position to lord over her."

I blinked at my little brother. People didn't give him credit for his brain because he was always joking around and smiling, and they did him a disservice. There was a wise man behind his gentle smile.

"You're right," I admitted.

"Is there something I'm missing?" Lex asked. I quickly shared the story Jenn had shared with me about her upbringing and the series of events that finally led her to be with us.

"That definitely sheds new light on the situation. Damn."

"What?" I asked as the Major rubbed his temple.

"I just wished Slater was here. He's our balance. Is that Molly?"

We turned to the sound of the Newfoundland's claws clicking in the hallway, followed by the scratching on the door.

"Guys? I'm lost." Jenn's voice said from the other side.

"Come on in, baby girl. Join us," Simon said, quickly opening the door for her. She was still in her pajamas, and her hair was a mess. She couldn't have been any cuter!

He hugged her warmly. "Did you sleep well?"

"Yeah. It was amazing. I thought you were still with me when I woke up, but you'd been replaced."

"Molly went upstairs and got into bed with you?" I was surprised. The dog hated the spiral staircase.

"I might have rigged the elevator so she could go up and down if she wanted," Simon admitted.

"There's an elevator?"

"It opens in the recess next to your doors which are currently off their hinges," Simon snickered. "Did you put my hammer back, by the way?"

"It would've been easier if you left me the key. Come here. Daddy needs a hug," I said, patting my lap. She hesitated for a moment and then joined me. "Are you still angry with me?"

"No, just embarrassed. I'm too old to have to be spanked like a child."

"Not in this house, you aren't," Lex stated. "Daddy was easy on you because it was your first introduction to the lifestyle, but from now on, if you misbehave, you'll be receiving your just desserts."

"I didn't like it."

"I didn't ask if you liked it now, did I? You've been here for over a week in close quarters. People who are snowed in have a chance to come to know one another more intimately than in any other circumstance. Do you honestly believe that we're going to do or say anything that will harm or break you?"

"No, but…"

"There are no 'buts,' Jenniebean. This is how it is. Yeah, we've got all the luxuries of a five-star resort and more gadgets than Comicon will ever see, but the bottom line is that we live a hard life up here in an unforgiving land. Mother Nature doesn't know the word 'mercy,' and if we're going to protect you, that goes for us as well."

Her eyes grew wet as she looked at Simon. "I thought you liked me."

"What makes you think I don't?"

"Jennifer, it's because we do like you that we have to be hard. None of us want to risk losing you to either the elements or an attitude," Lex explained. "We refuse to give you anything less than the love and passion you deserve. If you want to fault us for that, then so be it."

"I have an idea," Simon said, breaking the silence in the room. "Let's see if Lena is up for a sleepover. I think she might be able to help Jenniebean with some of these adjustments."

I bit my lip. "I love Lena, but don't you think she might be a little too much for Jenn to handle?"

"No, I think Simon's onto something. Lena's wild, yes, but her relationship with her daddies is also very strong and healthy. She might be the very thing Jennifer needs to break the ice and feel more at home. What do you think?"

"I have a choice?"

"Of course, you have a choice. We aren't running a dictatorship."

Jenn looked around the room at each of us, her struggling emotions reading like neon signs on her face. I turned her around to straddle my hips and look into my eyes as I held her face in my hands.

"This is all about you, sweetheart. No one is allowed to touch you except us, so you don't have anything to worry about. I want you to do this."

She bit her lower lip as she gazed at me with those gorgeous turquoise eyes. "Would it make you happy?"

"It would. Very much."

"Okay."

"That's my good girl." I kissed her between the eyes and smiled proudly. My praise clearly affected her as she blushed and then wrapped her arms around my neck and hugged me to her chest. I looked at Simon and Lex with relief. Our bound was forming, and I couldn't have been happier.

"I'm sorry I was such a brat to you. I deserved that spanking," she whispered with her head on my chest.

"You deserved much more than what you were given."

"I know. I'll try to be good. I promise."

"Just be yourself. Having a sore bottom isn't going to change the way we feel about you."

"It won't?"

"Not at all. In fact, it will allow us to know that we're doing our best to be good providers for our girl." I wrapped my arms around her shoulders and squeezed tightly. "I never want you to think that you aren't worth the time or effort it takes to make you the very best you can be."

Jenn tucked her head under my chin and sighed. "Do you think it's possible for me to feel like a little girl and a big girl at the same time?"

"You feel however you feel, sweetheart. It's not right or wrong. What's going on in that pretty little head?" Lex asked softly as he reached over and touched her knee.

"I'm so confused and torn and... and..."

"I keep telling you that you're going to hurt yourself one of these days when you play mental ping pong. Spit it out," Simon urged.

"I can't."

I met Lex's eyes. We've known each other long enough to anticipate each other's thoughts. *What would Slater do?*

"What did you learn last night when you were over Daddy's knee?" Lex asked firmly.

"Can we please not talk about this?"

"No, we will talk about it and will keep talking until you accept that there's nothing to be embarrassed about. If we have to, we'll even pass your little backside around the room until you realize that you have nothing to hide from us."

"You wouldn't!" She looked horrified.

"He would." Simon drummed his fingers on the arm of his chair. "Maybe that's what's needed here. We should introduce our little girl to a maintenance spanking from each of us so that she knows what to expect when she acts up. That will eliminate apprehension of the unknown."

"I don't like that idea at all." Jenn shook her head vehemently.

"We didn't ask if you liked the idea. There's an elephant in the room that needs to be slain if we're going to move forward. What are your hard limits?"

Jenn's lips quivered as she held herself tightly against me. "I don't know, Lex."

"How could she know? She's a novice. These are our hard limits," Simon announced. "We aren't into edge play, meaning no take-downs, asphyxiation, blood stuff, or any type of scarring. Sometimes we'll play a little harder with BDSM, but we generally are into D&S and kinky fuckery."

"Simon!"

"Will you please stop yelling at me? I'm trying to help here. Aren't you guys the ones who always say that life's too short to waste on playing meaningless games?"

"That's different."

"How, exactly?" Simon asked me. "Ordinarily, we wouldn't ever be having this conversation."

"Please don't fight because of me," Jenn begged. "I'll do whatever you need, just don't let me hurt your relationships. Please."

"We're not fighting, baby. We're guys, so sometimes we get a little hot under the collar when we're talking about important matters. Like it or not, you're the most important matter in our lives right now."

"I am?"

I kissed her soft lips. "You are. Now, I want you to go back to your room, take a shower, and throw on some sweats. We'll have breakfast, and then you're going to get a long talk from your daddies about what we expect. Okay?"

"Yes, sir," she whispered.

"We're hanging out around the lodge today and doing some chores. You'll help us as we see fit. Any questions?"

"No, sir."

"Good girl. Kiss and get moving." I dismissed her with a pat on the bottom. I waited until the door was closed and scowled as Lex grinned at me. "What?"

"That's the man I know. Good job. You too, Simon. We're united in this, okay? There's nothing that we can't do together."

"To the Brotherhood," Simon said, lifting his right forearm. We pressed ours to his and looked at the missing space where Slater should have been. We were incomplete without him.

****

"I got a call for a meeting in town tonight," Lex said as we sat for breakfast. "I thought it would be nice to take our little lady out for dinner and then head over to the Markford's and give her a chance to know them before the sleepover. Lena suggested having dessert at their place and bribed me with baklava."

I groaned. "Her baklava is to die for, but that girl on a sugar high is out of control. Last time she ran outside to play on the monkey bars in the dead of winter and got sick. Are her daddies going to allow that?"

"You know how protective they are. I'm sure they'll keep an eye on her or, at least, restrict how much she eats."

"Lena sounds like a lot of fun," Jenn said, nipping Simon's fingers when he stuck a piece of waffle into her mouth.

"No biting. Lena is wonderful, but she has no filter. She'll get you spanked if you aren't careful."

"Why?"

"Because that's what subbies do. They love to mess with each other. With Lena, it's never malicious. I can't say the same for all of them, though," I informed her. "We'll exercise caution with whom we expose you to in the beginning."

"I thought everyone here was nice."

"We're a community of people, not robots. Some of the girls come from troubled backgrounds and get very jealous. Others have criminal records and are being rehabbed. None of the guardians are blind to the flaws of their wards and will watch over the interactions to protect the more naïve members of the group."

"I can take care of myself."

"Can you, now?" Simon poked her side.

"Stop that."

"Make me, Miss Hard-Ass," he teased, poking her again. I raised my eyebrow. Jenn had a look in her eye that I hoped Simon noticed.

"Leave her be, Simon. Don't provoke her," Lex ordered.

"I want to know how she... fuck—"

"Put the knife down, Jennifer. That won't be happening again in our home," Lex ordered as Jenn slipped behind my brother with unbelievable speed and held the tip of a kitchen knife to his throat. She kissed his cheek and put the knife back down on the table.

"I told you I could take care of myself."

"Where did you learn that?" Simon asked, sliding the knife out of her reach.

"One of the clients had an escort who taught me some self-defense techniques. She said they might not save my life, but they would buy me time to escape."

"If you're interested, we can teach you all kinds of techniques. The rule, however, is you are never to use any of them against us," I said firmly.

"Are you mad at me?"

"No, I'm not angry. Your actions took me by surprise, but you did give a reasonable warning. Just don't ever do that again."

"I won't, Daddy." She climbed onto my lap and held the edges of my lips up into a forced smile. "Love me?"

Her question made my heart melt. I kissed her palms. "Yes, I love you, but I'm not happy with what you just did."

"I won't do it again. Cross my heart."

The slip into her Middle was natural and endearing. It was also my cue to show complete acceptance of that part of her persona. I pushed my chair back and stood, my hands cupping her bottom as she tightened her legs around my waist. She placed her cheek on my shoulder and hugged my neck.

"I think now is the perfect time for a long Daddies to Little Girl talk."

"Do we have to?"

"Yes. Gentlemen?"

"Let's go into the living room. Simon? Would you add some wood to the fire, please? Give me a couple of minutes."

"Where's he going?" Jenn asked as I sat on the couch with her on my lap.

"Daddy Lex believes that food makes everything all better."

"Is Daddy Simon sick?"

"Haha, funny girl," Simon grunted. "You want to be on my good side after that little stunt you pulled."

"You know I wouldn't hurt you. I thought that you'd respect my ability to take care of myself."

"There's a time and place. What you don't understand is that any of us could have disarmed you and caused some serious damage. I think you need to start watching us when we spar."

"I think she needs to get out of bed early and work out with us."

She wrinkled her nose at me. "I hate working out."

"It's good for you."

"So are lima beans, and I'll die before I eat those."

"You aren't going to die, and if I make lima beans, you will eat them. Food isn't wasted in this part of the world," Lex announced, placing a tray on the table.

"But I hate lima beans." Jenn pouted.

"Don't worry, baby. The only one who eats lima beans is Slater, and that's when he's feeling guilty about something and needs to suffer a bit."

"Slater sounds weird."

"I know you haven't met him, yet, but Slater is still one of your daddies, and you'll be respectful," Lex reprimanded.

"I'm sorry."

Simon nudged her arm and handed her a cup of hot cocoa. "Here you go, baby-cakes. Between you and me, I think Slater's weird, too; but that's why I love him."

"Don't encourage her. Name-calling is not acceptable."

"You call me names."

"Pardon?" Lex's expression was comical, to say the least.

"You call me Jennifer, baby, sweetheart, and other things."

"Okay, you got me." Lex laughed and sat back against the floor pillows. "No mean names. We build up, not break down. With that, Mr. Watkins, the floor is yours."

"Thank you," I said, adjusting her on my knee. "I've decided that it's time to take the next step in this part of our relationship. Have you been on your best behavior this week?"

"Molly thinks I have," Jenn said, scratching the dog on the top of her head.

"I didn't ask Molly. You've been here for ten days, and it's the perfect time to move forward. I want you to stand up in front of us."

Chapter Twelve
(Jenn)
∞ ∞ ∞

I wrinkled my forehead. "Why?"

"When I tell you to do something, I expect you to mind me. Go on."

I unfolded myself from his warm body and dragged my feet to the center of the room. I stared at the floor and fidgeted uncomfortably.

"How does it feel to be standing in front of us?"

"I hate it. It makes me want to cry."

"Why, baby?" Lex asked.

"I don't like being looked at. It makes me feel small."

"Would you be more comfortable if you sat down in front of us?"

"It's not like we're in a circle. Your eyes are on me, and it makes me uncomfortable."

"We don't want that. The only time you'll have to stand in front of us like this in the future is if you're in a family tribunal, okay? Sit wherever you want."

"Can I have a lap?"

"Not right now. Why the face?"

I scowled and plopped on the floor nearest to Lex. "I wanted to cuddle."

"You'll get plenty of cuddles, love. The point of this exercise is to show us what methods work best in communicating with you. You're a smart girl, and it's important that we treat your intelligence respectfully."

I looked at Lex with appreciation. "Thank you. That means a lot to me."

"What're your personal hopes and dreams, and how can we make them happen?"

"You've already given me everything."

"Answer his question and be honest," Ryder ordered.

Would asking for more make me appear ungrateful?

"I want to go back to school and maybe get a degree."

"That's an easy request. Do you know what you want to major in?" Lex asked.

"I'm not sure. I'm really good at puzzles and computers and stuff."

"You'll have plenty of help in any of those areas. The town even holds college classes in general ed. All that will start at the first on the year. What else?"

"This sounds really stupid, but I want to do something daring. I've been locked in a cage for so long and want to stretch my legs." I pushed my feet in front of me to make a point. "I'm so afraid of making a mistake and someone hating me."

"You can make as many mistakes as you need and no one's going to hate you here. We'll just spank you," Simon said with a shrug.

"Can I ask a question? Why is that so important to you?"

"It's important to all of us, especially you."

"No, it's not."

"You're here because you are a submissive, Jenniebean. Spanking is part of our dynamic. It's also a very effective means of clearing the air and opening up doors to the truth."

I frowned at Simon. Gone was the happy-go-lucky young man and, in his place, was a stern and focused Dom.

I felt anger starting to stir inside of me. "Are you saying that you'll beat me until I tell you what you want to hear?"

"I didn't hear myself say that? Did anyone else?"

"My question is why are you getting so angry? What are you afraid of, Jennifer?"

I jumped to my feet. "I'm not afraid of anything. You guys are instigating a fight."

"I don't see where we've done any such thing. Sit down."

"I'll stand, thank you."

"I said to sit down," Lex repeated himself.

I stormed to the other side of the room and sat on the bench next to the scenic window with my arms crossed. "You're infuriating."

"Jenn, I want you to unfold your arms and wipe the attitude off your face. Come sit next to me," Ryder ordered.

"I have an attitude because I feel trapped."

"Take a deep breath and count to ten. After you do that, you may speak to us."

"I can't believe neither of you have the brains to see what's really going on here," Simon said as he hauled his big body off the ground and marched over to me. He snatched me around the waist and football carried me to the ottoman where he sat down and pinned me over his thighs. I pounded his legs with my fists.

"Let me goooo! Ryder!"

"We're going to play a little game," Simon said, resting his hand on my backside. "I'm going to ask you questions, and you're going to answer honestly and completely. You'll only be allowed to pass one time, but it will cost you ten spanks. After that, I'll hand you over to one of the others."

"Oh, my God! This is so not fair!"

"Maybe not, but we'll get to the heart of the matter, and you'll get to experience a taste of your future."

"Help me," I pleaded while looking at Ryder. "Please."

"We're quite familiar with stubbornness in this family, and each of us have had to face the team when we've been particularly obstinate. We might not get our butt's blistered, but we've all had sore backs from hard labor on several occasions," Ryder said.

"Your best approach is to be honest and answer the questions, kid. No one's baiting you. We simply want you to stop pretending to be something you're not," Lex explained.

"I'm not pretending anything. Ow!" I gasped when Simon's hand landed sharply across my backside.

"Hurts, huh? I've already seen this lovely little thing, so this shouldn't be an issue," he said, pulling my sweats and panties to my knees. He held my right hand to my side, preventing me from grabbing my pants. "Isn't that the prettiest ass you've ever seen, boys?"

"You're embarrassing me."

"No, I'm not. You like it when we praise your appearance, don't you?"

"No. Owie! Stop," I yelped as his hand landed with four hard smacks. I couldn't believe how much they hurt!

"The truth, young lady."

"Okay! Yes, I like that you think I'm pretty."

"Do you believe we're telling the truth?"

A sob caught in my throat. "I want to believe you. I want to believe that you're attracted to me." He smacked me another four times. I kicked wildly to avoid the swats. "Why are you spanking me?"

"You know we're attracted to you. You proved that when you proudly left us all with hard-ons. Try it again."

"Pass!"

"That's pass, number one." The ten smacks that followed took my breath away, and I wasn't even being punished! "Who's next?"

"I'll take her," Lex volunteered. He positioned me on his lap and placed his hand on the back of my left knee. "How does all this make you feel right now?"

I sniffled. "Like no matter what I say, I'm going to be hit, so it doesn't matter whether or not I try."

"We're not trying to take your voice from you, baby," Ryder said.

"I know, but he asked how I felt and that's how I feel."

"Fair enough," Lex agreed. "I'm going to go back to the question of what are you afraid of. I'll also keep spanking until you've run out of answers."

His hand found the underside of my bottom in six fast, hard swipes. I wailed and tried to get away, but was no better off than I had been with Simon. The spanking then fell into a steady rhythm of determination.

I couldn't stop the tears. "I'm afraid that I'm going to fall in love with each of you and that I'll do something to mess it up. I'm afraid of my past catching up with me and ruining everything I could have with you. I'm afraid that Slater's going to hate me and I'll be sent away. I'm afraid of disappointing everyone, including myself."

There. It was out in the open. Lex gently ran his hand over my scorched flesh and soothed the pain. When I calmed a bit, he gave me to Ryder.

"How can we be the best daddies to you?" he asked as he rubbed my back.

I had no fight left in me. They were going to find out eventually, so why prolong the inevitable. "Be consistent and strong and let me know where I stand," I cried. "Just don't lock me in my room and not talk to me, and don't ever hit my face. I know you won't, but I need to be rocked and snuggled as much as I need to see your passion. Even if that passion comes in the form of spanking."

"Do you think this will be an effective mode of correction?" he asked.

"Yes, Daddy."

"I'm going to spank you in the way I should have last night. You said yourself that you deserved more."

"Please don't. You're scaring me."

"There's nothing wrong with a dose of healthy fear."

I couldn't decide which of the three hurt worse, but Ryder definitely had something in his swing that was different than the other two. I twisted and squirmed, but couldn't evade the punishing blows that seared my delicate skin. When he stopped, my sobs were out of control.

The other two men were by his side when he pulled me to sit on his lap. Each one stroked and caressed my arms, hair, and legs and planted kisses on my head and cheeks. I was surrounded by a giant hug in the arms of three strong, handsome men who wanted me.

They wanted me enough to show it. No one had ever done that before.

Lex gave me a warm kiss and pulled himself to his feet. "I've got to run some algorithms if I'm going to be ready for my meeting. Are you still up to going on a date with us?"

I nodded. "Yes, Daddy. Is it still okay that I call you that?"

"More than okay, darling. Be a good girl. Gentlemen? I'm locking myself in my office."

"Gotcha, Boss. We'll send in Recon if we don't hear anything come sundown," Simon said.

"Thanks. I'll call the Meat Locker and have them set up a room. Would you be okay sleeping in the same room with us? The town isn't equipped for visitors, so there isn't a large hotel. It's a place where we can hang if we get stuck in town overnight."

"I'll be fine. I belong to you, remember?"

"Yes, but we respect your comfort."

"My ass doesn't feel very respected right now."

"Your bottom received what it was due, so no pouting." Lex tapped my nose. "Sundown is at sixteen thirty. I want to leave here before fifteen hundred."

"Yes, sir, Major. Any other orders?"

"Fuel up the Skidoo. We'll go in that together."

"What's a Skidoo?"

"It's a modified snowmobile. You'll like it, trust me. We've got some chores we need to do. Simon?"

"I'll reload all the wood piles in the house and bring up some supplies from storage."

"Good. I'll bring Jenn with me to check for snow damage and then I'll ready the Skidoo. Don't stay out too long and don't let yourself overheat," Ryder ordered.

"I won't. See ya in a bit, Jenniebean."

"Bye, Daddy," I said shyly. The words felt good on my lips. I looked at Ryder. He was studying me. "What?"

"I was watching you. You really shine when you're in your Middle."

"I'm afraid to let that part of me loose," I admitted, curling against him. "I don't know how to act."

"You're not supposed to. We'll reel you in if it's too much, and also give you enough slack to explore. You'll have to trust us."

"I need to tell you something. When you guys did *that*, it made me feel something."

"By *that* I assume you're talking about the spanking. What did you feel?"

"You know."

"No, I don't. Explain."

I swear I was going to eyeroll myself into another universe! "It made me horny, okay? I know it shouldn't, but I had no control over it."

He chuckled. "Did you think we didn't notice? You already know it's a huge turn on for us. It would've been different if you were seriously disciplined—we take no joy in that—but for maintenance and less significant transgressions, we can't help ourselves."

I looked at him suspiciously. "You guys wouldn't spank me just to rev me up, would you?"

"I wish I could honestly tell you *no*, but I won't lie. You're in a house filled with healthy, red-blooded men who haven't been in a woman's arms in a long time. Once that step's taken, I'm afraid you'll be sitting on a red bottom quite often."

"That's so wrong."

"Then why are you smiling?"

"Leave me alone." I pushed him away, completely aware of the bulge in his jeans.

****

"Did you get everything done?" Ryder asked Simon as we set the table for lunch.

"Yep. We need to fill the meat locker. I tossed the last of the carcasses over the fence for Slater's puppies. He'd be pissed if he thought I forgot to feed them."

"They're wolves, and they know how to hunt."

"Yeah, but he also likes to know they're close by and safe. He's anxious about poachers after the hunting ban was lifted."

"I know he is." Ryder flipped a couple of grilled-cheese sandwiches onto a plate. "Jenn? Would you please bring this to Lex? He'll forget to eat if we don't make him and we don't want him getting grumpy."

"Yes, Daddy," I said cheerfully. I grabbed the plate and a mug of tomato soup and went to the far right wing of the lodge where Lex's room and office were situated. Molly followed with her eye on the plate.

"I'm not dropping this for you, you little pig. You act like no one feeds you. Daddy? I have lunch."

"Come in, sweetheart."

"My hands are full, and Molly's eyeballing your grilled cheese."

Lex opened the door and relieved me of my burden. "Molly has a nose for one thing and one thing only. Bacon. Taste."

"Oh, my God," I groaned when I bit into his sandwich. "This is delicious, but you guys are going to be walking coronaries if you keep eating this stuff."

"We only indulge during the winter because of the number of calories we lose to the cold. Molly, however, indulges year round." He gave her a bite of his sandwich and rubbed her head. "She misses Slater. You've been a big help, though. Ordinarily, she just lays on his bed and whines, but she's been your shadow since day one. Ryder said she's even sleeping with you."

"Simon showed her how to use the elevator. I didn't realize how smart she was."

"Don't judge the intelligence of someone by their appearance. Miss Molly is a search and rescue dog and has saved over twenty people from drowning and freezing to death."

"She has?"

"When Slater comes home, ask to see his brag book. This little girl has jumped out of helicopters into frozen water to save fishermen and dug under mounds of solid snow to pull out avalanche victims. She's pretty amazing."

"I never would've guessed."

"Things aren't always as they seem. Take Simon, for example."

"What about him?"

"You tell me."

"Well, I know he can do almost anything with his hands, so he's mechanically inclined. He's quoted stuff that the Markford's grandmother taught which was unusually poetic and unexpected. He also has a serious side that seems to come out when he's in his daddy mode."

"He's got a Ph.D. in physics with a specialty in projectile motion."

"Say what?" My jaw must have hit the floor.

"He's probably the smartest one of the bunch. His mind goes a million miles a minute, and the only way to slow it down is to play. We get on his case because it keeps him in check. He's a bit ADHD if you haven't noticed."

"Wow." I sat on the bed and shook my head. "What else don't I know?"

Lex laughed. "I ask myself that same question every day. Ryder is one of the world's greatest strategists. That's one, of many, reasons that we live here. There are a lot of countries who'd love to get their hands on him. He gives me all the moves that I code into these training games." He pointed to the computer. "Slater's the one that I find the most amazing out of the bunch. He's got an ear for languages which is beyond my ability to comprehend."

"I'd imagine other governments would want all of you as a unit."

"That's another reason why we live here. No one controls us, not even our own. Believe me; they've tried. We've even been ordered, and consequently threatened, by the recent administration to prove ourselves as Americans and give the US the means to lord over other countries. We refused. War's not a game, and until any of those people know what it feels like to take a life, we aren't giving them anything."

"I admire your stand. I had you guys pegged as mercenaries."

"We are, in a way, but we only fight for what will save lives, not help with a political agenda. Prior to you coming here, we worked with the DEA in different countries to break up drug smuggling rings. The day you joined us, I retired the unit."

"Why did you do that?"

"Because you're what we've been working for all these years. You deserve to have a healthy and happy home, and we want the same. We've been fighting for ten years non-stop. We've made a dent in some areas, but more criminals pop up. We're working on being efficient and learning to fight smarter. These programs that I'm developing will help train future soldiers in the war against drugs and human trafficking."

"What do you know about the place I was kept?"

Lex paused for a moment. "The information you gave us provided enough evidence to close in on them, but they weren't the headquarters."

"They weren't?"

"No. The cartel's enormous and one we've been trying to pinpoint for a long time. It's easier to hide facilities in areas like Canada because no one is looking for drug lords. We also believe that there's a large alliance located in Alaska that serves as a link between North America and Russia. They're well-hidden and very powerful."

"Lex? Do they know that I gave away their location?"

"Yes."

My heart started to pound. I stood and began pacing the floor. "I'm on their hit list. They won't stop until they get me."

"You're safe here, baby. I give you my word that none of them will get to you."

"How do you know? These people are expert subversives. They employ the best of the best. For each one of you, there are probably ten of them. They could be living in Northern Lights, for all you know."

"We take precautions against that possibility."

I started to panic. "Do you know what they'll do if they get their hands on me? I was so stupid! I—"

He stopped my rampage by pressing his lips to my mouth, not letting go as he carried me to his bed and laid me down. I groaned as his teeth found my throat and his warm breath sent shivers over my body.

"No one will ever harm what's mine," he whispered. His eyes were dark with lust as he hovered over me.

Chapter Thirteen
(Lex)

∞ ∞ ∞

I always believed that I possessed the most self-control in our team. I was the level-headed, prudent and rational member who everyone turned to when things got twisted. All those beliefs were tossed out the window when I peered into the frightened turquoise eyes of the woman I swore to protect.

She was more than that, now. Close quarters for any amount of time meant one of two things. People either got along, or they tried to kill each other. I could only speak for myself, but I was sure the other guys agreed. We could stay snowed in with this woman through eternity.

We never planned on who would 'get her first.' In fact, that was always the farthest thing from our minds since we shared everything without question or jealousy. To find her beneath me and pleading for comfort in a moment of terror, was something even I didn't have the strength to refuse. Her scent overwhelmed me—a mix of vanilla and lavender, reminding me of the promise of springtime when the sun caressed the wildflowers with warmth. I covered her mouth with mine and felt her tense in anticipation before she parted her lips and allowed me to explore her sweetness with my tongue.

She had never orgasmed before, and I would be her first. The trust she was offering me in her moment of need was humbling. I gently pinned her arms above her head and looked into her eyes.

"Yes?" I asked.

"Yes," she answered.

Her breath tickled my neck as I pressed my lips to her closed eyes and then moved down once again to take her mouth roughly. My hands tightened around her wrists as my tongue claimed her again, fiercely fucking her mouth and leaving no question as to whom she belonged.

With a single tug, I left her bereft of the layers of clothes that covered her torso. Impatient to see her breasts, I pulled the silky blue bra away from the porcelain mounds tipped with dark, pink nipples.

"You're perfection," I whispered, admiring the little buds that tightened under the chilly air. "Are you cold?"

"A little."

I swiftly added logs to the fire and stripped my shirt from my body. When I looked back, she had removed the bra and was waiting for me, her cheeks bright pink against her soft, pale skin.

"Molly, you need to leave," I said hoarsely, opening the door for the big animal.

"Don't you like an audience?" Jennifer asked as I climbed back on top of her.

"Not the four-legged kind." My mouth worked its way to her left nipple. A low sigh fluttered from her throat as I used my tongue to trace every ridge and pucker of her tight nub. Her hands trembled as they traced the muscles of my arms and back. With a growl, I snatched her wrists and held them, again, over her head.

"Tell me to stop now. If you don't, I won't be able to control myself."

"I don't want you to stop."

"I don't do tender."

She looked at me with both surprise and curiosity. "I trust you."

Never have those three words touched my heart so profoundly. "Keep your hands above your head," I ordered, slowly releasing her wrists. I placed my palms on the outer curves of her breasts and kissed between the valley before sliding my lips to her belly button. A little silver bell dangled sweetly in the tiny indent.

"You're so incredibly perfect," I whispered again, moving my hands to the waistband on her soft, blue sweatpants. I took my time, peeling the material from her flesh inch by inch so that I didn't miss a moment of the unveiling. Her sweats, panties, and Uggs fell to the floor with a muffled thump, leaving her naked before my eyes.

"It's not too late," I warned her.

She looked at my crotch and then back at me. A smile covered her lips. "I think it is. Show me what it's like to feel."

"I want a promise from you," I said gruffly. "If there is anything I'm doing that brings you back to that horrible place, you'll tell me."

She kissed me. "I don't think you're capable of bringing me there. In fact, I think you'll help me forget it."

"I want to look at you."

Her forehead wrinkled. "You do? Why?"

"Because you're gorgeous." I ran my hand along the inside of her thigh and felt her wetness. "Don't close your legs. You have the most beautiful pussy I've ever seen."

I wedged my shoulders between her knees and caressed her exposed folds. I could feel her thighs tightening as she tried to resist my attention. She wasn't accustomed to being the recipient of positive attention, and I needed to show her that she was worth it, but it had to be my way. I nibbled along the insides of her thighs and inhaled her arousal. Her body wasn't protesting my actions.

"Open your legs. If I have to tell you again, you're going to get spanked."

The instant glistening of her juices wasn't a figment of my imagination. She wanted to be dominated, not domineered. I waited for her defiance, the slight tightening of her knees as I ran a finger down the center of her ass.

"Did you just try to close your legs?" I asked, pulling away.

Her eyes twinkled. "Maybe a little."

"That was very naughty of you. You know what that means."

She squealed as I snatched her up and rolled her across my lap. Her heart-shaped bottom still held a faint shade of pink from that morning, but was otherwise flawless. I ran my hand over the swells and then dipped my fingers into the dark 'v.' She was soaking wet.

"I'm sorry, Daddy."

I was startled for a moment. I wasn't in the habit of mixing age-play and sex. I held the belief that by doing so, mixed messages were sent and often misconstrued by the ignorant who didn't take the time to understand the dynamics. But there was a tone in her voice that told me the term was one of trust and endearment. I needed to allow her to express herself how she felt most comfortable and view the moment as role play, not the lifestyle.

"I forgive you, but you need to learn to mind me when I tell you to do something."

"Please don't spank me," she said while wiggling her bottom under my hand. *Brat.*

"I have to; otherwise you won't learn your lesson," I announced.

"I'll be good. I promise."

"I'm sure you will." I raised my hand and clapped it down on the pale skin. An imprint of my fingers colored and then faded. My instincts were directing me, and they've never been wrong. That meant having to ask her one more time.

"Do I have your consent?"

"Do whatever you need to. I want to feel. I want to be okay with myself. Take away my fear. Please."

I held her firmly on the small of her back and felt her stiffen. "I'll do all that, but you have to completely submit to me and hold nothing back."

"I'll try," she whimpered.

"The harder you fight, the longer it will take. Give yourself to me," I commanded. My hand crashed against her upturned backside. I held nothing back, and I rained spank after spank across her cheeks, bringing them to a fiery red. Her cries changed to shouting, then pleas to stop. Finally, she ceased her kicking and twisting, and just sobbed silently into the comforter. I gave her a minute to process the pain and then turned her to her back.

"Keep your legs open."

There was no resistance as I tasted her juices. Her flavor was extraordinary and different from any other pussy I've explored. For a split second, I felt sorry for the other guys not being present to share my feast.

"What are you doing to me?" she gasped as I sucked, licked and flicked her clit.

"I'm going to make you scream, baby," I promised, inserting two on my fingers slowly into her tight sheath. Her panting grew more animalistic, and she lifted her pelvis off the bed.

"This can't be happening," she said in short, sporadic gasps.

"Don't fight. Accept pleasure."

She suddenly arched her back and released a wail that echoed off every wall in the lodge. I didn't stop finger fucking and sucking her until she came a second time.

"Fuck me, Lex. I need to feel you inside of me," she begged.

The rest of my clothes joined hers on the floor, and I crawled over her. Our lips melted together as the head of my cock sought her hot, wet passage. She let out a little yelp as I entered her.

"I'll go slowly. I don't want to hurt you," I promised, giving her muscles a chance to adjust to my size.

"You're so big. I don't think I can take you."

"Shh, don't cry. Relax," I urged. "Push out to meet me and then pull me in. There you go. Don't fight."

Her body was rebelling against the intrusion. "I'm sorry."

"Try this," I said, flipping to my back and tucking her knees against my hips. "Close your eyes and move when you feel ready."

I played with her clit as I eased her down on my cock. Her eye widened as she captured the rhythm of movement and worked me inside.

"I did it!"

"Are you still scared?" I asked, holding her still. Her tight muscles twitched around my shaft, and it was taking every bit of self-control not to take over.

"No. It feels—right. Can we switch places?"

I gladly obliged and turned her to her back. Her legs wrapped around my waist and she thrust her pussy toward me. There was no more holding back for me as her muscles clenched around my cock. I drove into her, and she clamped her tightness around me so much that I could feel each time I struck her g-spot. She bit my earlobe, making me plow even harder.

"Fuck!" I shouted as her intoxicating scent filled my head. I thrust in deeper and locked my hips before I flooded her with my steaming, hot cum.

We laid there breathlessly for several minutes as my cock finally relinquished its claim upon her body.

"Stay there," I said, kissing her eyelids. I went into my bathroom, cleaned up, and brought a bowl of hot, scented water and towels to gently cleanse every inch of her body that I had the privilege to know. Dressing the beautiful creature saddened me. I wanted to keep her naked and aroused forever.

"Are you okay?" I asked, smoothing her hair over her shoulders.

"I'm in a daze. It was ethereal. I thought you said you didn't do tender."

"I don't."

"Then your idea of tender must be much different than mine. Is this what it's supposed to feel like?"

"In my world, yes. How does your bottom feel?"

"Sore, but nice. I guess I'm a little kinky," she giggled.

"I'm a lot kinky, so there's nothing wrong there. I have to get back to work, and you need to go eat some lunch."

"Does this mean you're back to being a bossy daddy again?"

"That never changed." I grinned, tweaking her nose. "I'll see you in a couple of hours."

****

"Put a sock in it, gentlemen," I scolded when I exited my room that afternoon.

"We didn't say anything," Ryder announced.

"We didn't have to. The entire valley heard what happened in there."

"Simon!"

"What? You, too?" he asked Jennie. "I haven't seen you smile this much since you got here."

"Be nice, or I'm putting Hobo in your gym shorts."

"This little guy? He adores me."

"Hey! Give him back."

"Simon, don't tease. How are you doing, sweetie?" I asked, kissing her cheek.

"Good except for these two buttbrains. First, they wouldn't let me have any bacon on my grilled cheese because I took too long in coming back and Molly ate it all."

"Molly didn't eat it. Simon did," Ryder corrected.

"Why didn't you just go to the freezer and get more?"

"We were lazy."

"Sure you were. I'm more inclined to believe you were listening at my door like a couple of pervs," Lex scoffed.

"That, too."

Jennifer snorted. "Then they wanted to know how many times you ran 'algorithms' before you found the magic formula."

"We were just curious as to how your research was going, Lex," Simon said.

"Sorry about them. They can be such children at times."

"It doesn't bother me at all. They aren't totally mean, and the teasing makes me feel like part of a family. I'm still trying to wrap my head around the fact that my boyfriends are also my friends, daddies, teachers and big brothers."

"They're just names, little one. Just names. It's what happens here that defines them," I said, touching the center of my chest. "Are you boys packed up for our adventure tonight?"

"No one told me what to bring. I'm sorry."

"She's taken care of. The Skidoo's fueled, side-bags packed, and just waiting for us to board."

"I'm going to put Hobo back in his hutch if I can catch him."

"He adores Molly, but the poor dog keeps getting her nose pricked," Ryder chuckled.

Jennifer kissed Molly's big head. "I'll teach you Hobo's favorite game, and you'll never get your nose poked again. Simon? Go sit down. He's not going to come to you."

I winked at Ryder when she flattered herself on the floor and spread her long hair out around her head. We laughed as the four-legged sea-urchin ran straight toward her and rolled in the dark strands.

"Ow," she said, sitting up and untangling the hedgie. "I know you're getting frustrated because Mollypup doesn't know how to play your game. Let's teach her. She's smart and will pick it up right away."

"What are you doing, love?" I asked.

"Watch." She had Molly lay next to her and waited as Hobo went to touch noses with the dog. The second they made contact, he curled into a ball.

"Molly, you can't push him from the place he curled up. Take your paw and turn him around and then you can roll him like a ball."

I watched in fascination as Molly got the idea after three tries. Once she started to roll Hobo comfortably with her nose, she rose and went to the other side of the room. Hobo uncurled, turned around and ran straight to her. She hopped up, making him miss her and then flopped on her back and let the little animal climb onto her chest and snuggle into the fur of her neck. Simon was in tears from laughing, and Ryder was bent over and holding his stomach. I winked at our smiling girl.

"I haven't heard this much laughter in our home in years. Thank you."

"I've never laughed this much in my entire life. Thank you. Come on, sleepy head. Back to your hutch."

"My gut hurts," Ryder coughed. "Slater's going to shit bricks when he sees Molly's afraid of a rat."

"I already got it on video and sent it to him," Simon said with a smirk.

"Get geared up. It's time to go. We'll unload at the Meat Locker, and you two can occupy Jennie while

I'm at the meeting. I shouldn't be long so, when I'm done, we'll go for dinner and then over to Lena's."

"Are her daddies extending her bedtime?" Simon asked.

"Yes, but only as long as she doesn't get cranky. I pulled a box of cream puffs from the freezer to bring along. Do you have fuzz-faces gear?"

"Molly's coming?" Jennifer asked with excitement as she rejoined us.

"She's our unit mascot. Plus, she'll never forgive us if we deprived her of an evening of bacon."

"Ready to deploy?" I asked. Simon and Ryder ran to stand at attention in front of me. I looked to the right where the girl was filing a nail and to the left where Molly was scratching her ear. I lifted my chin like a proud commander.

"Is this what I'm to expect when we debark from now on?" I raised an eyebrow toward Molly. "I didn't ask for your comment, Miss Dog. Go to Ryder and sit at heel."

"That's one, Sir," Ryder stated, still at attention.

"Miss Hudson? Are you planning on joining our expedition?"

"Yeah, but I'm not doing that stuff. Ow. Simon! Let go of my ear."

"Stand straight next to me. Chin up, hands at your sides, eyes straight forward. You're at attention, Marine."

"I'm not a Marine and why do I have to be at attention?"

"Because that's what we do."

"That's what *you* do, not me. I'm going to grab a Coke while you boys play soldier."

"I guess she told us," Ryder said with a chuckle. "We could get her a pair of pink and purple Cammie's."

"I should start holding drills again," I grunted.

"She'd sleep through those. Lord knows, I did." Simon chuckled.

"I think we need to face the fact that the military presence in this house is going to be overrun with glitter stickers and stuffies, Major. We can't ever expect to win the war against entropy."

"That girl certainly is a whirling dervish of activity. Did you see the kitchen when she finished helping me bake?"

"You wanted a Middle," Jennie piped up as she plopped on a chair. I frowned and took her drink away.

"This isn't a Coke."

"I couldn't find them."

"There's a big difference between Coke and a beer," I scolded.

"Yeah, I'm sure she knows." Simon grabbed the bottle and finished it off in a single gulp. "Let's go before someone gets herself spanked. Arms." He worked her parka around her.

"We'll talk about this later, young lady," I promised with a wag of my finger.

She blinked her long lashes demurely. "Anything you say, Daddy."

Chapter Fourteen
(Jennie)
∞ ∞ ∞

I sat on Simon's lap and clung for dear life as the enclosed Skidoo flew over hills of snow and skidded across icy bends. Ryder cheered like a little boy on a roller coaster, Lex focused on the GPS and front cameras marking our trail, and Molly licked the condensation off the windows.

"Slow down, or I'm going to puke," I finally said, digging my fingers into Ryder's shoulder.

"Not one for adventure rides, huh?" he asked, slowing the vehicle until it leveled out and ran smoothly over the path.

"Not really. Why can't we take the time and enjoy the scenery?"

"Sorry, babe. Is this better?"

"Yeah. Look! Is that a caribou? It's huge." I jumped on Simon's lap. "I love how the snow covers the trees. It looks gold, doesn't it?"

"The sun's starting to set. Watch the horizon for the next few minutes," Lex suggested.

I pressed my face to the glass and stared breathlessly as the sun's rays shifted over the snow, coloring it with sparkling orange, red and pink. It started to settle to blue when we arrived in town and my face hurt from smiling.

"Did I order a pretty picture for you, or what?"

I hugged Lex from behind. "The prettiest picture ever, Daddy." I leaned over and kissed Ryder's cheek. "Thank you for slowing down so I could see the caribou. That was the best." I turned to lean in Simon's arms. "You're the most awesome booster seat ever. Kiss me."

The Skidoo earned several catcalls as Ryder drove it to the other end of town to a large building that, frankly, looked like an old metal Quonset hut.

"We're here!" he announced. "What do you think?"

My heart sunk. After driving through such a beautiful and animated town, ending here was a disappointment. *Suck it up, buttercup. Beggars can't be choosers.*

"As long as it's clean and warm, and I'm with you, I'm good."

"She's such a little liar. You should see this face. He's yanking your chain, Jenniebean. This is the garage for our snowmobiles and vehicles. We'll harness Molly to a cart and then stroll through the town."

"I'm going to get to my meeting and will meet you at the Meat Locker before dinner." Lex hugged his friends and then pressed his mouth tightly to mine. "Be a good girl for your daddies."

"Yes, sir."

"Molls! Let's get dressed," Ryder said, patting his thigh. The dog was beside herself and spun wildly before she slowed long enough to be placed in her harness and allowed her paws to be waxed. Simon opened a storage unit and dragged out a red sleigh complete with jingle bells and carriage lights and secured the dog's harnesses. He and Ryder then loaded the back with our supplies and lifted me to sit on the bench. Once I was snuggled under a bunch of blankets, they opened the door.

Light flurries of snow reflected the golden gas lamps that lined the street. The boys held Molly's lead and walked on either side of me as I gazed with wonder at the magical land that I now called home. The air smelled like fresh snow, pine trees, hot cocoa and peppermint, and Christmas music piped through invisible speakers. Several couples were having a snowball fight in a frozen park, their laughter filling the air with pure joy. A six-dog team trotted by with the Huskies yapping their greeting to Molly's elated bark.

I smiled and looked up as Ryder ran his hand over my head. "I love you, Daddy."

My eyes widened when I heard the words slip out of my mouth. His smile was brighter than the glittering lights.

"I love you, too, baby."

I turned my head toward Simon, feeling braver and more secure. "Daddy? I love you, too. I can't believe how good you are to me."

"We love you, Jenniebean. I know those are hard words to say and accept, but when they come from us, you have to believe they're true."

"I also don't think it's going to take much for us to fall in love with you, either. But those are big girl problems. Right now, you're a beautiful little girl who's about to experience an entire wintertime of Christmas."

"They're ice-skating over there! Look!" I squealed, pointing at the frozen pond with colorful lights that changed under the ice. I whipped my head around at the sound of a roaring fire. Two men sat on either side of a young woman on a bench and kissed her cheeks as she clapped gleefully at the multi-colored flame. A series of happy shouts announced the onslaught of a dozen people carrying long skewers topped with marshmallows.

"That fire is amazing. How do they get all those colors?" I grabbed Simon's hand and tugged eagerly.

"The core is made of loops of copper, and it's superheated with an underground pipe system where we've tapped into deep volcanic pockets. It oxidizes the metal and voila! Pretty colors."

"Can you make us one at home in the big fireplace? It's so romantical."

"Consider it done, love bug."

"You rock. Is it always like this here?" I asked as the boys parked next to the bonfire and placed me on a bench.

"When the nights are clear, we celebrate. Go play," Ryder said, releasing Molly from the sleigh. I chortled as she dove into deep piles of snow and then started to chase snowballs.

"I've never seen such a happy animal. Let me guess—everyone has bacon in their pockets."

"I wouldn't doubt it. I'm sure the Huskies will be joining her as soon as their haul is unloaded."

The yapping of the dogs made Molly spin around and stick her rump in the air as she prepared for the pack's arrival. They pounced on her, and the seven dogs went through a wild wrestling match. I grabbed Ryder's hand with worry.

"Is Molly okay?"

"They're playing. Nothing's going to happen to our fluff ball."

I watched one of the Huskies trot down the street and enter a store. "Do they let them run loose?"

"The dogs have sounding collars so they won't leave the parameter of the town. They're allowed in any of the shops, and we obviously have no traffic that will threaten them. This particular team is also comprised of S&R dogs, so it's important that they know all the people who live in their den."

"What's that place?" I asked, pointing to a tall house in the distance that glowed in warm, yellow light.

"Cinderella's Castle AKA Markford Manor."

"Wow. Where are the other houses?"

"They're around. Some are designed to blend in with the landscape; others are built underground or into the hills. We're the furthest away because of our specific logistics. What's wrong?"

"What if I want someone to play with when you guys are working?"

"You may stay at the *Zoo* if you don't want to be alone. It's an activity center for the girls when their daddies have to work."

"Are there any boys or mommies here?"

"Not yet, but that's not to say it won't happen one day."

"Would you refuse admission if one wanted to come?"

"Not at all."

"Uncle Simon!" one of the girls called. She dove at him and pushed him off the bench and into the snow. She sat on his stomach and kissed his nose. "Hi! I missed you."

I felt a frown form on my face. This woman was a little too familiar with *my* man. Ryder chuckled when I stood.

"Watch the little green monster, kid. The town is part of an extended family."

"But he's *mine*." I didn't understand where my possessiveness was coming from, nor did I like it. I also thought the girl was incredibly rude.

"Please sit down and listen to me. We are devoted and committed to you. Period. Northern Lights has one internal law, and that is no cheating is permitted in any way, shape or form. A girl who flirts inappropriately with another guardian is evaluated and monitored. If it continues, her family's discharged from town. The same thing goes for a guardian."

"What determines inappropriateness?"

"Any intimate approach like kissing on the lips, stroking inside of thighs, and exposing herself. Many guardians have permitted their close friends to spank their girls, but it's always witnessed and strictly disciplinary."

"I can't have you doing this anymore, Kit. I have my own girl now," Simon was saying as he pulled himself to his feet.

"I'm just playing."

"I know that, but you don't want to start any gossip, do you? Your daddies will have your hide if that happens again."

"You're no fun."

"I don't make the rules. Kit? This is my little girl, Jennifer. Jenniebean? This is Kit. She belongs to—"

"I don't belong to nobody. I'm my own person," the girl snapped.

"Be nice, Kit. She hasn't done anything to you," Simon advised.

"You were my friend long before *she* came along. There's no reason why I can't play with you."

"I want to show respect to Jennifer. You'd feel the same way if you were new to your family and someone came along and claimed one of your daddies."

"They can do whatever they want. Like I said, they don't own me. What are you looking at?" she hissed at me. I stood up.

"You. I haven't done anything for you to be so mean."

"Girls, stop," Simon ordered.

"I haven't done anything and you know it," I protested.

"Whine, why don't you?"

"Okay, that's enough, Kit." Ryder shook his head and pulled out his cell phone. "Hi, it's Watkins. Your Middle's on a rampage at the park. Yes, I saw it. No, problem. Bye."

"Did you just snitch on me?"

"I did. Your papa's on his way. Apparently, someone is supposed to be grounded for throwing a tantrum after being told she couldn't go to Anchorage with her two uncles."

"I can't believe you told on me." Tears glistened in the girl's eyes. She turned and glared at me. "This is *your* fault, you little bitch!"

I landed hard against the bench when she shoved me. Narrowing my eyes, I flew at her before Ryder could grab me.

"Oh, no, we don't," Simon roared, picking me up and dangling me under his arm.

"Put me down!"

"Are you going to cool your jets?"

"Yes!" I brushed myself off and stared at the girl who Ryder held firmly. "Are you insane? What the fuck is your problem?"

"Back off, Jenn. We'll talk about this during dinner, okay?" Ryder said softly. Simon wrapped his arm around my shoulders as a handsome man stomped toward us.

"Damn, it's cold. How are you guys doing?" he asked, hugging Ryder and Simon.

"We're great. How about you?" Simon asked.

"Doing very well. The new powerplant design was picked up by private industry two weeks ago and the bros are finishing up with their shoot in Australia. So, what's going on here. Kit? You're supposed to be grounded."

"I was bored and decided to go outside. This isn't a prison."

"No, but if you keep this up, you're going to wish it were. Gentlemen? I apologize for Kit's behavior. We still have a long way to go."

"We completely understand. This is Jennifer, by the way. She's our gift from the Graye's. Jack's the mastermind of our energy distribution through a geothermal powerplant he developed."

Jack looked genuinely happy to meet me and shook my hand. "Welcome to Northern Lights, Miss Jennifer. You've got yourself a houseful of incredible men who will love you more than life itself."

"Thank you."

"Thanks for giving me a call, Ry. The new system seems to be working. Maybe now that she knows she's being watched, some changes can occur. Let's go home, young lady. We need to have a long talk."

"But, Papa—"

"No *buts* out of you. March."

"What new system is that?" I asked after Jack left, dragging Kit by the hand.

"We have a daily newsletter with frequents updates. It includes the Naughty List and the names and levels of restriction for our mischievous subs. It makes all of us responsible for looking out for each other. Remember our motto."

"*It takes a village*," I said. "Doesn't it feel awfully intrusive?"

"We're military men. The only thing that we feel is intrusive is if someone outside of this family tries to control you." Ryder lifted his finger to answer his phone. "Is everything okay? Fabulous! We'll meet you in about ten minutes."

"Is Lex done already?" Simon asked, lifting Molly's harness. As soon as the dog saw the leather in his hands, she raced over and tried to wiggle herself onto the hitch. Ryder placed me back in the sled and tightened my balaclava to keep my face warm.

"He said the presentation went perfectly and they are going to offer him a deal in the morning. He's going to meet us at our room to get ready for dinner."

His words sounded clipped. "Daddy? Are you mad at me? None of you would take an unprovoked assault sitting down, so why should I?"

"I'm not angry. I'm just concerned that you'll react by fighting instead of trying to talk. That isn't good."

"At least she didn't have a knife at her disposal," Simon said with a chuckle. "If it makes you feel any better, Kit's tried to start a fight with nearly every gal who's come into this town."

"Why?"

"She's hurt, angry and scared. I thought we were going to wait until dinner to talk about this," Ryder said.

"I don't want my date ruined by talking about some other woman who has her eye on my boyfriend." I pouted

"Are we a little possessive?"

"How would you feel if some other guy did that to me?"

"They wouldn't."

"I didn't ask that."

"She's got you, Bro," Simon snickered. "You'd be pounding face in a heartbeat, and we both know it. Kit's background is a series of betrayal, pain, abandonment, and abuse. Add drugs and poverty to the mix, and you have a cauldron of bubbling explosives. Last summer, Jack and his two brothers found her face down in a puddle behind a building. She was cold, starving and in withdrawals. There was also a warrant out for her arrest on multiple charges."

"Shit."

"This is why we should never judge people by what you see on the surface. Jack contacted the Markfords for advice. Long story short, Kit was brought here. She was fattened up, detoxed, and is trying to work through her past. Lex and Simon have been a big part of her therapy program, which is why she was so expressive. She trusts him."

I looked at my big, beautiful giant. *Who wouldn't trust Simon?* "So why did she attack me?"

"It's all about trust. Newcomers are a threat to her. She still doesn't believe that she's got a home for life here, or that those three men love her to the moon and back. It's not unusual for an addict to act like this, so we all exercise patience and acceptance."

"I'm not going to accept anyone attacking me. I don't care what their excuse is. I will defend myself."

"That's reasonable, but just don't go looking for a fight."

"Can we drop the subject? It's putting me in a cranky mood," I requested. The bitch managed to take a magical evening and turn it to crap, and I was pissed.

"Don't allow people like Kit to steal your joy," Simon whispered. "Miserable people make people miserable. Avoid that trap."

"I don't want you touching her again. Not even in play." I couldn't help it. I needed to know that he wouldn't teeter-totter when it came to me.

"I won't be. You have my word."

"Thank you. That goes for you, too, Mister." I poked Ryder.

"I have very little interaction with Kit, so don't you worry. Lena's another story, though."

I frowned. I hadn't asked him to give up on the relationship with the Markford girl, and it bothered me that he brought her up. "How much of another story?"

"We're all very close to Lena. She'll always hold a special place in our hearts."

I wasn't liking this at all but chose to stay silent.

****

My mood lifted slightly when we walked through a tunnel of trees and were greeted by a cheery, two-story lodge that was decorated like a gingerbread house.

"This is adorable," I said out loud, basking in the warm glow of the amber lights.

"We've got the south side. Simon? Some help, please," Ryder said. They released Molly and hung the sleigh on a pair of long hooks under a shelter. The boys took my hand and walked me to the third level and around back. With the end of civil twilight and no sign of the moon, the grounds below were pitch black.

"Eery, huh? This time next month and you won't even see a bit of blue in the sky."

"I still can't get over how the sun rises and sets on the same horizon. It's pretty freaky."

"Speaking of freaky, look who's here," Ryder said, opening the mudroom door.

"I just arrived. Hi, baby girl," Lex said, giving me a hug and a brief kiss on the lips. "Did you like the town?"

"Most of it."

"What happened?" he looked concerned as he helped me take off my parka and boots.

"Kit," Simon said with a sigh.

"I'm so sorry. She didn't hurt you, did she?"

"If you guys know that this girl is going to accost people, why is she allowed to be unsupervised in public?"

"She was supposed to be grounded and got out. Northern Lights isn't a prison, Jenn," Ryder proclaimed as he removed his outerwear and turned on the heater elements so everything could dry.

"This is her first winter here, too. It's an adjustment, and she has issues with the dark. I'll take care of it. Don't worry," Lex promised, drying Molly with a towel after clearing her paws of clumps of icy snow.

"I don't want her touching you, either. You're mine."

"Hear this? We have a little alpha wolf who's claimed her pack. Slater will be so pleased."

"I'm not joking, Ryder."

"We know you aren't. You have my word that there's nothing to fear. There's only one girl in the town that we'll love on other than you, and that's Lena."

"What's so special about her?"

"We brought her here on a Recon mission. She was a prima ballerina for the Bolshoi Company in Russia and was taken hostage when her father refused to give his formula for a synthesized drug to the Bratva."

"That's the Russian mafia," Simon explained.

"They were going to break her legs so she couldn't dance again. She was in pretty bad shape when we got her out of there. They hadn't given her food or water for days, and she had pneumonia," Ryder said with sadness.

"That was another situation where Slater became invisible, and all the guards around her cage were wiped out by an unseen force," Lex said, opening the door to the suite.

"She must have been terrified."

"When we got to her, she was beyond that. We weren't sure if she'd survive. It was a very scary time for all of us. The Markford boys came to the hospital to help us stand vigil. Long story short, they fell for her. They got married a year later."

"All of them?"

"All of them. What do you think?" Lex asked as he opened the door to the room.

"Wow," I whispered. The wall length window overlooking a black landscape was alit with dancing flames that reflected off the glass and quickly warmed the room. The decor was sleek, modern, and very masculine with glass, black ebony, and stainless steel. I dug my bare toes into the soft carpet, enjoying the heat that rose from the floor.

"It's nothing that you'd expect, but it's comfortable and has the best view."

"I like it. As for the view, I beg to differ." I pointed to the window.

"I'm talking about you."

I blushed and looked down. "I've got a pretty nice view myself."

"Come see the bedroom," Simon ordered, catching me with one arm and walking into the adjoining area.

"Is this made for an orgy or something?" I asked, my eyes glued to the enormous half-moon bed. A party-size jacuzzi tub bubbled in the far corner next to another set of large windows.

"The town is polyamorous, remember? The owner designed the Meat Locker to accommodate multi-partner relationships. I don't know about you, but I'm getting hungry," Simon announced.

"You're always hungry." I poked his firm, flat stomach.

"That he is. Let's get prettied up for dinner. We'll be leaving for the Markfords at eight, so we've got plenty of time to eat and chill," Lex said, opening a bag and pulling out a midnight blue velvet dress with a satin tie.

"Let me dress her. Please?" Simon begged.

Ryder rolled his eyes. "She's not your dolly."

"She can be."

"Don't I get a say in this?" I asked, wrinkling my nose.

"No. Make her pretty. We'll be in the living room," Lex said with a chuckle.

Chapter Fifteen
(Jennie)
∞ ∞ ∞

"I noticed you didn't say anything after Lex told you about Lena. Arms up."

"There wasn't anything to say. I get it. I really can dress myself."

"I know, but I like doing it. Just like I enjoy feeding you."

"Have you ever wanted kids of your own? Like real ones?"

He tossed my shirt on the bed and shook out the dress. "Nah. First, my mother wished that one day we would have children to torment us in the same way we tormented her. I couldn't do that to Lex and Slater. They already have their hands full with us. Second, I'm incredibly selfish. Except for the Brotherhood, I don't want to lose any time with my girl."

"As in me?"

He kissed me hard, bruising my lips. "As in you. Finally, I couldn't expose a child to the horrible things we've seen in this world."

"Do the others feel the same way?"

"Completely. There's also the factor of who made the baby."

"Would it matter? All of you would be the daddy. I think you guys would make wonderful parents."

"You come from a big home. What was it like for you?"

I paused. "That was my norm. I've never known it any other way. Okay, being compared to my older brothers and sisters was hard on me, and I always felt as though I was living in their shadows. A lot of them resented me because they were stuck babysitting while my parents did things for the church."

"Do you want children?"

"I thought I did, but I realized long ago that it was something expected of me, not a desire."

"Do you think you'll change your mind one day? You're a lot younger than we are," he asked, lifting me slightly so he could pull a pair of glittery blue leggings over my bottom.

I was surprised, and relieved, with our conversation. "You're not that much older, but I agree with you. I can't keep doing things because I feel obligated. My parents' lives are theirs, and they don't influence mine. I mean, look at me! They'd shit bricks if they saw I was shacking up with four strange men."

Simon chuckled. "You haven't even met Slater yet."

"I have a serious question about this subject, though." I watched as he slipped my feet into white knee-high boots with two pompoms of white faux fur dangling from the top.

"You're wondering what would happen if you got pregnant."

"I'm wearing an IUD, but nothing is fail-safe except abstinence and sterilization. Would it be a deal breaker?" Worry started to tighten my throat.

Simon knelt on the floor and surrounded my hips with his long, heavily muscled arms.

"Sweetheart, if you got pregnant, that child would have the happiest life that her mommy and four daddies could give her. You come as a package, just like we do."

"Thank you. I'm still trying to find where I fit in your family, so I'm insecure."

"You fit in our arms, hearts, and our lives. We're yours, remember? By the way, next time, try peeing on a tree if you want to mark your territory."

"Sorry, Dude. I'm not into watersports."

"You two sound like you're having fun in there. Are we going to eat or do you want some alone time?" Ryder called from the door.

"Come in. We were just chatting. I saved this for you."

Ryder's eyes glimmered when he took the brush from his brother's hand and smacked it against his palm. "Do we need a reminder of how to behave in a restaurant?"

"No, no, no. That's to brush my hair, not spank me."

"I wish you would've called me before you dressed her up. I could've put the brush to good use." Ryder sat behind me to do my hair.

"Are we having a party?" Lex asked, throwing himself onto the bed.

"Everywhere we go is a party. Finished," Ryder said proudly.

"I'm afraid to ask how you know how to braid hair, Watkins," Lex said.

"We had a little cousin who lived with us for a while during her parents' divorce. She had long, red hair and screamed every time Mom tried to brush the knots out. Ryder hates the sound of screaming."

"It hurt my ears."

"You do explosives. How can screaming hurt your ears?" I asked.

"It was high-pitched and reminded me of nails dragged down a blackboard. I was in a chat room when one of the guys told me to braid her hair to keep it from knotting. He emailed me instructions of the styles his daughter liked."

"Was she cooperative?"

"Hell, no, but Ry was prepared. The folks weren't home, and he was ready to take his first step into Domhood. He reddened her backend until she whined more about sitting that getting her hair brushed. He never had a problem after that. Are you ready to go?"

"Right after you get changed," Lex said, holding his hand out for me. Ryder took the other one, and we walked into the living room.

"Show us how pretty you are," he ordered, sitting on the couch.

Even though the ensemble was rather pre-teen, it did make me feel adorable. I spun around for them and struck a pose.

"You like?"

"All she needs is a tiara, and she'd be a perfect little princess," Ryder stated.

"A tiara like this?" Lex asked, producing a sparkling little headpiece. I couldn't help but squeal with excitement.

"Will you put it on me?"

He grinned after fixing it in my hair. "You're so beautiful."

I hugged him. "I love you, Daddy. Thank you."

His return embrace was filled with affection. "I love you, too, Princess. Simon? Get the led out."

"I'm ready. Well, will you take a look at that sparkly thing on the princess' head?"

"Is it pretty?" I asked, twirling again.

"Only the best for our girl. Just don't lose it."

I froze mid-turn. "Whoa. Is this real?"

"Why do you look surprised?" Ryder asked, pulling me onto his lap.

"This must have cost a fortune. It's too much."

"It's never too much." His eyes smoldered when he looked at me. I started having thoughts that were as far from being a little girl as one could get. "You're squirming, and I can't be responsible for what happens."

I whispered a word in his ear that I never thought I'd say. "I'm horny."

"We don't have time right now. Let's talk about this when we get home, okay?"

"Man, you look like you just yanked out a tooth," Simon teased.

"It feels like I did. The last thing I wanted was to refuse an offer like this one," Ryder said apologetically.

Lex clapped my thigh. "Even if you agreed, I would have intervened. When we're in town, we are Northern Lights Daddies."

"Does that mean I have to be like this, even when we go to bed?"

"Yes, ma'am. When you become more adjusted to your Middle, we can consider switching. Right now, just focus on you being a princess."

"Look, Jenniebean. Molly's a princess, too."

I looked around to see the Newfoundland wearing a collar of jingle bells around her thick neck. On her head, she wore a pair of cloth reindeer horns joined together on a flashing, plastic tiara. She thumped her tail on the floor and yapped.

"That dog is strange. What a show off," I commented with a smile as she presented herself in front of Ryder so he could take pictures.

"Slater hates us doing this to her."

"Then why are you sending him all these pictures? Are you sure you're best friends?"

"We're more than best friends. We're brothers and irritating one another is what brothers do. Isn't that right, Ry?"

"Yup." Ryder hung some small Christmas bulbs from Molly's ears and took more pictures.

"Boys. What about our coats?"

"We don't need them. We're going underground. After you, my lady." Simon held his arm out for me.

****

The four of us walked through twinkling tunnels paved in cobblestone twenty feet beneath the surface of the town. The Christmas theme continued, and the air smelled like fresh pine, sugar cookies, and peppermint. Lex pointed out the storefronts and eateries, each opened for whatever the community might require.

"Is the town above functional, or it is just a decoy?" I asked as Simon pulled me into a shop and grabbed a giant lollipop off the shelf. He signed his name on an item list and took my hand.

"It's completely functional and is there for both the ambiance and convenience. Sometimes we just want to grab something, like I did when I picked you up," Ryder explained.

"How big is this place?"

"The *Party Hall* is approximately three times the size of the town. Some of the houses nearby have underground access, particularly those who house scientists and the agriculturists. The laboratories, workshops, warehouse, and the hydroponic fields cover about half of the facility. The primary purpose is storage and safety. We want to be as independent of the outside world as possible, so we're developing a means to be self-sustaining."

"So it's a giant grocery and hardware store."

"Partially. We also have emergency housing in the event of a volcanic eruption or avalanche."

"Volcano?" I gripped Simon's arm. "What volcano?"

"Relax. We have state of the art monitoring equipment for anything that might come our way, and this place will house four times the amount of residents and feed them for over a decade."

"Great, but you didn't say anything about a volcano. Is Denali mountain a volcano?"

"No, it's a volcanic granite made of a blob of cold, solid lava many feet beneath the surface. It's also the tallest mountain in US territory and is still growing," Lex answered.

"Hey, that's my lollipop!" I protested as he took it from my hand and slid it into the pocket of his dinner jacket.

"You'll spoil your dinner. The bunker protects us against volcanic ash."

"So we aren't going to turn into crispy critters?"

"It's doubtful. Avalanches, extreme temperatures, flash floods, and blizzards are always our concern."

"What if we're home and can't get here?"

"We have the same construction under our house and enough supplies to feed Simon for twenty years."

"That's a lot of supplies. Ow!" I yelped as Simon smacked my backside.

"We'll show you it all later. Ladies first," Ryder said, opening a door that was labeled *Moosehead Steak House*.

We walked up the stairs and entered a dark, rustic room warmed by a blazing fire from an enormous hearth. I stared between the colossal roof beams to the glowing wood floors as we were led to a window table overlooking the town. The guys greeted several diners and briefly introduced me.

Ryder held the chair for me to sit down and placed a napkin on my lap before he sat next to me.

"This is so pretty. How's the food?"

"The best in the world. The chef and his three brothers came here several years ago after receiving their sixteenth Michelin star and opened the restaurant."

"Didn't people wonder where they went?"

Ryder glanced at Lex. "They told the media they were ready to retire, and cashed in all their assets and sold all their restaurants. As far as the media is concerned, they were flying from the UK to Japan when the private jet crashed into the ocean."

"That's terrible. How could someone be so deceitful?"

"They had no other family, so the only people affected were diners and the media. Several residents here have done the same. The world doesn't honor the request of celebrities and would be as quick to judge as it is to praise. The Ramseys wanted to fulfill their dream of living in peace with a special girl."

"Did they?"

"Yes, ma'am. They were introduced to their little girl shortly after their arrival."

"Did Mr. Graye give her to them?"

"No. They found her after a skiing accident and nursed her back to health. The five of them have been together since."

Lex ordered dinner for me and smiled from across the table. "What do you think?"

"It's surreal. Beautiful, heavenly, and so magical. It doesn't even look real," I said, watching the ice-skaters on the frozen pond and horse-drawn sleighs jingling down the warmly-lit street.

"I felt the same way when we came here," Lex admitted. "Northern Lights became my sanctuary and helped me find peace."

"I think it did the same for all of us. Except for Slater," Simon said quietly.

****

"That was incredible," I sat back and rubbed my tummy.

"Are you done?" Simon asked.

"Yes. You can have the rest," I said, slipping Molly the scraps under the table.

"It takes so little to make that man happy." Lex chuckled while sipping his coffee. "Did you want to go to the Markford's underground or above?"

I looked at the golden lights of the distant manner. Before I could respond, Ryder intervened.

"I forgot to tell you. They're sending a horse-drawn sleigh for us. I already called to let them know we were almost done with dinner and would meet them at the hotel."

"A horse-drawn sleigh?" I couldn't contain my excitement.

"I'm pretty sure that it will be all decked out for us, too. Simon? Lena said to tell you that she baked a tableful of pastries for you."

I laughed at the look on the big man's face. "He looks like he's about to come."

"Jennifer!"

"Whut?"

"Brat. Let's get going," Lex said. "Simon, there's nothing left on that bone. Time to fall in."

"Yes, Sir, Major Becker," Simon answered, standing and pulling my chair out for me. I hooked my hands in the crooks of Ryder and Lex's arms and left for the hotel. We finished bundling up just as the sleigh's driver announced his arrival.

"Where's Molly going to sit?" I asked as we settled ourselves.

"Molly's going to do what she does best."

"Eat? Sleep? Leave big piles of puppy stuffing?"

"No, she's going to trot along the side. The road's soft, and it's only about a half mile away."

"Won't the snow hurt her paws?"

"Her paw wax will protect her. She won't wear boots like the mushing teams," Ryder said, placing his hand on my thigh under the heavy lap blanket. I turned my head toward him and received a brief kiss on the mouth. His fingers inched toward my inner thigh, and I spread my knees in response.

"Damn snow pants," he whispered in my ear.

"I'll make it up to you when we get home," I whispered back.

"Do you know how to ski?" Simon asked, oblivious to his brother kneading my inner thigh.

"No. I can't even ice-skate."

"We'll teach you," Lex promised. "See that? The Markford's built that for Lena so that every time she comes home, she feels like a princess."

In front of us was a tunnel of trees covered with thousands of tiny lights. The horses slowed to a lazy walk as we entered the twinkling passageway, giving me time to ogle the fairyland around me.

"What are you doing?" I asked Lex, who sat behind me.

"I'm covering your eyes. I want you to see Markford Manor all at once."

When he removed his hands, my eyes slowly followed the line of the fantastic house.

"It's a real castle," I whispered.

"Yup. Come summer and I'll build you a castle in the trees, okay?" Simon asked, lifting me out of the sleigh and placing my feet on the ground.

"Daddies! The uncles are here! They brought Mollypup," came a screech from the tall, double doors.

"Lena, get back in the house." One of the men ordered. "Come in! Come in! It's too cold out there. I have the Dragon's Lair blazing for you."

A firm hand led me to stand before the largest fireplace I've ever seen. It was made to look like a cave and had two dragon eyes staring from the back.

"It really looks like there's a dragon in there!" I exclaimed.

"You'll find surprises everywhere you look, sweetheart. I'm Tony. These are my twin brothers, Sean and Stefan. You've met our wife, Lena."

Lena squeezed my neck. "I'm so happy you're here. Come and see my room."

Before I could utter a sound, she was dragging me through the house and up the staircase. I barely was able to take in my surroundings before she opened the door and clapped excitedly.

"This is my room. Isn't it fun?"

"Wow," I whispered, watching as Molly went straight for the bed. The room looked as though it belonged to an eight-year-old. Everything was pink and white, with frills and sparkles. Stuffed bears sat in each of the three rocking chairs next to an enormous dollhouse, and a long bookshelf housed beautiful music boxes with graceful ballerinas in different poses. The far wall was made of mirrors with a ballet barre attached.

"Do you like it?"

"It's so pretty," I said, taking a long look at the young woman. She was dressed in pure white with sparkling crystals sewn into the material of her tutu. White satin pointe shoes and a shimmering headpiece with white feathers completed her attire.

"I know it can be a little scary in the beginning, but you'll love it here. Especially with the uncles," she said with a strong Russian accent. "Tea? It'll warm you up."

"Yes, please." I joined her at the little round table that held a beautiful china tea set.

"Cream and sugar?" she asked.

"Thanks. I'm sorry that I'm so quiet. I'm a little overwhelmed by all this."

"As you should be." She handed me a cup. "You're very lucky, though. The uncles are wonderful men and will treat you like a queen."

"Does that include Slater?"

Lena sighed and sipped her tea. "I don't see Uncle Slater very often, but when I do, he's kind and polite. He's just different than the others."

"Different as in how?"

"He's mysterious and unpredictable. He also has a way of looking at you that makes you either jump with joy or break out in tears. I mind my manners when he's around. Do you know when he's coming home?"

"No. I guess that's good, though. It's giving me a chance to know the other three first. This way when he comes home, I'll be able to focus on him. I just hope he likes me."

"If he acts like he doesn't, please don't be hurt. He doesn't let people into his life until they prove they're worthy."

"That sounds a little stuck up."

"Slater? Stuck up? He's the most humble man you'll ever meet. His standards for those who are part of his life are high, and he has no patience for foolishness."

"I'm really afraid to meet him."

"When you come face to face with him, you will fall to your knees. I've never seen a more beautiful man in my entire life—and you've seen my daddies and the uncles."

I sipped the tea and wrinkled my nose. "What's in this?"

"Oh, nothing. Rooibos red tea with cream and sugar." She winked. "There might be a splash of vodka, too."

A grin stretched across my lips. "Do your daddies know?"

"No way!" She shook her head. "I'd be sitting on a pillow for a week if they found out I broke into their liquor cabinet."

"I won't tell. Promise."

"I know you won't. More?"

"Please."

We chatted as we finished the contents of the teapot. She shared all the ins-and-outs of the town and her excitement of the upcoming camping trip. I didn't know if it was her genuine warmth, or the vodka, that made me relax. Either way, I felt welcomed and comfortable in her presence. All trepidation I had regarding her and my guys was gone.

"Lena? Will you please bring Jennie down so we can have dessert? Uncle Lex is already in your Baklava."

"Coming, Daddy!" she called back.

"The dishes?" I asked.

"I'll wash them tomorrow. We have a room filled with handsome men who want to be around us, and I'm not going to make them wait."

I watched her run and leap into the arms of one of the twins. He spun her around and then flipped to cradle her in his arms.

Ryder beckoned to me and patted his lap. His warm arms felt good around my shoulders. "Did you have fun in Lena's room?"

"It was nice. I can't believe how pretty she is, and so nice."

"She certainly is. Would you like to see her dance?"

"Would she be okay with that?"

"Of course. Gentlemen? Since Miss Lena is already dressed for the occasion, could we ask for a dance?"

Tony chuckled. "She's always dressed for the occasion. I've lost count of how many costumes she has at this point. Sweetheart? Would you like to dance for your uncles and Miss Jennie?"

The big, blue eyes brightened as she gracefully nodded her head. "May I do Swan Lake? It's my favorite."

"Being that you're already in costume, I would insist upon it," one of the twins answered.

"Take your cups, and we'll go into the theater."

When I heard the word 'theater,' I immediately pictured a home theater with a large screen TV, but I was wrong. There was an entire stage, complete with long, red velvet curtains and plush seating of red and gold. A grand piano sat on a raised platform to the side.

"Did you build this just for Lena?" I asked.

"Yes," one of the twins, Sean (I think) said. "We didn't want her to stop dancing when she left Russia. It's in her blood."

"Being musicians, we understood the need to create and perform, so we started a tradition where we come in here every week to play music for her to dance to," the other twin said.

"Lena's also been teaching dance classes to several of the women in town. She's even put together a little troupe so they can do recitals for their daddies," Tony added.

"She's not only amazing on stage, but is stunning on ice. If you want, she could give you lessons," Lex said as he wrapped his arm around my shoulder.

"That would be fun. What are they doing?" I pointed to the piano.

"Stefan's our pianist, and Sean plays the woodwinds. They'll perform the music for Lena to dance to."

"These guys are musical geniuses," Ryder said. "I don't think an instrument exists that one of them can't play well."

"There are a few, mainly aboriginal." Tony laughed. "There are others that make Lena scream and run away with her hands over her ears. She doesn't care for Asian music. It's too atonal and drives her batty."

"What's that?"

"The tonal center isn't based on westernized music scales. It's a lot like Slater's monk music."

"We haven't forced that on her yet." Simon laughed. "We figured we'd wait until she gets grounded and then make her listen to it as punishment."

Tony chuckled. "You know damn well that Slater would be right there trying to teach her to meditate. When's he coming home, by the way?"

"Hopefully before the camping trip. It all depends on how successful he is with his assignment and the weather," Lex answered.

"I think he's going to try to spend some time at the temple. He's really been struggling lately," Ryder added.

Tony nodded. "That's understandable. Are you ready?" he asked me as the lights started to dim.

I have never watched a ballet. Truthfully, the whole concept bored me, but I wanted to show my new daddies that I had good manners.

New daddies? Where did that come from?

I dug my nails into Simon's arm as I was sucked into the performance. Lena transformed into a graceful bird on the stage, flying to heights that were humanly impossible, and spinning so rapidly that a normal person would have fallen to the floor. I held my breath and felt tears prick my eyes.

"What do you think?" Lex whispered in my ear.

"I've never seen anything more beautiful in my life."

We gave her a standing ovation when she ended her dance and bowed low upon the stage. She kissed the twins and then walked over to us.

"That was amazing," I said, hugging her. She wasn't even out of breath! "I can't believe how flexible you are."

"Thank you. My daddies enjoy my flexibility a lot," she giggled mischievously.

"You're bad."

"You have no idea."

"Thank you for that performance, my darling. Get changed into your nightie and then come back down. I'll let you stay up until ten, and then it's off to bed with you," Tony ordered

"That's only thirty minutes. I don't want to go to bed. I want to stay up and play with the uncles and Jennie."

"No pouting, young lady. Come," Stefan ordered, rising as he held his hand out to her.

"We won't be staying much longer, either. Sean? I forgot to ask, but didn't you say something about your computer glitching?" Lex asked.

"Yeah, I did something to it."

"He always does," Tony said.

"Let me take a look at it."

I watched Lex and Sean leave and then gazed at the remaining men. "Can I ask a question?"

"You may ask anything your heart desires, sweetheart," Tony said.

"Does it get confusing when she calls all of you 'daddy?'"

"Not really. She refers to us in the collective most of the time, but if she needs to differentiate she calls us by name."

"Are you guys my uncles now, too?"

"We'd like to be. Your daddies are very close to this family and consider this a second home. We want you to do the same."

"My second question is how do you tell the difference between the twins?"

"Stefan's right-handed and has a dimple on his right cheek. Sean's the exact opposite. They are mirror imaged," Tony answered with a laugh.

"Thank you. Uh oh." I lifted my eyes to the upstairs.

"It sounds like somebody is getting herself spanked," Simon chuckled. "What do you think she did?"

"Maybe she's another little girl who likes to argue with her daddy about bedtime," Ryder stated.

"All that just because she didn't want to change for bed?" I asked, horrified.

"No, I think what we're hearing is the consequences of someone who broke into the liquor cabinet and helped herself to some vodka for her tea party. I just noticed the cabinet was open when we walked by it." Sean said, walking back into the room with Lex at his heels.

"Back so soon?"

"He didn't have the extension cord plugged in," Lex said as he plopped in front of the fire.

"Back to the vodka. Jenn? Is this true?" Ryder asked.

I bit my lower lip. "It wasn't that strong, and it really helped me relax."

"No more alcohol for you without permission. Understood?"

"Yes, Daddy." I lowered my eyes.

Simon patted my thigh. "We don't want you snitching, either. If something like this happens, politely refuse it."

"If I had known that Lena was drinking, I wouldn't have allowed her to dance. It's too easy to break something if you don't have full control of your body," Tony said, drumming his fingers on the chair. "Did Lena clean the dishes when you finished, Jennifer?"

"No, sir."

"Stefan can read her like a book and probably noticed something and checked the teapot. He's the strictest of the three of us and puts up with no nonsense, especially when she puts her safety at risk."

"I'm sorry. Is there anything I can do?" I asked, wrinkling my forehead as I heard Lena cry.

"Yes. Be aware that Lena enjoys being naughty and will try to drag you in with her. Unless you want a taste of that," Tony pointed up, "you'll be careful of what you get into. Understand?"

I swallowed dryly as Simon squeezed my thigh. "Yes, sir."

"Good girl, because that would mean a family tribunal for you," Ryder warned.

"Aw, there's our little Lena the Ballerina. Come to Uncle Lex," he said, holding his arms out for the red-nosed girl. She climbed onto his lap and held him tightly as she cried into his shoulder.

"I'm sorry, Uncle Lex."

"All is forgiven, baby. Did you still want to do a sleepover?"

"You'll let her?"

"Of course! Perhaps next week if the weather permits. Would that work for you, gentlemen?"

"It sounds perfect. We're visiting Grandma next Sunday morning and staying with her overnight. If you don't mind, we can take Jennie with us and let her visit the tribe. Lena loves it there, and it might be a lot of fun for the girls," Stefan said, kissing the back of Lena's hand. She transferred over to him and curled up in his lap.

"Then can she spend the night here?" Lena asked with a sniffle.

"Only if your daddies want her for two whole days," Ryder said.

"We'd love to have her. What do you think of that, Jennifer?"

"It sounds amazeballs!"

"Okay, then it's settled. I'll update you with the details later on in the week."

"Perfect. I think we should get going. We have a long day tomorrow and someone's tired." Lex pointed to me as I yawned.

"No, I'm not."

"We're not going to go through this again," Ryder said sternly. "We'll take the tunnel back to the hotel if that's okay. I'm too lazy to bundle up again."

"I'll call for a cart. I'm glad you came," Tony said, kissing my forehead. The twins repeated the gesture before Lena hugged me tightly.

"We're going to be such good friends. I promise."

I hugged her back. "I can't wait. Night, and thank you for everything. I'm sorry you got in trouble."

"I'm always getting in trouble," she shrugged. She looked over her shoulder as Stefan placed his hand on her shoulder.

"This is true, and we love her more and more every time. To bed with you, young lady."

"Can I sleep with you tonight?"

"Yes. Go on. Don't forget to brush your teeth and have your hairbrush ready for me," Stefan said warmly, kissing her temple.

"He brushes my hair every night before bed. It helps me sleep. *Spokoynoi nochi*."

"A peaceful night to you, too, sweetheart," Ryder said with a final hug.

****

"This is nice," I purred as the four of us got into the huge bed. I had my head on Lex's stomach, Ryder was on my left side with his arm over my tummy, and Simon on my right with his arm across my thigh. Molly refused to be ignored and curled up in the space between Lex's leg and Simon's back.

"It's been a long time since we've foxholed together," Ryder chuckled, glancing over at Lex.

"I think the last time was when we got caught in that snowstorm years ago. Simon gave off so much body heat that he melted the snow."

"It's cool that you guys are so comfortable with each other. I hate it when men are afraid to be affectionate."

"We're brothers and have been through hell and back together. We don't jerk each other off, but we don't care about getting naked together."

"Simon!"

"What did I say wrong now?"

"Nothing," I said, stroking his hair. "I love you, Daddies."

"We love you, too. We'll go sledding tomorrow after I'm done with the final meeting, okay?"

"That sounds perfect." I yawned. "Night."

Chapter Sixteen
(Ryder)
∞ ∞ ∞

"Did you have a good time in town?" Lex asked as we sat for an early dinner the following day.

"I did," Jenn nodded enthusiastically. "I felt bad about Lena, though."

"Why? Because she got spanked? I wouldn't be surprised if that little girl got her backside whacked at least once a day. We love her dearly, but her little side has no boundaries," I said, handing her a bowl of rolls.

"Do you feel more comfortable about the daddy element?" Lex asked.

"I do. It was so natural for her and I felt her pulling me in. Her room was so much fun, too."

"The Markford's designed the manor to keep her in her little mode as much as possible. She thrives in that place," I said. "We'll be updating your playroom as soon as we figure out what you like best."

"I have a playroom? Where?"

"It's a secret," Simon said with a snicker. "There are lots of hidey holes and invisible doors around the lodge."

Jenn giggled. "It's like the Alaskan version of Wayne Manor and the Batcave."

"Exactly."

"Did you put your tiara away?" I asked.

"Yes, Daddy. I can't believe you got me something so pretty. I didn't want to take it off."

"It's for special occasions, like when we go on dates and get to dress you up," Simon said. "So, are we going to play together when we go camping?"

"Dear God! Will you give it a rest?" I asked my brother. "Go jerk off or something if you're that horny, but stop bothering the poor girl. We'll play together in due time if she wants to. You know the rules. Individual before we go together, and she calls the shots."

"It would be fun, though. Right?"

Jenn smiled. She lowered her voice and traced her finger down his arm. "I didn't make the rules, but I do know what will help make you feel better."

"Yeah? What?"

Jenn glanced at me and winked. "I would start by taking off your clothes."

Simon's grin nearly split his face. "I love getting naked."

"I'm sure you do," she said sexily. "Bet you can't guess what happens next."

"You jump my bones?"

"No, not at all." She brought her glass of water to her lips and sipped. "I was going to suggest that you take a run in the snow and cool yourself off. If that doesn't work, maybe this will."

"You brat!" Simon jumped out of his chair when she dumped the water on his lap. If it had been anyone else, I'd be worried about a fit. But not Simon. Jenn seemed to know that, too.

"Did it help?" she asked innocently.

"Lex!"

"Don't look at me. Ryder? Can I get you anything else?"

"I'm good. I'm in the mood to curl up with a book in front of the fire tonight."

"I'm going to hit the rack. Come give Daddy a hug and kiss good-night, you," Lex ordered. Jenn obeyed, kissing him full on the mouth.

"Thanks for dinner, Major. We'll do the dishes," I offered. "It's your turn to take Molly."

"No problem. Come on, fuzz-face. I'll catch you guys in the morning. Make sure she gets some sleep so she isn't cranky tomorrow. I don't want her getting into trouble because of you."

"Yes, sir, Major Becker, Sir! Good-night." I grabbed Jenn by the waist and hauled her off his lap and then dismissed Lex with a wave. "You look like a drowned rat, little brother. Go jump in a warm shower."

"I'd rather hit the hot tub."

"You have a hot tub? Where?" Jenn's eyes widened.

"We have a very large hot tub. We also have a steam room, sauna, and tanning booths." I said.

"Tanning booths?"

"It's pure vanity. We don't like looking like pasty-ass Pillsbury doughboys, plus it makes us feel better," Simon stated.

"It also forces us to take a few minutes to relax and meditate, which Lex insists is important for our mental health."

"I'm still not convinced," Simon added. "Old Slater snuck in some of his monk music to play during our downtime, and all I wanted to do was kill him. There's nothing relaxing about that."

"Monk music is an acquired taste. He promised not to do it again when I threatened to pipe Kenny G into his room when he sleeps." I snickered.

"Did I just witness a bit of mischief?"

"Don't let Mr. Perfect fool you. Big brother here is the biggest prankster of the lot."

"I don't believe that for a minute." Jenn snorted half-heartedly. "Do tanning booths help with the light adjustment during the winter?"

"No, that's a different light spectrum. The house lighting is programmed to counter effects of the circadian rhythms and combat possible seasonal depression," Simon explained.

"The clamshells have an option for blue light. Lex has us sit under it every morning during the winter because he doesn't want to be stuck in the house with homicidal maniacs," I added.

"Now that Jenn's a seasoned hiker, she should start working out with us," Simon suggested.

"Seasoned hiker? I walked up a hill to go sledding with you three times before you decided to show me the ski lift thingy."

"You were exhausted, which is even more reason to work out."

"I think that's an excellent idea," I grinned as the girl moaned. "I won't let her in a tanning booth, though. Her skin's way too soft and pretty."

"I agree with you, there," my brother commented. "I also like the way her bottom lights up during a spanking. I'll hook her up with a blue light bed."

"Don't I get an opinion about this? I'd like some color, too."

"The only color you're going to get is that red backside Simon enjoys so much if you try to argue with us," I said firmly.

"The lady does like to put up a fight. It's part of her charm. Back to the subject at hand. I need to warm up and want to hit the hot tub. Do you two want to join me?"

"I don't have a bathing suit," Jenn said.

I chuckled. "Neither do we. Are you game?"

Jenn nodded and scrambled to her feet to help me clear the dishes.

"I'll be right back. I need to open the lock so we can program her in."

"We'll be done here in a flash," I said, putting the dishes into the dishwasher. "We'll meet you in the hallway."

After we cleaned the kitchen, I wrapped my arm around Jenn's neck and wrestled her playfully toward my side of the house.

"Ow! You bit me."

"Don't try to choke me. Where's the entrance?"

"We have several. Simon rigged them to be invisible."

"Why?"

I turned her to look at me. "You know what we do in our other life. The gym is a little more than a training facility."

"Spit it out, big brother. We already mentioned it's a bunker similar to Northern Lights, but we have some things other than emergency shelter and food."

"I know your gym's down there. What else?"

"A full weapons and ammunition arsenal and a shooting range."

"Are you crazy?"

"We told you about the hydroponic farms and labs under Northern Lights. We have our own facility that's not for public knowledge."

"Let me get this straight." She put her hand on my chest. "The town is made of mercenaries and freedom fighters, and you all have hiding places in case one of the bad guys come after you."

"No, of course not. Our unit is the only contracted team, and we only go after drug lords and human trafficking. Others serve different purposes outside their contribution to the town."

"Like Top Secret espionage?"

"You've been watching too many spy movies, baby girl. No spies, I promise. As for the top secret stuff, if we don't have a need to know, then everyone's business is their own.

"We don't have to tell you about keeping quiet about this stuff, right?" Simon asked.

"Of course not! I should be insulted."

"You should be, but you're not. Here's the panel."

"This? It's a picture of the four of you." She gazed at the 'family photos' on the wall. "Is that Slater?"

"That's the Wolfman."

"Lena was right. I live in a house with uber hot men."

I chuckled. "Don't tell him that. He gets embarrassed."

"I'm the hottest," Simon grunted. "This is a touchpad lock. Pick a password and use two fingers to write it in, and then underline it with three fingers."

She scrunched her face and followed his direction. "Do you do this instead of fingerprints or a retina scan in case someone chops off an arm or pokes out an eye to get in?"

"No more unapproved movies for you, young lady. It's a prototype security system that Lex just sold to private industry for mega bucks. That's what his business meeting was about in town."

"This is so cool," Jenn said as we trotted down the metal staircase and the gym came into view.

"It's Simon's pride and joy. The wet section is over here."

"That's an awesome pool! It's huge."

"It has a wave simulator in it that we use for rough water training and body boarding when we're bored. This is the fun part."

"Oh, man..."

I winked at Simon. We mutually agreed to make the recreation area tropical for a change of scenery. The hot tub was built to resemble a spring surrounded by black boulders of volcanic rock and had a small bubbling waterfall trickling through the natural holes. Orchids and giant ferns bloomed between the crevices while air plants and colorful bromeliads sprouted in the hollowed trunks of fallen trees.

"It's chilly down here. Give it a couple of minutes to warm up," Simon suggested as he activated the heater.

"No way! Volcanos?" Jenn exclaimed as flickering tongues of multiple colors blew from rocks that surrounded the water.

"I'll turn down the lights and put on some nature sounds. You'll never know we were in underground Alaska."

"Did you design this?" she asked Simon.

He blushed and nodded. "The four of us stumbled on a hot spring when we were in Chile near the Villarrica volcano. This is as close to what it looked like as I could make it."

Jenn sat on the moss bank. "I love it. I can't believe how romantic it is, especially since you didn't have a girl around. Were you planning on taking Molly here?"

"Ryder, she's teasing me again."

"You're a man. Grow a set and stop whining," I taunted.

"Come here, Simon. You make it so easy to pick on you." She patted the ground.

"You need a spanking."

"Maybe later. Right now, I just need a kiss."

"From me?"

I held back my laughter when I saw my brother's face. He was trying so hard to behave himself and not show his excitement.

"Would you prefer if I had hair all over my face and doggy breath?"

Simon growled and caught her in his big arms before he pressed his mouth to hers. Her face was flushed when she pulled back to catch her breath. They gazed at each other for a minute and then she looked at me.

"I think I need another kiss. What do you think, Daddy?"

"I'm not your daddy right now, babe," I growled as I dropped to my knees and leaned forward to kiss her. Her mouth was soft and hot against mine, and I felt my heart pound when she parted her lips to receive me. I felt her linger before she rose to her feet. We watched with our mouths hanging open as she peeled her clothing off one layer at a time until she stood naked before us.

"Fuck. I've never seen anything so beautiful in my life," Simon muttered hoarsely.

"I'm yours if you want me. Of course, it means breaking the rules." She turned and strolled to the edge of the hot tub and then looked over her shoulder with a smile. "Are you coming in?"

Simon and I looked at each other and smiled.

To hell with rules!

Chapter Seventeen
(Jennie)

∞ ∞ ∞

I stepped boldly into the water and glanced over my shoulder. I was filled with a new sense of confidence after Lex stripped me of shame and his hands clothed me in pride. He said I was beautiful and the two men before me reinforced their friend's words. Simon looked as though he was about to turn somersaults with excitement while Ryder's hooded eyes reminded me of an animal stalking its prey. They hesitated for a moment as they struggled with the ingrained notion of obedience to their commander, but it didn't take much once I invited them to join me in the water.

I watched as they shed their clothes and instantly felt my mouth water. Except for their coloring, there was nothing physical that made them look like brothers. Ryder was the tallest with a lean, muscular physique that was hardened by years of running, swimming and climbing. Simon, a couple of inches shorter, was built like a mountain after spending countless hours lifting weights and wrestling. The use of the tanning beds turned their skin a deep gold which accented the ridges and angles of their muscles. The bold tattoos on their right side gave both a menacing look as they stood naked in all their glory.

My eyes shifted ever so slightly as I noticed that the brothers displayed more than their coloring as proof of their shared genetics. Their beautiful long, thick cocks swayed back and forth with minds of their own. I smiled and beckoned for them to come to me.

"I wanted you so badly last night. Sleeping with you between us was torture," Ryder admitted as he sat next to me. I looked demurely at Simon.

"Did you want me, too?"

"Uh, huh."

His sudden shyness was adorable, but I wasn't in the mood for cute. I felt Ryder press my thigh under the water and followed his cue.

"How badly did you want me?" I rasped, easing my body through the hot water to face him. Hunger flashed over his face as I straddled his lap and wiggled. I felt his monstrous cock growing harder against the inside of my thigh as his hands crept up the outsides of my legs. His dark blue eyes focused on my face as his fingers inched toward my breasts.

I moaned when I felt Ryder's mouth on my neck as he pushed my thick hair over the opposite shoulder. He ran his hand down the length, and I imagined him knotting it in his fist while I went down on him. I tilted my face to kiss him as Simon buried his face between my breasts. Sandwiched between the two, I got my first taste of what it was like for the Watkins' brother to work as a team.

Ryder's hand ran down my hip and made its way to the inside of my right thigh. I shivered as he touched the smooth, slick entrance of my pussy while kissing the back of my neck, shoulder, and side of my throat. I wrapped my hand around Simon's swollen cock and admired the girth.

"Oh, God," he groaned as I nestled it between my breasts and leaned forward to kiss the mushroom shaped head.

"Simon..." His name was barely a whisper. "I want you."

"Take her out," Ryder ordered his brother. I wrapped my legs around Simon's waist and tongue-fucked him as he lifted me with his hands cupped under my ass. Ever so gently, he stretched me on the mossy embankment where the soft, velvety plants caressed my back and ass. I purred as four hands touched every inch of my body. Talented fingers found erogenous zones that even I was unaware of and made me writhe with want.

"Hard-limits?" Ryder asked in my ear.

"None. I'm yours to do anything you want."

"To any hole?" Simon asked. I looked at him straight in the eyes.

"To any hole. Just go slowly."

"We'll take it easy this time. We don't want to hurt you."

"Ryder..." I breathed his name, slowly undulating under his gaze. I opened my legs for him. "I need you in me."

His shoulders were much broader than I realized as he settled between my thighs. I beckoned to Simon and reached for his swollen cock and stroked it gently. My nipples grew tight as Ryder's mouth descended upon my wet pussy and Simon's teeth nibbled along my neck.

"Come here," I ordered, turning my face to the side. I licked the edges of Simon's cock and then took him into my mouth.

"Holy shit," he hissed as I filled my throat with his hardness. I breathed slowly through my nose to control my gag reflex and sucked him as happily as I did the lollipop he had given me. He gently pinched my nipples as he fucked my mouth, making me coo with pleasure as I lifted my legs over Ryder's broad shoulders.

With Simon in my mouth, I used my hands to guide Ryder. He lifted his mouth from my mound and watched as I rubbed the head of his cock in the juices that spilled from my pussy. His dark blue eyes bore into mine as I urged the tip into my wetness.

"I don't want to hurt you," he whispered, slowly inching his way past my tight walls. I wanted more. I pulled him closer to me, encouraging him to push until he was buried to the hilt in my hot, hungry body.

I freed Simon's cock from my throat to catch my breath.

"Take me, Ryder. Hard. Please," I begged.

Simon's mouth was pinned to my breasts, suckling each one until the nipples stood high and proud. He groaned as my mouth enclosed around his cock again. I could feel it swell and throb against my cheeks.

I gasped as Ryder followed my command and pushed, slipping his thick pole deep into me.

"You're so tight," he whispered, rolling his hips so I could take him even deeper. He slowly moved in and out with thrusts so hard that they pushed the air from my lungs. "You feel so good, baby."

He took me slowly as though he was measuring my ability to handle whatever he had in store for me in the future. I wrapped my legs around his back, drawing him in, and moaned around Simon's cock, sucking hard to keep him in my mouth.

I felt Ryder's muscles tighten. He suddenly stopped and looked at his brother. With a nod, they changed places.

"On your knees," Ryder ordered, capturing my hips and flipping me over.

"What are you doing?" I asked.

"Hush." He pushed my head down while Simon lifted my hips and raised my ass high in the air. "Open."

I obeyed, looking up at Ryder as he pressed his cock against my lips. He gasped as I swallowed him.

"Fuck, Jenn. You're amazing." He held my face and guided me over the length of his cock. I sucked and then released, ticking his sensitive, velvety skin with my tongue. My groan vibrated in my throat as Simon took me from behind, stretching my pussy to the tightrope of pleasure and pain. I lifted my ass higher, inviting him to thrust in me with as much strength as possible.

I never believed I'd feel such powerful emotions as both ends of my body engulfed the brothers' cocks. My body responded apart from my mind, feeling more sensation than I thought possible. I could only imagine what it would be like with Lex there as well.

I met their rhythm and felt every nerve in my body tingle. I wanted to cry out their names and tell them how good they were, but my lips remained wrapped snugly around Ryder's thickness.

"Damn," Simon swore, and he pounded into me with so much strength that his heavy balls slapped against my clit. I looked into Ryder's glazed-eyes as he watched his brother fuck me from behind. I suspected Simon also watched the cock that slid in and out of my mouth, driving him to fuck me with a furious passion.

"Let me inside of her again," Ryder demanded as his fist curled around my hair. I yelped as Simon smacked my bottom before pulling out, and then spun me around instead of exchanging places. Ryder repeated the smack and then rammed into me.

I pulled Simon from my mouth. "I'm so close. Please. Together," I panted.

They matched each other's speed and thrust and swelled with me. A scream rose from somewhere in my throat as I was thrown into a violent, mind-rendering orgasm. They joined me, both releasing animalistic growls as they poured their hot seed into my mouth and pussy. Simon slid from my throat and finished on my lips.

"FUCK!" I shouted as my body continued to spasm from head to toe. I quivered from head to toe, desperately trying to catch my breath as I became a limp blob of post-orgasmic flesh.

They collapsed on either side of me, both covered with a sheen of perspiration.

"Noooo. Don't leave," I whispered as Ryder's cock slid from my body.

"Amazing," he whispered, looking at the ceiling.

"Ditto that, bro. She's perfect," Simon agreed. "Did we hurt you?"

"Only in a good way. Is this really my life?" I asked dreamily as I closed my eyes.

"You're going to love the four of us together," Ryder said, running his finger along my breast. "We work like a well-oiled machine both out of bed and in it."

"I'm floating."

I moaned as Simon carried me to the hot tub and lowered me into the water. He held me against his chest as the heat soothed my sensitive flesh and enveloped me in a womb-like embrace.

"I'm glad you broke the rules."

"We are, too." Simon kissed my cheek.

"Have you two done this a lot?" I asked with curiosity.

"Only once, but we couldn't find the rhythm," Ryder told me. "With you, it came naturally."

"Yeah, Slater's his usual fuck buddy. So we haven't had many opportunities."

"Simon!"

"What?"

****

When I woke, I was in Ryder's bed, still naked under the blankets and crushed between two large, hot, muscular men.

"Good morning, cupcake."

I tilted my face to look at Simon. "Good Morning, Daddy."

Ryder turned to his side and draped his arm over my waist. "Did you sleep well, Princess?"

"I don't remember," I laughed. "Did you do something unspeakable to me between soaking in the hot tub and waking up here."

"We thought of it," Simon stated.

"No, you thought of it. I told him it's more fun when you get to participate. That pretty pink mouth wouldn't work the same if you were in a sex coma."

"I'm so sore," I announced as I sat up. "Every muscle feels like a rubber band."

"We'll work it out in the gym. Hop to it," Ryder said, smacking my thigh before leaving the bed. He pulled on a pair of sweats and a t-shirt and stood with his hands on his hips. "Simon, let her go."

"But she's warm and cuddly."

"Like Molly?"

"I know the perfect way to get your blood moving," he said as he sat up.

"Sex?"

"No, Jenniebean. A spanking."

"No!" I protested as he flipped me across his knee and tossed the blankets to the side. His hand clapped against my naked flesh hard enough to make me call out.

"Daddy! Daddies! Help me!"

"What's all this racket about?" Lex asked, walking into the room with Molly at his heels.

"No! Yuck!" I protested when the dog started slobbering all over my face. "Stop it, Molly! I'm not Simon. I don't like making out with you. OW!"

"Bare-assed and over my knee, and she still makes fun of me."

"That's because you make it so easy. You might want to let her go. She's going to cry," Lex said, sitting on the edge of the bed. Simon smacked me three more times and then handed me over to Lex.

"Good morning, my darling. Did you have fun last night with the boys?"

"It was amazing. Thank you. All of you."

Lex hugged me. "You're not the only one who's happy about this arrangement. Do you think you'll be able to handle the demands of four men?"

"If Slater is anything like you three, I'll do my damnedest."

"That's music to my ears. Simon? Would you mind grabbing something for her to wear while working out?"

"I don't want to work out. I'll watch."

Simon ignored my statement. "Sweats or shorts?"

"Shorts, and I hate working out."

"You'll grow to love it. It's a family thing," Ryder promised.

"Does that mean if I want to have a tea party, you'll have to participate?"

"We wouldn't have to. We'd want to. Arms up," he ordered as Simon handed him a t-shirt.

"Legs out," Simon commanded. I kept them tightly crossed. "Come on, give me your foot."

"No."

"She just told me 'no,' even though her bottom is still pink and tender." Simon shook his head.

"Gentlemen?" Lex said, standing.

I shrieked as he grabbed my ankles and turned me upside down. Simon held me by the waist and growled as I pounded his bare foot with my fist.

"Put me down, you beasts." I scissored and twisted my feet to make it as difficult as possible for Ryder to dress me.

"Let her fight. She'll wear herself out soon," Lex advised.

He was correct. Within a couple of minutes, I was completely dressed and sulking. Simon flipped my lower lip.

"The face isn't going to change things. Put your butt in gear. Did you just stick your tongue out at me?"

"See what two hours with Lena did to her. Can you imagine what we're going to get after she spends two whole days with that monkey," Lex said with a laugh. He pulled me off the bed and pushed me out of the room with his hands on both my shoulders.

"Let's put her on the ski machine. She'll like that," Simon suggested.

I scowled at the guys as I clung to the two poles on the side of two long gliders. Lex set the program and then went to the free weights with the other two.

"What the... cool," I said as a shield emerged in front of me. Several options materialized on the screen, and I touched the one that said Denali. The machine started to move slowly on its own, and the snow-covered peak of the mountain appeared with a countdown. The next thing I knew, I was cross-country skiing in virtual reality.

"This is incredible!" I proclaimed as cool air blew on my face and the scent of pines and snow surrounded me.

"I think she likes it," Ryder said from behind me.

"At least it will get some use," Lex agreed. "I'll load some more programs in there for her later."

"Don't work her too hard," Simon requested. "I don't want her passing out on me like she did last night."

"Simon!"

I giggled as I tried to tune out their comments as they waited for the program to end.

"That wasn't half bad, was it?" Lex asked.

"No, Daddy. It was kind of cool."

"We're going to spar for a bit and then clean-up for breakfast. You're welcome to watch."

"Are you going to teach me stuff?"

"Slater's the best one for that. It would be a good exercise in bonding."

"What if he doesn't want to teach me?"

"He'd never refuse. Trust me," Ryder stripped off his shirt and headed toward the large sand pit. Lex and Simon followed. I sat for the next hour watching gorgeous man-meat flex and dance as they practiced hand-to-hand techniques against each other.

Maybe working out wouldn't be so bad after all.

Chapter Eighteen
(Ryder)
∞ ∞ ∞

"You be a good girl for the uncles. Hear me?" Lex asked when the Markfords arrived with three sleds pulled by Alaskan Huskies. I frowned as he fussed over our girl like she was as fragile as a petal.

"Yes, Daddy."

"We'll take good care of her. No worries, okay?" Tony said, helping her on his sled.

"We're gonna have so much fun," Lena announced.

"You behave, too. Don't get our girl into trouble," I ordered. I saw Lex speaking to Stefan and studied my friend's face. He was worried about something.

"Do you want to tell us what's going on?" I asked him as the yapping dogs took flight over the snow.

"We have a problem. Let's go inside."

"Is Slater okay?"

"He's fine. I asked him to come home."

I looked at my brother. Something was brewing. "Out with it, Lexington. This is about Jennie, isn't it?"

"Yes."

He remained silent until we were back in the house and sitting around the fire. We were used to him taking a few minutes to gather his words before we received an assignment or debriefing, but something was different this time. He was genuinely frightened and fighting to stay calm.

"She was spotted. They know she's in this area."

"What? How?"

"I don't know the details yet. I got a call from Graye Manor this morning and spoke to Elias, the chief of security. The house Jenn was in was a fly-by. While they managed to arrest everyone for illegal drug use, they didn't get the top dogs. He intercepted a call that Jennifer was recognized and they know the direction her plane went."

"Who recognized her and where?" Simon asked.

"We don't have a name, only that it was a woman. He's assuming it happened when she was waiting for the transport. That puts them at about three weeks ahead of us in their search."

"Did you discover the interception point for their exchanges?" Simon asked.

"We were only able to trace the calls to the general areas of Juneau to Anchorage."

"What's the plan, Major?" I asked.

"We talk to Jennifer and see if she knows anything. Obviously, the person who recognized her visited the house in Canada and was around long enough to point her out. It could be anybody."

I've never witnessed Lex get ruffled. "What aren't you telling us?"

"There's a price on her head. The cartel is offering one million dollars to whoever brings her in, dead or alive."

"Fuck," Simon hissed. "We shouldn't have let her out of our sight. Should we go get her?"

"No," I corrected. "No one would suspect she was one of two women on a mushing team or that she'd be in an Athabaskan village."

"Ryder's correct. Right now, she's in a safe location, and we can use this time to up our security."

"The weather sucks. How's Slater going to get here?" Simon asked.

"He's resourceful. He'll find a way home even if it means riding on the back of a caribou."

"I'd laugh except he's done that before." Lex sighed.

"You don't think he'd try to walk here, would he?" Simon asked.

"Slate's not stupid. If he can get to the army base, I can finagle a Ripsaw to take him to the ranger station," Lex said. "In the meantime, I think it would be a good idea to start laying some man traps."

"We don't know what type of bush skills any of these people have, so we've got to make sure we funnel outsiders where we want them to go," I responded. "Send up a drone and get me an aerial map."

"What about the animals?"

"They are smarter than people and will be able to detect our scent, but I'll rig up the ultrasonic repellants to keep the big game and wolves away just in case."

"I'll put up extra surveillance cameras and in-house alarms," Simon offered. I touched my brother's hand.

"If anyone comes within eye-distance—"

"I'll do my job. I won't let anyone live to hurt my girl." His eyes were dark and angry.

"Let's hope it doesn't come to that, but it's best that we're prepared. They've got a huge time jump on us, so we've got to be ready for anything."

"That's my biggest concern. We don't know where they are," Lex said, drumming the arm of the chair with his fingertips. "I'll get you the pictures and maps right away."

"Thanks, Major. I'm going to hit the lab and start working on the layouts for the traps."

"I'm going to chop some wood," Simon said, quickly leaving the room.

"Simon?"

"He's worried," I said. "He always chops wood when he feels out of control. It helps him clear his head and come up with ideas. Lex? Have we ever lost a fight or failed a mission?"

"No, but the stakes are the highest we've ever faced and time is against us. We were careless. I should've considered placing more decoys."

"All this means is that we will fight harder than ever. I'm going to ask Simon to teach Jenn how to use a gun."

"Good idea. I know she's safe in the lodge, but she can't stay inside forever. We need to stop these assholes before they have an opportunity to find us."

"There are only three ways to reach the lodge. Air, the road, and the lake. Do I have your permission to go top gun?"

Lex thought about it for a moment. "We can't take the chance that innocent civilians will be harmed. Rig the lake and the road, but keep it low to disable any vehicles coming in that way. The monitors will notify us if the trap is tripped."

"I can also place under-ice explosives at the neck of the lake to trigger if a vehicle lands. They'll crack the entire line of ice."

"Good idea. I'll notify the town to keep all vehicles off our line of site. Let's get to work."

****

I went underground to the munition labs and closed the door behind me. Before I started anything, I needed to talk with my best friend.

"Hey, Slate. What's your ETA?"

"I'm going to get home as soon as I can. It's a twenty-hour flight from Tokyo to Alaska."

"I wish you were here already. I'd feel so much better. They've got almost a three-week jump on us."

"Not good. That's enough time to get a feel of the area."

"A good week of it was a white out, but we don't know if we've been under surveillance. We got comfortable and careless. If anything happens—"

"You couldn't have planned for this."

"If you were here, we would've been on our game."

"You don't know that."

"Bullshit. You've always had a sixth sense for danger and would've nagged the fuck out of us until we secured the area."

"Sometimes things aren't what they seem."

"What do you mean?"

"The only thing you can be sure of is to expect the unexpected. Trust your instincts and don't second guess yourself. How's the girl?"

"The girl's name is Jennifer, and she's doing well. You need to give her a fair chance."

"You know my feelings and why," he said gloomily.

"She's nothing like your ex. She's sweet and innocent and open to anything new. She even wants to learn self-defense."

"So, teach her."

"That's your job, buddy," I said, flipping a pen in my hand. "I also think you're so full of bullshit that I can smell you from the other side of the world."

"Oh, really?"

"Yes, really. If you didn't care, you wouldn't be coming home."

"My family needs me, and there's a young woman in danger. It has nothing to do with me caring."

"Keep telling yourself that, Slate. Let's be real. You know Simon and I applied for the program in response to the pact the four of us made years ago. We promised to share everything, including a wife if the right woman came along. That's never changed."

"Until Sarah."

"What about her? We need to forget about Sarah. She wasn't right for you, and we should have knocked some sense into your head before it got as far as it did. You have to stop beating yourself up over it. We all make mistakes, bro."

"Not this bad."

"The point is that she's out of the picture and we've been given the chance to have the type of family all of us have dreamed of having. You know Dorian Graye would never send anyone our way who wasn't trustworthy."

"I'm not in a place to be in any kind of relationship. I have nothing to give, and I certainly have no desire to receive."

"Hear me out. The poor little thing escaped a horrible situation and needs our help as much as she needs our love and protection. These people want her dead. This is the only place she's ever felt safe, and I want to keep it that way. When the shit hits the fan, her world is going to be shaken and she's going to need all of us. You're the most intuitive, and she's going to instinctively lean on you. The kid's been horribly damaged and abused, and she's going to need a daddy who can help her heal."

Slater was quiet for a moment. His voiced softened. "I didn't realize she was an age-player. Where did they find her?"

"I know that tone. Disband with the paranoia, Slate. She's clear and has nothing to do with any of your government opposition. We ran a background check on her for the town, as well. You know how stringent our rules are."

"That's all well and good, but I'm not interested in a relationship."

"Then just work on being pleasant. I know that's a major request, but it's not fair for her to be completely displaced and live in a home where she doesn't feel wanted, especially after this shit comes to a head."

"I'll fuck this up like I do everything else."

"You have to stop being so hard on yourself. You were conned. Sarah lied to you because she saw you as a means for self-gain. She was greedy and knew you had deep pockets. It could have happened to any of us. You need to let it go."

"Easy to say. My stupidity could have exposed our town and what we do. If I had brought her in and told her about us, it could have hurt all of you."

"Yes, it could have, but you cut her off before anything significant happened. I'm not going to allow you to deny yourself happiness because you made a mistake. As I told you, we're just as responsible for breaking our promise and not calling you to account."

"You probably would have needed a GI party to make me listen. I can be a little thickheaded."

I chuckled. "Even if we could get past your ninja moves, I think we've grown beyond tying you up in a blanket and pounding sense into you."

"Does this girl have the fortitude to live in an environment like ours? I dread being stuck with a whining female through the winter. Simon's bad enough."

"This girl's endured more than anyone her age could even imagine. Fortitude isn't the issue. It's a matter of compatibility and trust on both ends. Either way, as her guardians, we're to serve her needs first and provide her with whatever she requires to be happy."

"I guess I can always live in the ice-house."

"No, you're going to live here where you belong."

"Am I obligated to be involved with her?"

"You're obligated to protect and do what's best for her, nothing more. If your relationship doesn't happen organically on both sides, then so be it."

"You're having sex with her already, aren't you?"

I sighed. "It's hard to explain, but she fits. There's something in her that clicked with each of us and it was so natural."

"She's been with all three of you?"

"Yeah."

"Ry, you know I don't have anything to give and, frankly, I'm gun shy. I don't want to cost you guys a chance to have what you want."

"Tough shit. It's all or nothing—that means you, too, buddy. Listen, you've got plenty of time to develop a connection if that's what's meant to be.

Right now, let's just focus on her safety and getting rid of the scumbags who are looking for her. You'll have time to get to know her and teach her what she needs to know later."

"But..."

"Do I have to get Lex involved?"

"Are you threatening me with the boss? That's never worked in the past, why do you think it'll work now?"

"Okay, since you want to play hardball. I'll contact your masters at the temple and tell them that you're being prideful and stubborn."

"You wouldn't."

"Try me. I'm not above emotional blackmail."

Slater released an audible sigh. "I'm not in the mood to continue an argument I won't win. I guess Molly will be okay with a house guest for a while."

"Molly adores her and has taken over her bed. Jenn's softer and smells better than you, so your dog might have a new best friend."

I received a grunt in response. "That would only happen if the girl kept her pockets filled with bacon. Molly would never replace her daddy with a stranger. I'll always be her favorite."

"Just try to be nice. We don't want Dorian Graye showing up to kick your ass."

"No, but I wouldn't complain if his gorgeous wife stopped by. She's as pretty as the mountain at sunset."

"While Mrs. Graye would love getting that type of compliment, I'm certain she's a force to be reckoned with if anyone screws with one of her girls," I said with a smile. "They're very protective of this young lady. That should tell you something."

"We'll see. I'm going to grab some shut eye. What's the weather look like?"

"Snowy with limited visibility. There shouldn't be a problem when you land, but no hoppers are going to be flying anytime soon. If you can make it to Fort Wainwright, Lex can get you in a Ripsaw to take you to the ranger station. I'll pick you up from there."

"Where's the girl now?"

"With the Markfords visiting their grandmother. They're going to spend the night there and then go back to town so the girls can have a sleepover."

"She's out of the line of fire for the time-being. Good. Keep her there. You do realize that Lena's probably going to get her into hot water."

"We warned her, but she has a bit of a naughty streak in her. I think you'll find it amusing."

"Stop with the hard sell. I'll talk with you soon."

I chuckled as the phone disconnected and then started to draw out plans for my traps. Anyone who was after my girl won't know what hit them. I just hoped I had the time I needed before the cartel found her.

Chapter Nineteen
(Jenn)

∞ ∞ ∞

I hung on for dear life as the dog sled zoomed over the knolls and through the trails. Tony stood behind me, leading the team, and communicated to his brothers with loud whistles. When we arrived at the tiny Athabaskan village, several boys ran out to greet us and took charge of caring for the dogs.

"*Bitsoo!*" Lena shrieked happily in Koyukon when the tiny, old woman approached. After a big hug, the woman held her at arm's length.

"Child, you are skin and bones. Don't those boys of mine feed you?"

"We feed her plenty, but she dances it off. How are you, Grandma?"

"I am well. Who is this beautiful creature?"

"Jennifer Hudson. She belongs to the Squad. Jennie? This is Grandma Markford."

"Call me Bitsoo. Lovely, absolutely lovely." She held my face in her hands and studied my eyes. "Such an unusual color for a deep soul. Intelligence and wisdom live within your eyes. Your spirit's filled with passion and fire, but there's a bit of a trickster that wants to come out and play. You push it down for fear of hurting others."

"Our grandmother's a medicine woman," Sean explained. "She's very wise and we've learned to heed her counsel. I've never seen her read anyone this quickly."

"What does it mean?" I was confused.

"You'll know when it's time. Your spirit animal will reveal itself to you when your heart is ready to receive what it has to say. Come, children. We have food prepared."

I was overwhelmed by the welcome and warmth I received from the tribe, and Bitsoo's stories were mesmerizing, especially when she danced as she told them.

"Are you having fun?" Lena asked as she played with a doll one of the women made for her.

"This is wonderful. I love it here. It's such a happy place."

"Do you want to see the potlatch storage?" she whispered in my ear.

"What's that?"

"Every year the bands come together for a huge celebration where they exchange gifts. Bitsoo's village holds all the gifts in a storage room so they don't get ruined. It's just across the village, like ten minutes away. We'll be there and back before anyone notices."

It was stuffy and warm in the longhouse, so I welcomed some fresh air. I followed her outside where we quickly threw on our parkas and headed down the short road. We arrived at the storage house just as I started to become uncomfortably cold.

"There are lots of blankets in here we can use. Here."

"Did you break into your daddies liquor closet again?" I asked as I took a long swig from her hidden flask.

"No. I picked this up in the top store and hid it under my bed. Good, huh?" She wiped her mouth after taking a drink.

"It certainly warms you up on the inside. I guess the spanking you got from Stefan wasn't enough to discourage you."

"He spanked me for breaking into the cabinet and risking my safety. He didn't say anything about not drinking."

"Ah, a loophole!" I laughed as I took another sip. "You're a girl after my own heart."

"Did your daddies say anything to you about it?"

"I'm not supposed to have any alcohol without permission, but who's going to know? Vodka doesn't have an odor and there isn't enough here to get that drunk."

"*Za nashu druzjbu*! To our friendship," Lena said, raising the flask.

We finished off the contents quickly and then looked through all the beautiful artwork, clothing, and carvings.

"Did I hear something?" I asked, lifting my head.

"*Gav-no!* It's my daddies. I'm in so much trouble."

"Oh, shit."

"That's what I said." She looked at me and then broke into a giggle fit. Next thing we knew, we were snorting and rolling on the floor.

"Girls! What are you doing in here? You know you're not supposed to wander after dark," Stefan scolded.

"He doesn't want a grizzly bear to eat us," Lena stage-whispered.

"Guys! They're over here!"

"Are they okay?" Sean asked, sticking his head through the door.

"What's this?" Tony lifted the flask from the ground and sniffed it. He then tipped it back. "Vodka. Who does this belong to?"

We both remained silent for a second and then started to giggle again.

"Let's get them to bed. We'll deal with this tomorrow."

"I'm so cozy inside," I sang as Sean pulled me to my feet.

"I'm sure you are. Stefan? Could you call her family and see what they want to do about this?" Tony requested, lifting Lena into his strong arms.

"Don't call my daddies. Please?" I begged.

"If you didn't want us to call your daddies, then you would have behaved yourself. I'm very disappointed in both of you," Sean scolded as he slung me over his shoulder when my legs decided to stop working. Lena and I giggled all the way back to Bitsoo's hut where we were put on a thick-furred floor mat and covered with several blankets.

"Are you coming to bed? We're cold," Lena asked as Stefan pulled our boots off and placed them near the fire to dry.

"We will later. Do I need to get someone to guard the door or can I trust you to stay put?"

"You can trust us, Daddy."

He frowned. "No, I can't. You disappointed me again."

I looked at Lena's face in the firelight. It lost all its joy. "I'm sorry," she whispered as she started to cry.

"Save those tears for when we get home, young lady. You're going to need them."

Lena was still crying when he left.

"Are they going to sleep with us?" I asked. It was becoming more difficult to form words.

"They must, or we'd freeze to death. He's so mad at me."

"I think he's more disappointed."

"That's even worse. I don't know why I do such stupid things. It hurts them. They deserve better."

I put my arm around her. "They love you. They know that getting into trouble is part of the package."

"Yes, but all the time? I got you in trouble, too. I'm sorry."

"It was bound to happen eventually," I forced a fake laugh. I couldn't tell her how scared I was about being called before the family tribunal, or my fear of them changing their minds about wanting to keep me.

"I'm glad you're my friend," she sniffed. "No one ever wants to play with me from the village, and I get so lonely."

"Why? You're so sweet and fun."

"They think I'm the princess of the town because of my daddies. They also know that I do stupid things like this and their daddies don't want them to associate closely with me."

"That's horrible!"

"Don't be surprised if they are the same way toward you. Your daddies are the town's security force."

"So? What does that have to do with me?"

"You'll be a princess, too."

"I don't want to be a princess."

"You won't have a choice. Uncle Lex is probably the most powerful man in this community. What he says, goes. His influence with the military and the government is tremendous, and he knows how to get us what we need."

"I didn't know that."

"There are lots of secrets in Northern Lights," Lena said with a yawn. "Not all of them are good."

"What do you mean by that? Lena? Lena?"
She was fast asleep in a drunken stupor.

****

"Does this mean no sleepover?" Lena sniveled as the Markfords harnessed the dogs to the sleighs.

"Not tonight. We aren't going to reward you for bad behavior," Stefan said firmly as he buckled her in.

"Daddy!"

"Not another word out of you, young lady."

"I'm sorry," I said softly to Tony as he adjusted my buckles. "Do you hate me now?"

Tony kissed my forehead. "Don't be silly. Little girls get into trouble all the time, but that doesn't mean we love them any less. We'll plan a sleepover some other time after Lena's restriction is lifted."

"I called your daddies last night and told them what happened. They aren't happy with you," Stefan added.

"Are you the mean one of your family?" I snapped. "All you do is snitch, spank, and threaten."

He looked surprised. "No, I don't."

"Yes, you do. I just met you and haven't heard a single sound of praise from you toward Lena."

"Jennie, please don't yell at Daddy," Lena asked softly. "He's very protective, that's all."

"There's a difference between being protective and being a bully. He's a bully." The look on Stefan's face made me instantly regret my words. He was hurt. "Stefan, I'm sorry. I shouldn't have said that."

"You know nothing about me, only what you've seen in the limited time we've been together." His voiced sounded choked.

"I didn't mean to hurt you. It's just that I haven't even seen you smile or show any affection toward Lena," I said softly.

"He's very private, that's all," Lena said. "He's been there taking care of me since the moment they brought me home. I was very sick and he refused to leave my bed for more than a few minutes. Every time I opened my eyes, Stefan was there holding my hand. He became Daddy before the others."

I felt my face heat. "I didn't know. I'm so sorry. I misjudged you, Stefan. Please forgive me."

"I'm sorry, too" Stefan squatted in the snow to look at me and placed his hand on my arm. "I didn't know I was coming across as a jerk and I'm glad you pointed it out. I don't want you to feel I'm unapproachable. I'm here for you if you ever need me. I promise."

"Thanks," I said shyly. "Does that mean you'll call my daddies and talk them out of being angry with me?"

"No, it does not, you sly little mouse. Are you ready?" he asked his brothers as he stood and braced himself behind Lena on the sled. With a shout of *mush*, we were off.

The reception that waited for me upon our arrival made me want to turn around and go back to the village. Each had his arms folded over his chest and looked very cross. Even Simon appeared peeved. I turned to Tony.

"Are you sure I can't go home with you and live there for a few months?"

"If you think that those faces are reserved just for your daddies to use, you're wrong. I'll take her in," Tony shouted to his brothers. I quickly hugged Lena and Sean and then paused in front of Stefan.

"Again, I'm really sorry," I said, still feeling guilty.

He hugged me tightly and planted a kiss between my eyes. "Don't be. I'm glad you had the guts to say something. Good luck in there."

"I'm going to need it."

"She's all yours, gentlemen. I'm sorry that this happened again on my watch. We need to keep a closer eye on Lena from now on when the girls are together."

"Don't worry about it," Lex said warmly as he hugged his friend. "We expect stuff like this to happen. We'd be suspicious if they never got into trouble."

"You guys have been involved in the lifestyle much longer than we have. We've never faced this kind of defiance before." Tony sounded sad.

"Lena's never had a friend to play with before, either," Ryder said, patting him on the shoulder. "The important thing is that they're safe."

"I still feel horrible."

"That's the curse of being a Daddy Dom. All we can do is be consistent and love them through the mischief. The truth is that we're both very fortunate with our girls. Their baggage is minimal compared to some of the others."

"That's true. Thanks. I appreciate the understanding."

"I'll give you a call later, okay? Jennifer? Thank Uncle Tony and go inside," Lex said firmly.

"Thanks, Uncle Tony. I'm really sorry. I'll do better next time. I promise."

"I know you will, sweetheart. Bye, guys."

I waited until he returned to the sled before I said anything. "I screwed up. I'm sorry."

"Take off your gear and go upstairs to change into your pajamas."

"Pajamas? But it's only eleven o'clock in the morning."

"Do as you're told," Lex spoke with a low voice.

I hung my head. "Yes, Sir. May I take a shower? It was kind of dusty and smoky in the village."

"Go on and be quick about it."

I bit my lip and looked at them. The fact that they didn't hug me showed how angry they were. It broke my heart.

"What are you waiting for?"

"Are you going to send me away?"

"That's never going to happen. You have our word. Go."

I trudged upstairs, took a quick shower, and then put on the pair of pink flannel 'Hello Kitty' baby-doll pajamas that had been left on my dresser.

I picked up Hobo and scratched his tummy as I sat on my bed. Since meeting Lena and observing the relationship she shared with her three husbands, I found it easier to embrace my guys as daddies. I just wished I was as secure as my friend. No matter how bad she was, the thought of her three husbands sending her away never crossed her mind. I wondered if I'd ever get to that point.

I looked up as the three entered my room and stood in front of me with their arms still crossed.

"I don't think it's necessary to discuss what happened yesterday, do you?" Lex asked.

"No, Daddy. I'm sorry."

"Weren't you told to refuse things that you knew were wrong? Like getting stone-cold drunk?" Ryder lifted his eyebrow.

"Yes, Daddy."

"You've disappointed us so badly," Simon scolded. "What possessed you to follow Lena's lead?"

"At first I went outside with her because the longhouse was too hot and stuffy. She told me about the potlatch stuff, and I was curious, so we walked over to the place where it was stored. It wasn't far."

"Did you tell an adult where you were going?"

"No, Daddy. I didn't think anyone would miss us in all that chaos."

"What's your excuse for the drinking?" Ryder questioned.

"We got really cold when we went inside even though we cuddled under a ton of blankets. Lena offered me her flask to warm up."

"Alcohol doesn't warm you. It only dilates the blood vessels and fools the brain into thinking that everything is okay. It also stops you from shivering which is what keeps you warm," Lex lectured. "People die when they drink in this weather."

"I didn't know that."

"You only took one sip, right?" Simon frowned.

"No, Daddy. We finished it off. That's when the uncles found us." I decided it best to use the terms Lena taught me.

"I see. Tell me, something, Jennifer." Lex leaned against the edge of my desk. "What would have happened if the Markfords hadn't found you?"

"We were going to go back right away."

"You were drunk and could barely stand straight. How long do you think you could survive in this weather if you had passed out on the street?"

"We were wearing our parkas."

"If the parkas didn't keep you warm in the storage shed, what makes you think they'd keep you warm when you were exposed to the elements?"

I could see the veins pulsing in his neck. He was furious!

"I don't know, Daddy," I whispered. "I didn't think of that."

"Let me tell you. In these conditions, the temperature and wind chill factor would have wiped you out in less than twenty minutes. A blizzard can also strike at any given moment and produce a white-out. You didn't know that, either, did you?"

I winced as Lex grew louder. "Please don't yell at me. It scares me."

"You should be scared! That foolish decision could have gotten you killed." Lex inhaled. "Go downstairs. You're going to stand for a family tribunal."

I looked at Ryder and Simon. Their silence was deafening. Hanging my head, I went downstairs with the three men on my heels.

Even though the fire was behind me, I was shaking like a leaf as I stood in front of my family. Their facial expressions meant business.

"All of us use this method if we mess up. It's humbling and forces the transgressor to be accountable for his or her actions. We decide together what should be done and how to execute it."

I looked at Lex with confusion. "You guys stand up here?"

"I've probably been there the most," Simon responded. "Last time was because I forgot to check the ax-head and it flew off the handle while I was chopping wood."

"Was anyone hurt?"

"Thankfully, no. But the guys decided that I would finish the woodpile using a handsaw. It took me forever, and I had blisters all over my hand."

"You've never forgotten to check the ax-head since have you?" Ryder asked.

"Nope. The point I'm making is that we've all been in your shoes after doing something stupid. The only difference is that you're not going to be doing any hard labor as punishment."

"Start with an opening statement about the situation and how it could have been avoided," Lex ordered.

My lip quivered as I retold the story and finished it by telling them I needed to become more of a leader than a follower. They seemed to be satisfied with my narrative.

"Opinions, gentlemen?"

"I'll start," Simon offered. "Our goal is to teach her how to survive in this land. The minute you told her how quickly she could've died, she turned pale as a ghost. She's a smart girl, and I believe she learned a valuable lesson."

"You forget that she directly disobeyed my orders that she wasn't to have any alcohol without permission. The defiant action of getting drunk proves that she didn't take me seriously." Ryder looked straight at me. I quickly looked back down and bit my lower lip.

"She also broke house rule number one—not to put herself in any dangerous or precarious situation and go nowhere without telling someone." Lex looked at me. "These rules apply to all of us without exception. There's no excuse for disappearing, especially in this weather. Comment?"

"No, Sir." *What was the point, anyway?*

"Simon?"

"A long OTK using the hand, followed by corner time and a week's grounding to the house with no video games or online chatter."

"Ryder?"

"I second Simon's suggestion, and add the number of strokes that equal the temperature last night to include the wind factor."

"It was fifteen below with ten miles per hour winds. That's makes it about minus forty degrees." Simon calculated in his head.

"The suggested sentence is a long over the knee spanking with my hand, forty strokes with an implement, corner time and a week's restriction. Correct?"

"I think that's reasonable," Ryder announced. "Jenn?"

"Do I have a choice?"

"No, but you can tell us whether or not you agree with the sentence and why."

"Will that change anything for me?"

"Probably not," Lex answered. "The sentencing stands. We only need to decide on one more issue- the implement I should use."

"The strap, for sure," Ryder said.

"I disagree. Use a paddle, Lex."

I looked back and forth between them as though they just grew a second head.

"You're her official guardians and have final say. What will it be?"

Ryder looked at his brother. "About that, Simon and I decided that it wasn't right for us to claim primary guardianship. We're all equals in this family when it comes to our girl, and all of us should have the same authority when making decisions involving her."

"We also don't want any dissension in the ranks. You run this house, we're in your unit, and you're the head honcho. Except when you've been called before the tribunal, you've always been in charge. Ry and I want to continue in that dynamic. It's something we've done for over ten years and it works for all of us."

"Are you certain about this?"

"Yes. All we did was fill out the paperwork, but it was for this family. If I strongly disagree with something, I promise to take you aside," Ryder added.

"You're putting a lot of trust in my hands."

"We've put our lives in your hands for all these years. We have no intention of changing," Simon announced.

Lex nodded. "Thank you. Ryder? Would you mind bringing me her hairbrush, please?"

I wanted to throw up.

He nodded and left the room.

"I seriously hope that I won't have to deal with this issue ever again, Jennifer. If I do, it won't fair well for you."

"Here you go," Ryder said, handing Lex my hard, broad-backed plastic hairbrush.

"Thank you. Have a seat," Lex ordered, rising to his feet. He grabbed a straight-back, armless chair from the dining room and set it to the right of the blazing hearth. He scooted himself far enough away from the fire that it wouldn't be too hot. I suddenly realized where this was going.

"Nononono...." I protested as he patted his lap. "You're really going to roast my ass!"

"It will be uncomfortably warm, but nothing more. You'll also have to look at Ryder and Simon. Over my knees, young lady."

I burst into tears and dropped to the floor to hug his leg. "I'm sorry! Please give me one more chance. I swear I won't do anything dumb again. Please."

He stroked my hair and tilted my chin to look at him. "No, honey. I love you too much to let this go."

Hearing him say he loved me should have comforted me, but I only sobbed harder. "You deserve better than me. You've been so kind and supportive. I try to be good. I really do, but then I do or say something stupid. I can't stop worrying about what I'm going to do that'll finally make you get fed up with me."

"Sweetheart, come here." He pulled me onto his lap and wiped my eyes with his hand. "You're perfect for us, naughtiness included. You know we'd never harm you, right?"

"Yes," I wept. I didn't doubt that statement for a moment.

"Sending you away would harm you. It would also harm us. Do you understand that no matter what kind of trouble you get into, we're always going to be around to pull you out and make sure it never happens again."

"I'm sorry, Daddy," I cried.

"This is part of living in a household like ours. None of us enjoy it, but would you rather us give you the silent treatment and ground you to your room for a month?"

I shook my head. "No. I'd feel abandoned. It would break me."

"A spanking hurts, and it's humiliating, but it's also over quickly. It proves we care enough to take time out of our day and give you what you need. Let's do this."

He positioned me with my bottom in the air and skimmed down my panties. Within a few seconds, my bottom and thighs started to heat up from the fire. He gave no warning when he began to pepper my cheeks with hard, precise spanks falling in rapid succession right after another.

It was terrible. I never imagined his hand could hurt so much.

The speed and intensity of the spanking kept me kicking and struggling, and I cried so hard I couldn't make out the expressions on Ryder and Simon's faces. Just when I got to the point that I couldn't breathe, he stopped.

My rump felt like it was on fire. Even his hand resting on my cheeks gave me no solace.

"It hurts." I wept. "Daddy, it hurts."

"I know. Do you need a drink of water? Here," he said softly, taking the bottle from Ryder.

"She's going to be sitting softly for a bit, Major," he said, running his hand along my flesh.

"That's the idea. Now for part two. Forty strokes of the hairbrush for putting yourself in danger."

I didn't think anything could hurt worse than his hand, but I was wrong. The swats fell in a blur of agony, each focusing on the soft crease between my bottom and thighs. He locked my ankles in place with his foot and held me tight enough that I couldn't move.

"You're killing me! Daddy, stop! Daddy!"

"Ten more to go and then we're done." His voice was muffled and sounded forced. The final cracks of the hairbrush seemed to take forever and convinced me that I'd never be able to sit again. When he finally stopped and loosened his hold, I folded onto the floor and sobbed.

How could I have been such an idiot to want this kind of life?

My answer came seconds later when I was in Ryder's arms with my body pressed against his chest. My tears soaked through his shirt as he caressed my back and told me how much he loved me. When I started to calm down, I was transferred to Simon who embraced me in his bear-like arms and told me how beautiful and sweet I was, and that I made his life better by being in it. Finally, I was returned to Lex.

He said nothing. He didn't have to. I looked up to see tears on his cheek. That was the moment I knew I was home for good. He loved me. Really loved me. They all did.

Except Slater.

Chapter Twenty
(Jennie)
∞ ∞ ∞

"We need to talk with you about something, Jenniebean."

I looked up from my place on the floor where I was laying on my tummy and coloring. My ass was still throbbing, so I didn't care that it was visible to all eyes in the room. I didn't want anything, not even a blanket, to touch it.

"Did I do something else wrong?"

"No, honey. You trust us to protect you, don't you?" Ryder asked, laying down next to me and picking up a gel pen to color with me.

"What's wrong?"

Lex joined us. "We don't keep secrets in this family. It's not good. Someone reported seeing you."

My heart felt like it stopped and I began to panic. "Oh, my God. They've put out a hit on me! What am I going to do? They're going to kill me."

"Try to keep calm. We've got this under control. First, we need to know where you might have been recognized. Did you see anything on your trip over here?"

I thought for a minute. "Yeah. At the Fairbanks airport. When Mr. Murphy and I were waiting for the hopper, I saw a woman in a red coat and glasses who I swore I saw at the house."

"Do you think she might have gotten her hands on the flight schedules?" Simon asked.

"It's very possible. We have to assume that they know Jennifer's somewhere in Denali," Lex said. "This woman—is there anything you can tell us about her?"

"If she was at the house, then she had to be a bigwig of some sort, and probably fairly wealthy. She had a funny accent, too. Like they were talking about the new president and she couldn't pronounce the word *nuclear* correctly."

Ryder looked at Lex. "Didn't Slater say something about Sarah's accent?"

"That's impossible. It's too coincidental." Lex shook her head.

"Is it? Sarah lives in Anchorage, had money coming out of her ass, and is the Chief Customs Officer. Maybe seeing Jennie was coincidental, but if she's involved with the cartel, then hooking up with a guy who is a member of an elite force that crushes drug cartels wasn't a coincidence. She might have been using him to find us and take us down."

"Fuck." Simon rubbed his neck. "When's Slater going to be home?"

"Hopefully within the next couple of days. I haven't heard from him, so he might be stuck on a layover. After he lands, I told him to go to the army base so they can take him to the ranger station the following morning."

"We need to abort those plans. If Sarah's been watching him, he'll lead her straight to us," Lex said grimly.

"Do you think she connected Jenn with our unit?" Ryder asked.

"She's a greedy, two-face bitch, but she's not stupid. Think this out. She sees the girl who was in the drug house in Canada and subsequently calls her report to the ringleader. They informed her that the girl escaped and the house was raided minutes later by the DEA and SWAT team. The girl would naturally report everything she knows to the authorities. The next step would be to place her in witness protection until she testifies against them."

"Slater mentioned that she knew he lives around Fairbanks and used to work as a contractor with the military," Simon added. "He wouldn't have revealed any confidential information, so she had to have another source."

"She's a government employee and probably has some insiders confirming Slater's involvement in crushing the cartel. Given our present administration and how pissed off they are about our refusal to cooperate with their political agenda, they might have given her information out of spite," Ryder said. "They don't have our coordinates, so that's a plus."

"Denali's a big place. How could anyone find Slater without an address?" I asked.

"That's why I'm concerned about him being followed. She's got the customs card which means her people will notify her as soon as he walks through the line. You know what this means, gentlemen?" Lex asked.

"They're not after Jenn. They're after us," Ryder answered.

"We'll make it impossible to get anywhere near here. Even if they flew a drone overhead, they wouldn't see the lodge. We're camouflaged from above," Simon commented.

"What about the town?"

Ryder looked at me. "There are fail-safes that protect Northern Lights. I need to let the Markfords know that we're activating them."

"What kind of fail-safes?"

"The kind that the trespassers won't walk out alive. I need to run a check ASAP and make sure everything's running. Simon? We need the secondary mode of defense."

"On it."

"Be quick. You don't have a lot of light left, and they've already got the advantage of time," Lex ordered. The two kissed me on the cheek and ran out of the room.

"I'm going to go activate the motion detectors. Anyone who slips by the other two defenses won't make it through this one," Lex said as he stood.

"What good will that do?"

"They specifically target human beings and operate the same as the lake barrier. Anyone walking through will be sliced in half by lasers."

"Oh, my God." I covered my mouth with my hands. I couldn't conceive how any of my guys could be such cold-blooded killers.

"I know this is hard for you to understand, but it's them or us. I'll be damned if I let those criminals hurt my family."

"Where are you going?" I grabbed his arm.

"I'm need to go outside and do another parameter check. Stay put. I'll be back as soon as I can."

"Yes, Sir."

My chest tightened as I watched him leave. Panic made my heart pound painfully in my chest. I felt powerless and terrified, not just for myself but for the three men who were my daddies, lovers, and friends. I knew the fuckers who kept me captive followed their own rules and wouldn't hesitate to destroy everything in their path.

After pacing the floor for several minutes, I went up to my room to change into sweats and then hunkered down in front of the dying fire. Molly laid next to me, occasionally nudging me with her nose. Without the sound of boisterous men, the lodge was as quiet as a tomb. I checked my phone constantly, waiting to hear from them, but got nothing.

Hours ticked by and my fear grew with it. Civil twilight had ended, leaving behind endless shadows covering the deceptive white blanket. The temperature had dropped drastically, and Lex's words haunted me. *Could they survive in this weather if they were separated? What if one of them got caught in an avalanche?* Lex was only supposed to check the parameter, but he hadn't returned yet.

What happened to him?

My stomach turned over and twisted in knots. I held Molly close, thankful I had her to keep me company. Being alone was my worst nightmare, and her big, warm body soothed my nerves. I started to doze when she suddenly stood and growled.

"What is it, Molls?" I asked, looking outside. "Did you hear a wolf? They aren't supposed to be able to come here. Oh, you need to go out. Okay, let me throw on my parka and boots."

I walked outside with her and was slapped hard in the face with the icy wind. Tightening the hood over my head, I stomped onto the deck and looked around. She started to growl again.

"What is it, girl?" I asked, squinting to see if I could make out anything. With a bark, she suddenly broke away and disappeared into the darkness. "No! Molly! Molly, come! Molly! Come back!"

I walked down the steps, catching myself as I slid several times and stepped thigh-deep into the snow as I desperately called for the dog. The air around me was deathly silent except for the howling of the wind over the knolls.

"Molly, where did you go?" I whispered, my eyes welling with tears. I was alone. Utterly and completely alone. I kept walking, sinking deep in the snow and calling for her. My teeth were chattering, and I started to ache. If I stayed out any longer, I knew I wouldn't make it back inside. I trudged through the path I made, feeling the inky darkness enclose around me. My legs were numb when I finally made my way to the stairs, and I used all my strength to climb them.

I collapsed on a bench in the mudroom, turned up the heater and tossed my parka and boots to the side. I couldn't stop shivering as I removed my soaking wet sweats and briskly rubbed my legs and hands to circulate my blood. I needed more warmth. It felt like I was walking on pins and needles as I entered the lodge and limped into the living room.

Something was wrong.

When I left, the fire was low and the embers red. I stared at the high flames and then saw a set of large, wet boot prints marked the floor. Relief filled me. One of the guys was home!

"Lex? Simon? Ryder? Where are you? Molly took off and won't come back. Guys?"

I turned around to the sound of footsteps. A tall, bearded man dressed in black snow gear stood in the doorway to the kitchen. He was holding a long, silver knife.

"Well, well, look who decided to come inside. It's foolish to go out in the snow by yourself, girly. You can get hurt."

He took a step forward, and I stumbled backward against a wall, terror making it impossible for me to breathe. "We wouldn't want that to happen now, would we?"

A piercing scream escaped my throat as he lifted the knife...

****

OH, No!
Where are the boys?
Who is this intruder?
What happens to Jennie?
Does Molly get any more bacon?
(Yes, this is a little bit of my sadistic side coming out)
Don't worry! I won't make you wait -
Billion Dollar Daddies: Jennie 2 is coming next!
Make sure you sign up for my newsletter, so you don't miss the pre-release sale.

Would you like to know more about the characters you fell in love with- or learn about the ones you just met?

Lonnie, Max and Mik:
- Billion Dollar Daddies: Lonnie 1&2
- Book Trailer- http://breannahayse.com/billion-dollar-daddies-book-trailer/

Dorian and Meredith Graye:
- The Whip Master
- Mastering Annie
- The End Zone (Game Plan Series Book 3)
- Touch Down (Game Plan Series Book 4)
- Unnecessary Roughness (Game Plan Series Book 5
- Calliope's Little Conquest (Saddlesore Ranch, Book 1)
- Book Trailer- http://breannahayse.com/book-trailer-whip-master/

Coming Soon!
Billion Dollar Daddies: Jennie 2
Billion Dollar Daddies: Dorothy
Game Plan Series, Book 6: Half-Time
AND Northern Lights Series starting with Lena!

Breanna Hayse

**#1 BESTSELLING/INTERNATIONAL
Multi-Genre Author in categories of:
ROMANCE***BDSM***WESTERN***
VICTORIAN***
CONTEMPORARY***MYSTERY***HUMOR*
HISTORICAL*
ACTION AND ADVENTURE***HORROR***
SCI-FI***URBAN***EROTICA
NonFiction- Women's BiographyPolitics and Social Science/Pornography *** YA/Women's Social Issues**

BDSM/AP lifestyler Breanna Hayse strives to give her readers truth and reality of the BDSM/Age-Play/Total Power and Erotic Exchange lifestyle.

Who am I?

I'm a native Californian gone 'wild' and had the opportunity to travel the globe and discover the world through the eyes of both a Marine Intelligence specialist and a BDSM lifestyler. I left the service to go into hospice nursing and grief counseling, eventually working as a marriage and family therapist for those involved in alternative lifestyle development. This experience has allowed me to gain unique inspiration for my books and offer realistic plots and relatable characters.

In 2004, my husband, John, and I joined forces to work with both submissives and dominants- teaching, training, listening and loving. Our goal was to take the mystery and fear out of the lifestyle and mentor people in safe, consensual and healthy relationships.

My first book, The Game Plan, was originally published in 2012 and opened the door to the now-booming world of Age-Play literature. Since that time, I've devoted my 'spare' time to writing, researching, community involvement, and private and group pro bono counseling in deviant behavior, alternative lifestyle, and addiction recovery.

I was formally 'dungeon trained' as a Domme before discovering my submissive side when I joined the service. My scenarios are pulled primarily from either personal experience or observation, including spending time in BDSM clubs as the safety/medical officer. My multi-faceted background allows me to glean from many avenues and give a unique and intelligent literary experience through elements of fantasy and fiction. I also discuss the questions and psychology of the lifestyle in a manner that is fun and informative, and based on 'the real deal.'

I live with my husband, musician, and fellow-author, John Hayse, and two border collies in southern California. We practice a 24/7 D&S relationship with speckles of AP (and many trips to Build-A-Bear), and happily spend every moment together that we can. My hobbies include my puppies, hiding my vanilla salt-water taffy where John can't find it, exotic art, collecting inspirational trinkets, and developing my own paddle line. You can also see me as a featured author/instructor in professional conference settings and as a Sexpert for kinkyliterature.com.

Questions?
Write to me (breannahayse@gmail.com) or
    Visit our Blog: http://www.breannahayse.com

Titles by Breanna Hayse

Age-Play (Contemporary/Victorian)
Billion Dollar Daddies: Lonnie
Billion Dollar Daddies: Lonnie 2
Sweet Little Devil
Skylar's Guardians
Playing A Little
The Reformer
His Lordship's Lap
A Little Play Day (nonfiction)
The General's Little Angel (nonfiction)
A Little Discipline (BVS)
The Game Plan (Game Plan Series- Book 1)
Time Out (Game Plan Series- Book 2)
The End Zone (Game Plan Series- Book 3)
Touchdown (Game Plan Series- Book 4)
Unnecessary Roughness (Game Plan Series- Book 5)
Two Guardians for Little May (Little Lake Bridgeport- Book 1)
Dr. Daddy Dom (Little Lake Bridgeport-Book 2)
Daddy's Little Lady (The Adventures of Little Lady Jane, Book 1)
Daddy's Little Courtesan (The Adventures of Little Lady Jane, Book 2)
Daddy's Little Adventurer (The Adventures of Little Lady Jane, Book 3)
Moving a Little Heart (Little Hearts- Book 1)
Loving a Little Heart (Little Hearts- Book 2)
A Little Wish Upon a Star
Judging His Little Girl
Chastity's Belt

A Little Journey

DD/BDSM
Meeting Her Master
Painful Consequences
The Defiant Heiress
Blindfolded
Guardian Domination
The Whip Master (Fifty Maids of Graye, Book 1)
Mastering Annie (Fifty Maids of Graye, Book 2)
Small Town Sass
Liars & Tigers
Eight Little Letters
Ryann's Revenge (with Rai Karr)

Anthologies
First Submission (Black Velvet Seductions)
Uniform Desire (Black Velvet Seductions)
Love, Lust and Scary Monsters (MS Anthology)
Capture 2 (Enchanted Anthologies)
Without Limits (Interracial Anthology)

Sci-Fi
Disciplining Myyst
Loving Logan
Lost and Found
The Submission Games
The Siren (General's Daughter Series- Book 1)
Up A Notch (General's Daughter Series- Book 2))
Caught in the Net (General's Daughter Series- Book 3)
Convergence (Generals' Daughter Series- Book 4)
Under Cover (General's Daughter Series- Book 5)

Plus More!

Fantasy
Dare to Defy
Her King's Command
Beauty

Western (Contemporary/Historical)
Cowboys Know Best
Serendipity Ranch
Over the Barrel
Switched in Time
Saddlesore Ranch (Calliope's Conquest)

Mystery/ Suspense
Protect and Correct

Horror/Paranormal/Post-Apocalyptic
Spyder's Web (Darkness Series 1)
Ravyn's Cry (Darkness Series 2-coming soon)
The Bad Girl Corner (Darkness Series 3- coming soon)
Two By Day, Three By Night
Between Satin Sheets: Series (coming soon)
Payback's A Witch (short story)

Historical
Servant of Salem
Breaking Chains©: Justice for Liberty

"Coming soon" works are in production with the editorial staff and are not to be copied, distributed or

shared without the author's written permission. The intellectual property in the stated copyrighted series are not to be duplicated/photographed/copied or otherwise distributed by penalty of law.

For exciting new books, meeting authors and discovering what's going on in the Hayse Household-

Please visit our Blog and sign up for our newsletter for special announcements, new releases and give-aways!
breannahayse.com

"Be Good--- or else!"

Printed in Great Britain
by Amazon